# FATE AND THE EXOGAMES

## G. A. JØHN

# FATE AND THE EXOGAMES

To the wild rebels out there,

this one is for you.

Don't ever stop fighting the good fight.

The Council of High Judges

— the leaders of Second Earth —

provide all prisoners with

the single opportunity

to earn their freedom.

More so, to win it.

This event occurs once

every two years

and they call it

the Exogames.

# PART I

# THE CRIME

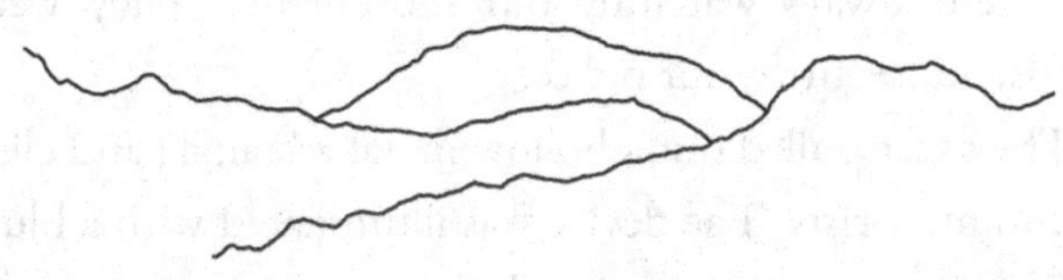

## ONE

**B**EFORE **I** **REALISED** **I** **WAS** **STANDING** a bit too close to the triple-pane glass window of the holding bay in Second Earth, my breath fogged it up and covered the moon. It wasn't the first time I was allowed to see the stars at their brightest or the sun when it shined most. But it was the first time I saw Earth, the real planet, below us, at its darkest.

Humanity escaped Earth centuries ago and settled in a colossal space station orbiting the planet. The survivors never returned to Earth, and I don't think anybody really wanted to go back. I'd heard stories about why we left. Most of them were just theories that had changed over hundreds of years or stories to scare the ones who asked questions. Ghost stories, that is. But I don't believe in ghosts.

Second Earth was as wide as a large city and a hundred

storeys tall. Over one hundred thousand humans populated it, and everyone had their own specific role. For the moment, it was my home.

The door behind me slid open with a loud beeping noise. If it weren't for my throbbing headache, the sound wouldn't have bothered me. One of Second Earth's guards walked in, a helmet covering the top half of his face and a laser gun attached to his magnetic holster. We called them 'gazers' because we realised they were always watching our movements. They were our guards, our security, our police.

The gazer pulled out a hollow metal rectangle and clicked it around my wrists. The device was illuminated with a blue light to signal its activation. My hands froze, and no matter how hard I tried to wiggle my fingers, they wouldn't budge.

He grabbed me by my jacket and pulled me out of the room without a care in the world. We followed the maze of hallways through the station. I caught side eyes and ugly glances from people who walked past; some even turned around and walked the other way. I wasn't sure what level we were on until I saw the giant word — THIRTEEN — painted in a circle on the wall. Level thirteen was what we considered the unlucky level. I was pretty sure the levels between twelve and fifteen were always sectioned off for the criminology departments.

The floors of Second Earth began at the bottom with level one and stretched as high as level one hundred. My role was in aerospace, and my department was way up on level eighty. But my brain was in far too much pain to figure out why I was being escorted through level thirteen with handcuffs around my wrists. I searched the depths of my mind for a logical reason, but the answer was always clouded with confusion, like a deep fog with no possible way out.

We walked down a staircase into a half level below thirteen. The corridors here were much narrower, and the hair on my head scraped the ceiling.

The gazer paused in front of a door and hovered his hand over a square panel where the handle should have been. The door raised up, and he shoved me inside the room. There were no windows or any other doors inside; it was tiny and empty. Fluorescent white strip lights along the walls lit up the room in a lined pattern. A glossy black metal table and chair morphed from the floor and clicked into place.

I made my way around to the other side and pulled out the chair. It felt wet, but perhaps it was just because I was sweating. I could even feel the sweat on the inside of my pants when I sat down.

The door opened again, and Anyma entered with a smile on her face. Anyma had been my best friend since we were children. We did everything together. We teamed up on a multitude of projects in the aerospace department. Her hair was caramel-coloured and never tangled, and her hazel eyes always glowed when she was jovial.

"What have you done now, Fate Artemis?" she asked as she leaned over the table.

"Honestly, if I knew what I did, I don't think I'd be here."

"They're gonna be asking questions. I'm scared for you," she said as she rubbed my hair. "Your hair hasn't grown in a long time."

My hair never grew fast. I thought it was a brunette thing, but it turned out it was just me. I had otherwise grown fairly quickly. I was nearly two metres tall — the tallest of all the boys in my department.

"What are they saying out there?" I asked.

"They were talking too fast for me to understand. I just needed to see you before you stood in front of the Council of High Judges," she answered.

The Council of High Judges was our government. We didn't have a monarchy or a democracy on Second Earth. The Council of High Judges were five leaders who governed in agreeance with each other. It was a system that worked and wasn't going to change, no matter how much the people wanted it to.

The door opened again, and a tall, ivory-skinned man with his hair slicked back, and a tablet in his hand walked in.

"Just pretend I'm not here, Fate," Anyma said as she moved to the side of the room and sat on the floor.

"Alright," the man sighed loudly, not making any eye contact. "Fate Artemis... age twenty... crimes against Second Earth."

He waved his hand over the table, and another chair morphed from the ground where he stood.

"Would you care to elaborate?" he said as he placed the tablet on the table and took his seat.

"I'm sorry, but who are you? I'm not entirely sure what's going on," I said as I tried to move my arms, forgetting they were cuffed.

"My name is Tethys, and I will be representing you in front of the Council of High Judges tomorrow. You have committed a crime against Second Earth, and your sentence will be confirmed at the hearing," he answered without hesitation, as if it were a speech he had rehearsed a hundred times before.

I looked over to Anyma, who twiddled her thumbs and shook her head before she leaned against the wall. Tethys tapped the screen on his tablet twice, and a hologram of my head appeared just above it, spinning slowly. I almost didn't recognise my own face because the entire hologram was blue. At least my eye colour was accurate.

Tethys flicked his fingers over my holographic head, and words appeared above it that read:

## CRIMES AGAINST SECOND EARTH

I waited for a further description to appear on what exactly those crimes were, but nothing did. The words kept circling around my holographic head like a halo, although it wasn't exactly a peaceful moment. I sat with my head down, expecting the words to find their way out of my mouth.

"Fate?" Tethys said in a tone that suggested he didn't want to wait for a response.

"What crime have I committed against Second Earth?"

"That's the question we need the answer to. Just think hard. Think back to what happened on the Comett," he said.

The Comett was the spaceship I had been promoted onto. I

wasn't sure why it was spelt with a second 't', but I kind of liked it. I wasn't supposed to start any journeys for another few days. I wasn't even allowed to go near it, but he assumed I had already been on the ship.

"The Comett?" I asked, raising my head. "I don't know. I haven't been on the spacecraft."

Tethys tapped my hologram head again, and more words appeared in a giant column, like a news headline:

JOURNEY: ASTEROID BELT
DATE: 30TH SEPTEMBER 2498
      (DELAYED EIGHT YEARS)
SPACECRAFT: THE COMETT
PASSENGERS: SEVENTY-EIGHT (78)

Tethys pressed on the 'passengers' tab, and the entire list of seventy-eight passengers appeared. Down at the very bottom was my own name, Fate Artemis, staring me directly in the face as if I were the enemy.

The more I tried to think about it, the more my head hurt. I couldn't possibly understand why, or even how, I could have been on that ship before the probationary period ended.

"Are you certain you don't remember being on that ship at all?" Tethys asked after he closed all the holograms back into his tablet.

"Positive. I never went near it. I've never been to the hangar before, except once to fix a malfunction, but I never stepped foot on any of the spacecrafts," I answered.

My legs shook, and my boots tapped on the floor softly. I

heard my own heartbeat over the tapping. I hoped Tethys couldn't hear it — the tapping that was, not my heart.

"Can you tell me everything you did yesterday?" he asked.

The more I remembered the previous day, the deeper hole I would have dug for myself. I didn't show myself to work even though the shift was on my usual schedule.

"Um," I didn't want to explain myself because it would have made me look more guilty than I already was, so I made up a new story. Although, I was terrible at lying. "I ate my morning meal in the main hall. I was with Halley until around lunchtime, again in the main hall. Then I continued with the research assigned to me."

"What kind of research?"

"That's confidential," I said, shaking my head.

"Alright, what else did you do?"

"My work, until it was time for dinner, again in the main hall. I met up with Halley, and we split off into our separate dorms."

Tethys exhaled loudly and pressed pause on a device beside his tablet. I realised he had been recording the conversation.

"Look, buddy—"

"Fate," I corrected abruptly.

I despised anybody who called me 'buddy'. It reminded me too much of my father.

"Fate. Nobody else survived."

*Survived?* I thought in confusion — it wasn't a word we used very often on Second Earth.

Anyma crossed her legs and leaned slightly forward, turning

her ear towards Tethys' voice.

"Survived what?" I asked.

"The explosion. The Comett is no more," he continued as he stood up and moved behind me. "The ship blew up moments after it left Second Earth."

My heart dropped to the very bottom of my torso and twisted my stomach twice over. I felt my hands sweating through the cuffs, and my legs shook harder. I moved my hands off the table and placed them in my lap, hoping it would stop them from shaking, but it made it worse. I pondered why nobody knew how this had happened, why I didn't know. The Comett was one of the largest ships in Second Earth's possession. Our spacecrafts didn't just explode like that.

The last time our department was in possession of a larger ship was thirty-five years ago when we had sent a crew to Titan, one of Saturn's moons, to analyse the potential for life. However, their communication systems had disconnected shortly after. The crew never returned to Second Earth, and we were never able to contact them. We didn't even send out a rescue team because it was deemed too dangerous. Titan had no life; everybody knew that, so the expedition was terminated, and the entire crew was declared dead.

"The Comett was equipped with all safeguards," I said.

Tethys didn't respond, and I didn't turn to face him.

"It couldn't possibly have exploded. The stop switch would have activated."

"Stop switch, you say?" Tethys asked as he leaned against the table and reached for his tablet. He pulled up a report of the explosion and scrolled. "Ah, here we are. Stop switch... missing," he read.

"Nobody could have removed the stop switch on their own. I would know; this is my department."

"Precisely, no doubt about that. But what doesn't sit right with me is how you seem to have your name on the passenger list but weren't present at all when the ship took off," he said after he shut off the hologram.

"I'm confused. It doesn't sound like you are on my side here. I told you already; I don't know why my name was on the list. And I was nowhere near that ship. You can ask everyone I work with. You can ask Halley."

"We questioned her already," he said as he picked up his tablet and recording device. "She said that you told her to put your name on the list."

"No, that can't be right. Halley would never... I would never have told her to do that, to risk both our jobs."

"Her words, not mine. I will submit these for tomorrow's case. You better get some sleep — it might be your last night here on Second Earth," he said before he walked out of the room.

Anyma followed him out and half-smiled at me without her eyes. The same gazer from earlier walked in and unlocked the handcuffs. I rubbed my wrists from the irritation they caused; my fingers took a second to regain their movement from the pins and needles. He placed a new device that attached to the back of my neck, again with the blue light to signal its activation. I had never seen this device used on anyone before.

"What is this?" I asked.

"Your tracker," He said, motioning his hand for me to exit the room. "When this sirens, it will be time for judgement."

I gulped, and my eye twitched.

"Where do I go now?" I asked, expecting him to transfer me to another holding bay.

"Anywhere on Second Earth. We will come find you when it is time."

I knew the gazer was lying. Even I, a person with some authority in aerospace, was restricted from travelling in many parts of Second Earth. Secrets were being kept from us all. Of course, we all wanted to know what they were, but nobody had the courage to find out.

I made my way to the glass drop pod closest to me. It was hard to find because it was tucked away in a strange gap between two walls. Most drop pods on Second Earth were only big enough for one person, but they were extremely fast. I squeezed myself into the compartment, and the ground lit up. The glass door closed, and I saw my reflection in it. My face was drooped, and my lips were sealed tight as the whites of my eyes became increasingly visible. Even though the drop pod was made of glass, the shaft it ran through was black, so there was no spectacular view.

A tiny gold sphere fell from the roof and hovered in front of me. It scanned my entire body twice with a blue light and shot back into a hole in the roof. I was secured in a hard plastic shell, and my head was cushioned at the back.

"Please enter the level you wish to travel to," a clear robotic voice announced.

There were no buttons in this drop pod. In the old system, circular lights appeared on the door with each level and one would have simply pushed their desired floor to travel to it. That was quite a while ago, before the upgrade.

I needed to get back to my department to figure out what had happened.

"Eighty," I said, loud and clear.

The drop pod remained motionless, and there was no announcement. I was confused, so I tried again.

"Eig—"

"Unfortunately, you have been restricted from travelling to level eighty," the robotic voice announced. "Please enter the level you wish to travel to."

*Why can't I go back to my department?* I thought.

I shrugged it off as a malfunction and realised that it was probably dinner. I needed to get to the main hall, find Halley and figure all of this out.

"Level fifty," I announced.

Immediately, the drop pod was sucked up with a lightning-fast blast of air, and all my organs fell to my toes. It came to a sudden halt, and the plastic encasing me fell away. My eyes took a second to adjust, but I shook my head and squeezed my eyelids, and after a second, the white sparkles disappeared. My stomach didn't feel normal though, vomit rose up my throat, but luckily nothing came out. I always felt the same way after taking the drop pod. I didn't think I could ever get used to it.

I took the left hallway because the one on the right was too dark and I was far too preoccupied to deal with any monsters. Just to make sure I was on the correct level, I looked for the painted 'FIFTY' on the walls and thankfully found it. Level fifty was where the main hall was. Everybody received their meals on this level, but some people took their food to their dorms to eat in peace and quiet. I couldn't blame them; the hall often became too crowded, but I supposed it was why the Council of High Judges allocated specific meal times for each department. Even so, thousands of us still couldn't fit in the same space.

I heard loud conversations further ahead and voices that overlapped one another. The door automatically opened as I approached it, and instantly the noise grew a thousand times louder. My head still throbbed, and my ears couldn't handle it, but I had to find Halley in the deep ocean of bodies.

I glanced over to the giant digital clock on the pillar in front of me — there was one on every pillar. Second Earth still recorded the time as it was on the real planet Earth in twenty-four hour time. It was easier to keep everything consistent. The time ticked over to 18:14, which meant the aerospace department was in the hall. Everybody between levels sixty and eighty-five was allocated dinner from 18:00 until 18:30.

The hall was divided into sections for each level. Directly in front of me was the section for level sixty-one. That meant everyone from level eighty was at the very back of the hall. To make it all the way over there would take at least ten minutes, five and a half if I ran, though I wasn't particularly fond of exercise. I dodged people who carried their food trays, and I slid underneath tables, accidentally knocking over people's drinks. Some even threw a tantrum, but there was no time to worry about that. Gazers who patrolled the hall looked at me with raised eyebrows and probably wondered why some maniac was sprinting through the entirety of level fifty.

Alas, I made it to the other side of the main hall and recognised some of my team. Vesta and Juno sat on the tables and laughed at each other. They were twin siblings and had earned themselves the title 'Troublemakers of Level Eighty' because every opportunity they had to wreak havoc, they grasped tight and didn't let go. Pallas was the only one in our allocated section who didn't talk. She simply kept to herself and ate the mash of vegetables in her tray.

"What happened to you?" Juno asked as he leaned forward and laughed, almost falling off the table.

"Yeah. Where have you been?" Vesta said as she nudged Juno and grabbed onto his leather jacket.

I had no idea what they found so funny all the time. I just wasn't the type to laugh at everything, especially since my career and future were in jeopardy.

"Have you seen Halley?" I asked with a straight face.

Vesta pointed behind me and laughed hysterically.

"Turn around, idiot," she said.

"What's up with those two?" Halley said as she came up from behind with her tray in one hand and a small black cube in the other.

"They've lost the plot," I said as I turned to face her. "Halley, what the hell is going on?"

"Shut up and listen to me," she commanded as she twisted the cube under her elbow, and broke it into two pieces.

"What?"

She passed me one of the pieces, and the very moment it came into contact with my skin, the entire hall went dead silent. Everybody's mouths moved, but no sound came from anywhere. For a second, I thought I'd lost my hearing, and I panicked because I was worried I wouldn't get it back.

"You've been caught out, Fate," Halley's voice echoed as she moved her auburn hair away from her face.

"What just happened? Why can't I hear anyone else?" I asked with concern.

"It's the afticuvos," she answered as she held up her piece of the cube. "It's the project I was working on to reduce the noise during take-off. No one can hear us."

"Why can't I remember anything, Halley?"

"I don't know. The gazers came and took you after the explosion."

"I don't remember any explosion. I was just interrogated by some Tethys guy about it. I couldn't have possibly been anywhere near the Comett."

"Fate, I got your message. You told me to put your name on the passenger list. I confirmed with Supervisor Hoba if it was alright because I knew you were still on probation. He said it was fine."

The time clicked over to 18:28 and flashed twice to remind everyone that our meal time was almost over. Halley passed me her food tray so she could show me her message bank. She pressed a button on the small handheld device, and an array of messages lit up on the screen. She scrolled to my name and showed me the most recent message:

HALLEY,

PUT MY NAME ON THE LIST OF PASSENGERS FOR THE NEXT TIME THE COMETT JOURNEYS OUTSIDE SECOND EARTH. IT WOULD MEAN A LOT IF YOU COULD DO THAT FOR ME.

THANKS,
FATE ARTEMIS

"That's impossible. I didn't write that," I said as I handed her tray back.

"I don't know what to say, Fate. Seventy-seven passengers and crew were on that ship, and all seventy-seven died."

"You have to believe me, Halley. You can clear my name. Tomorrow at the trial, you can tell them."

"There is one thing I'm not, and that's a liar. I'm sorry, Fate, but this is too far out of my control."

"What about Supervisor Hoba? You said he approved it. He can tell the High Judges that he gave the thumbs up."

"It doesn't work like that, Fate." She took back the piece of the afticuvos and walked to the exit.

The hall immediately boomed with noise again, and everybody scrambled to the exits and the drop pods as the time clicked over to 18:30.

"Are you coming with us?" Juno asked. "We're getting drinks."

"Not right now, guys," I replied.

Something sinister was going on in Second Earth. I felt it deep in my stomach, churning and twisting every time I thought about it. I just needed to figure out exactly what it was before it was too late.

**T W O**

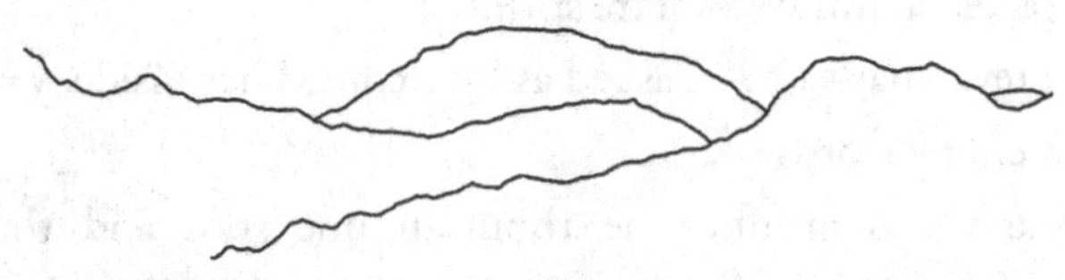

**M**OST OF THE DORMS IN Second Earth were tightly packed between one another. I was lucky that mine was nowhere near the others; it also had a window. But that was about the only luck I ever had in my life, and I was not sure I would have even called it luck. My window always faced the darkness of outer space and never the planet below us. In the distance, tiny stars flickered like fireflies on a stretched-out dark, navy blanket, twinkling to gain our attention, and sometimes I wanted to join them.

I wasn't sure how much longer I had until the hearing and didn't want it to be the only thing that took up space in my mind. I kicked the boots from my feet and tossed them into the corner furthest from my bed. The lights that lined the walls faded to a soft amber so they would not strain my eyes.

My heavy head landed on the soft pillow, and I half expected all my thoughts to disappear. But they still lingered, as if my brain was their own private playground.

Just as my eyelids were about to shut, I was pulled back into reality with the sound of the doorbell. Nobody really used the doorbells on Second Earth. Everyone just knocked hard to get into places. I heaved myself out of the floating bed and ambled to open the door. It was Anyma, puffing as if she had just completed a hundred-metre sprint.

"Hey, what's up?" I asked as I welcomed her inside, yawning between my words.

She paced around the room in one spot and then sat abruptly on the stool by my bed. I slid my hand on the matte control panel to turn up the brightness of the lights and sat on the far end of my mattress with a pillow wedged between my arms and chest. She threw her hands around my neck and squeezed comfortably tight. Her heartbeat pounded through her ribcage, and I almost felt it on mine but the pillow muted the pounding.

"I'm... I'm just worried about you, Fate," Anyma whispered into my ear.

"Stop it. You'll stress me out even more."

"Do you know what's going to happen tomorrow?" She pulled her hands away from me.

"No. I don't want to think about it," I responded, rubbing my eyes to stay awake.

"I want to be there tomorrow—"

"No," I interjected. "I don't want you to see me get a terrible sentence. You know how harsh the High Judges are."

"I'm going to support you. Nobody else will," she said firmly.

"I went to see Halley not long ago to see if she had any information about all of this."

"Was she any help?" Anyma asked.

"She showed me a message that I apparently sent her. It doesn't make any sense that I'd ask her to put me on the list."

"We will figure this out, Fate."

"I was hoping Halley could back me up tomorrow, but she's confident that the message came from my tablet," I said.

"Do you have your tablet now? Check if it really did come from you," Anyma suggested.

I scurried through the drawers in the wooden bedside table, moving books and inanimate objects out of the way to find the tablet. It wasn't in the top drawer, so I checked the second one, and it was also empty.

"It's not here."

"Did you leave it at work, maybe?" Anyma asked.

It felt like a light bulb turned on inside my head, and my eyes widened. "It's on my desk."

"Get up." She snapped her fingers and gestured for me to start moving. "We're going now. We need to find out the truth."

For a moment, it seemed as though Anyma was more determined to solve this case than I was. I followed her out of my room and shut the door carefully behind me to avoid waking anybody.

"What floor is this?" Anyma asked.

Surprisingly, I blanked out. I couldn't remember which level we were on, so I crouched down and ran my finger under the lip of the illuminated path. Every level was labelled with its corresponding numbers, and since this floor had no obvious painted number, I used the second most useful method. It was a bit more tedious, but for the life of me, there was no easier way. Underneath the pathways were buttons, and when pressed, they revealed the number of the level.

I slid back slightly, and my finger found the button. I pushed firmly, and a robotic voice spoke through the speakers in the ceiling.

"Level seventy-six," it announced.

"Right, we have to go up four levels," I said as I pushed myself up. "I don't know why I forgot that."

"Drop pod is the fastest way there."

"No, it won't work. I tried going there before, and I don't have access. We have to take the stairs."

"I haven't taken the stairs in forever," Anyma scoffed.

"Yeah, because you always get the early shifts. There's always drop pods available," I laughed.

Anyma and I sped to the nearest staircase, which was tucked behind a set of dorms towards the centre of level seventy-six. The door raised up, and the individual lights lining the edge of each step turned on one by one. My legs already ached, and walking up four levels when I should have been asleep didn't help at all. We paused in front of the door that had an etched 'eighty' on a small silver plaque. I expected it to raise up and let us into the level, but nothing happened, not even the whirring sounds the doors usually made before they opened.

"Use your key card," Anyma suggested.

"It's back in my room." I moved my hands around the door to see if there was a latch that would manually open it.

Quiet murmurs echoed from the other side of the door, gradually increasing in volume as they moved closer. I immediately grabbed Anyma and held her against the wall, away from the light. The door shot open, and I heard Vesta's nasally voice.

"I can't believe they turned off the drop pods. Maintenance must be *so* important," she said sarcastically.

I tried to peak to catch a glimpse of the person she was with, but their voice was also distinct. Halley.

"The stairs aren't so bad," she said. "We needed to start doing more cardio anyways."

Vesta laughed mockingly as their footsteps receded to the lower levels.

"See you tomorrow then?" Halley asked.

"Sure. I won't be at work, though. I'm going to Fate's hearing," Vesta answered.

I was positive I heard her correctly, that she was going to attend my sentencing. They were a few levels down, and their voices weren't echoing as loudly. I knew Vesta didn't like me much. Perhaps she wanted to see if I was going to be served a horrible sentence.

"Quick, Fate," Anyma said as she pointed to the door.

We hurried to catch our only opportunity to get into our department; otherwise, the door would have locked us out.

Most of the lights were off, but I was still able to navigate through the piles of machinery and broken parts. We sneaked behind nib walls and dodged the people who were working this late. My desk was within sight, pressed against the closest wall in an open area. It looked lonely, and dust was beginning to gather because I hadn't been at work in a few days.

My tablet sat on the desk above a small box. Someone must have moved it, because I had left it flat on my desk the last time I was here, and the small box had been on the floor.

"I'll go get it," Anyma offered.

I quickly pulled her out of sight and pointed at Pallas, who sat quietly at her desk, drilling into pieces of metal. She had been working on her project for months. I wasn't exactly sure what it was, but I had a hunch it was something extraordinary. Pallas always worked on incredible projects, despite being so young. She was facing away from us, intensely focused on her work.

"I will go," I insisted quietly.

I tiptoed in the shadowed parts of the room, doing my best to be stealthy. I carefully placed my feet away from scraps of metal and wiring scattered across the floor, but I missed a piece and tripped on a small aluminium sheet. My eyes widened, and my entire body froze, as cold as ice. I was stuck in an awkward position which gradually became more difficult to hold. I lost my balance and crash-landed on a crate that smashed into large pieces, and I prayed that Pallas hadn't heard the noise over her drilling. Thankfully, she didn't look up from her work. I paused for a few seconds and continued.

Even in the dimly lit room, Anyma's worried face caught my attention. She looked more worried than I was, but I was determined to know if the message came from me. Just as I reached for my tablet, a voice echoed softly from behind my ears.

"What are you doing here?"

*Oh no.* Pallas had caught me. My heart pounded so fast I thought it was going to pop from my chest. My entire body rushed with a cold shiver, and sweat built up underneath my arms.

"I came to get my tablet," I said honestly.

There was no point in lying. I didn't want to be in any more trouble than I already was.

"What do you need your tablet for?" she asked, trying to squeeze a real answer out of me.

I didn't want to tell her the truth. It was probably the third time in a whole year Pallas had actually spoken to me. At first, I thought she disliked me, but then I realised it was her personality. She rarely spoke to anyone in our department.

"I need to finish the project I was working on," I lied.

"Oh yeah? What's that?"

"I'm not saying. What project are *you* working on?"

"It's a project for Halley," she answered.

"Halley isn't supposed to be doing any group projects this quarter. What has she got you up to?"

"She wanted me to finish off a few things for her. It's no big deal."

"Alright, well, you take care. Don't stay up too late." I

abruptly ended the conversation. I didn't expect to avoid trouble so easily, but Pallas wasn't one to get involved in drama.

I swiped the tablet from the top of my desk and walked back around the crates of junk to Anyma. We took the staircase back down to level seventy-six and made our way to my room, walking past the giant window to our right.

The door to my room detected my body immediately and unlocked without any hassle. Anyma sat on the stool again, and I laid down on my bed. I tapped the screen on my tablet to unlock it, but the battery was completely drained.

"Don't tell me we have to go back to get a charger," Anyma complained.

"Don't worry. I have one here," I said as I pulled one from the bedside table. "I have a spare as well. I think I accidentally took Vesta's."

"She'll get over it," Anyma laughed.

"I don't think she knows I have it." I laughed too.

My tablet took less than a minute to reboot, and once it did, it was pretty straightforward to navigate. It wasn't as fancy as the tablet Tethys used when he interrogated me, but it did the job just fine.

There was an array of unopened messages that dated back a few years, but Halley was the most recent contact on my tablet. I was too nervous to press on her message. It could prove my innocence or prove that I had really sent the message. My finger double-tapped Halley's name and the most recent thread appeared. It read:

HALLEY,

PUT MY NAME ON THE LIST OF PASSENGERS FOR THE NEXT TIME THE COMETT JOURNEYS OUTSIDE SECOND EARTH. IT WOULD MEAN A LOT IF YOU COULD DO THAT FOR ME.

THANKS,
FATE ARTEMIS

For the life of me, I still could not remember sending her that message. I didn't always use my tablet to message people because it wasn't its primary purpose. My job in aerospace was to write some of the system codes for the spacecrafts, and that was the main use for my tablet.

"Fate, what is it?" Anyma asked.

"The message did come from my tablet," I answered with disappointment.

"Shit. But that doesn't mean you sent it."

"I'm the only one who can unlock my tablet. Nobody else has access," I said, still pondering the possibility that I had sent this message.

"Wouldn't our department have access to your tablet? Not the whole department, but the leaders? Supervisor Hoba?"

"They would. But they'd have no reason to get into it. Plus, they would have needed to ask for my permission."

"Get some rest, Fate. Go back to it when you wake up."

"I can't. The hearing is tomorrow. I need to figure this out tonight."

"Trust me, Fate. You're tired. I'll see you tomorrow, first thing. And we can try and figure out who logged into your tablet."

"Okay. I am tired. You've got that right," I giggled.

"Alright, I'll see you tomorrow," Anyma said as she headed towards the door.

"Anyma," I said.

She paused and turned around.

"Can you stay with me tonight?" I said softly.

"Anything for you."

I tried not to smile too much, hoping to play it cool. She tucked me into my bed like a little baby and dragged a pillow to the floor.

"No, I mean here," I said as I tapped on the mattress lightly.

"This feels illegal, you know." She laughed as she slid underneath the covers.

There was no law prohibiting us from sleeping in the same bed, but Anyma was very honest about her morals. I promised no funny business. I just needed comfort. I needed to feel safe, and Anyma was the closest thing to it.

Sleep took us both the same way darkness overtakes the light, and in my dreams, I was free. That was where I wanted to stay, never needing to come back to the reality of my supposed crimes.

# THREE

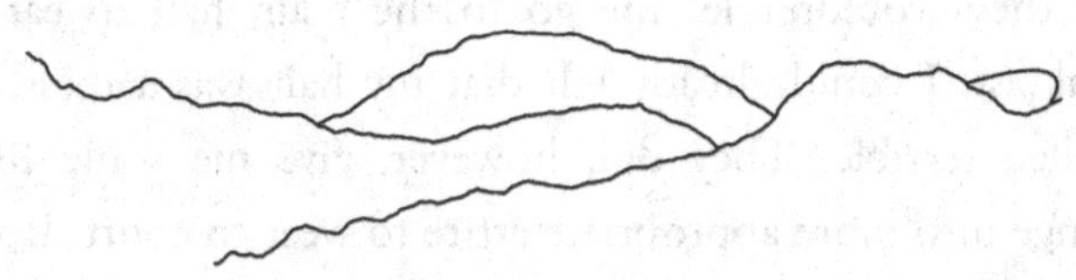

**M**Y EARS BURNED with the sound of the siren on the back of my neck. I had completely forgotten the gazer had attached it to me. It was only loud because it was so close to my ears. I rolled over on the bed and found it empty on the other side. I assumed Anyma was in the bathroom, but the door was wide open, and the light was off. She must have left during the night without saying anything.

The clock by my bed flashed 10:10, a time I rarely woke up. I was more of a morning person. A fist pounded against the door to my dorm. This was the day I dreaded, and I had only found out about it a few hours before. Everybody feared the court hearings on Second Earth. The Council of High Judges always prosecuted harshly and sometimes without proper reasoning or evidence to back up their claims. I hoped only to get suspended from my job or have to forfeit my position. Anything but death — but I also knew there were far worse things than death.

I dawdled over to the door, still struggling to wake up. It must have been too long for the gazers to wait because they pounded the door much harder the second time. I waved my hand over the control panel, and the door shot up, revealing the two gazers waiting to take me to court.

I didn't even get time to brush my teeth or wash my face, and they wouldn't let me go to the main hall to eat some breakfast. I could already tell that my hair was a mess, and I smelled terrible. They did, however, give me some time to change into more appropriate attire to wear to court. It wasn't any fancy suit or tie, just my regular cargo pants and a plain shirt.

We took the elevator to the legal floor just above my department. The gazers were the only ones with access to the larger elevators that could fit more people. I assumed they didn't want me to use the drop pods because they probably thought I would have run away to delay the hearing, but I honestly just wanted it all to be over much earlier.

The doors opened, and for the second time in my life, I saw the legal floor. The first time I was here was eight years ago, during my father's court case. My body didn't want to step off the elevator, and I didn't want to relive that moment. For some time, I had tried to forget about everything that had happened with my father, but it wasn't easy to disregard such integral moments of my life.

The gazers pushed my legs off the ground and forced me to

walk to the first door on the right, leading me into the courtroom. It looked the same as I remembered from eight years ago: the half-circle panel with five extremely tall chairs for each of the High Judges, and a large sitting area opposite the panel that stretched to the ceiling for the audience. There was no seat for me; there never was for the defendant. I was simply required to stand on a circular light in the very centre of the room.

*Here we go,* I thought.

The entire courtroom was already filled with people waiting to watch the hearing. It was embarrassing to walk to the centre with everyone's haughty eyes glued to me. After all, they were only there to mock me and witness the sentencing. My feet locked into place on the centre circle, and I glanced over at the audience. Some co-workers from my department sat in the row of seats to my left: Vesta, Juno, Pallas and Halley. Anyma sat in a seat directly behind them and smiled at me as she nodded her head for encouragement.

Tethys was nowhere to be seen. I thought he was supposed to help defend me in here. But by the same token, my father had stood here alone and defenceless as well. I needed to do this by myself, and I wasn't ready for it.

"All rise," the gazer who stood at the door announced.

Everybody stood up straight, silently, and watched the High Judges as they made their way to their seats. They were all very tall and very old. Their beady black eyes were like marbles surrounded by their pale skin. Over their slightly hunched shoulders, they wore long red robes with a purple stripe that dragged on the floor. I caught a glimpse of gold tassels before they disappeared behind the panel.

The High Judge in the centre propped an electronic reading monocle on his eye and scrolled through the tablet in front of him.

"Fate Artemis?" he asked as his low voice reverberated through the court before he looked directly at me.

"Yes, Your Honour."

"Today, we are here to witness the sentencing of Fate Artemis for his crimes against Second Earth. How do you plead?"

"Not guilty," I answered.

The audience booed with conviction, but another High Judge raised his hand to stop them. I didn't have any time to think about the 'crime' I'd committed because all of this had happened so quickly. Of course, I would never plead guilty without knowing the consequences, especially when I was innocent.

"Of the seventy-eight passengers and crew scheduled for the journey, all but one died." He spoke calmly and slowly with random increases in volume.

"I don't know how my name ended up on the list of passengers, but I was not involved in the explosion," I responded much too quickly.

"Eager, are we? Do you know what could have caused the ship, the Comett, to explode?" the High Judge in the far-right seat asked.

"I know the stop switch should have activated. But Tethys,

during the interrogation, stated that it was missing. The stop switch most certainly would have prevented the explosion."

"Why did you step onto the ship?" the centre judge asked. "You must have been aware that your probationary period had not ended yet."

I already told them that I shouldn't have been on the passenger list. It seemed as though they were trying to get me to say the wrong thing.

"Yes, I was still on probation. I wouldn't have risked that to enter the ship."

"Your father did, eight years ago," the High Judge in the leftmost seat said. "Scorpius Artemis."

"I cannot speak on behalf of my father," I said.

I didn't want to talk about my father's crime. There were too many unfortunate memories attached to that moment.

"From our understanding, you were recently restricted from entering level eighty. However, it was brought to our attention that you snuck into your department last night."

I turned and faced Pallas. She was the only one that had seen me. I watched as her lips mouthed the word, "Sorry." There was nobody on Second Earth I could trust anymore. Pallas, the one who kept to herself and remained content, had snitched me out for no reason at all. Perhaps she needed a promotion at work, but other than that, there was no logical reason for her betrayal.

"Fate Artemis, for crimes against Seco—"

"Wait a second," I interjected in frustration, pleading with any excuse under the sun. "This is hardly a court case. I can prove that I'm innocent! I just need some more time."

All five of the High Judges gave me a menacing look as they tilted their heads down at me. The centre judge pushed a button underneath the table, and the circular light on which I stood turned to blue. My body lost all its weight as I began to rise. My feet kicked off the floor, and I hovered about a metre in the air, unable to get back to the ground. The High Judges whispered to each other for a few minutes, but it seemed much longer as I felt the stares from the audience.

"Fate Artemis," the centre High Judge said as he took off his monocle. "For crimes against Second Earth, we hereby sentence you to fifty revolutions around the sun on Mars."

The audience grew loud with murmurs, and Anyma yelled out, "No, you can't!"

Everybody ignored her.

Mars was the location of our most secure prison, and only those who committed the most disturbing crimes were sent there. Fifty revolutions equated to approximately ninety-four Earth years. That was an entire life sentence; there was no point serving it. How could I, a simple nobody from aerospace, be sent to Mars to serve a life sentence? I'd be leaving behind everything and everyone I knew.

"What about the prison here on Second Earth?" I asked.

"Alternatively," the High Judge began as he ignored my question.

A wave of relief rushed through my body, and my eyes lit up. *Please have something better for me,* I hoped.

"The biennial Exogames are approaching. Do you wish to compete for your chance at freedom?"

No. Definitely no. I withdrew my plea. A tournament of five games that increased in difficulty each round, the Exogames were not something to be taken lightly. Freedom was granted to the winners who survived to the end. Only prisoners were allowed to play; nobody in the general public could enter the games. However, the chance of making it through any of the games was exponentially low, practically impossible. My father had competed after his court hearing. I never saw him again.

"I choose to spend fifty revolutions on Mars," I said confidently, knowing either option would result in death.

"Right then," the centre High Judge said. "Fate Artemis, you have been sentenced to fifty revolutions around the sun on Mars. That is final." He struck a metal plate with his gavel to conclude the proceedings.

The gravity around me returned to normal, and I landed abruptly on my feet. The gazers who stood at the entrances marched in my direction and grasped my arms tight. I tried to fight back by throwing my hands around to break away from them, but it was pointless. They would have never given me back my life. They dragged me to the exit, but I wanted to see Anyma once more. She was the only one who had helped me try to figure this out.

"I get to say goodbye," I cried, and my voice cracked. "I have to say goodbye."

"Not this time, buddy," the gazer replied as he jolted me closer to the door.

My head throbbed, and my heart became heavy as it sank to the bottom of my stomach. I shook with fear, unsure if the decision I made was the correct one. My throat tightened, and I felt myself on the verge of crying, although I tried not to show any emotion. I needed to be stronger than this, and if I couldn't, then I had to make it seem like I was.

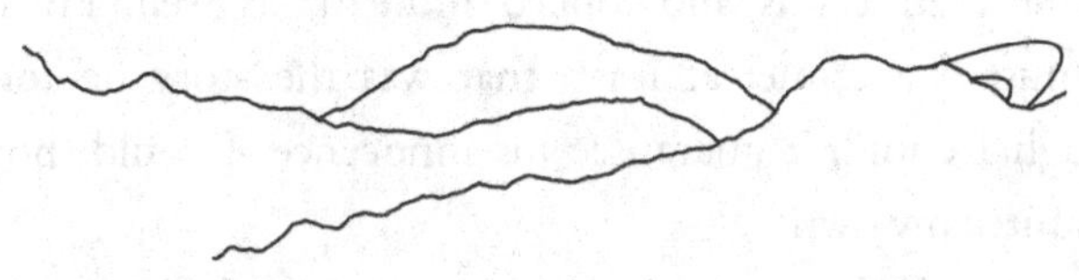

## FOUR

**K**NOWING **I** **ONLY HAD** forty-nine revolutions around the sun remaining until the end of my sentence wasn't all that calming. Almost two entire Earth years spent on Mars were more than enough to drive me insane. I empathised with the people who had been here for almost an entire lifetime. I saw my future in them, the way my spirit would only continue to diminish.

The prison reminded me of Second Earth. It was made from the same metallic materials and had a similar design — an entirely metallic facility with narrow hallways and fluorescent light strips along the walls. My cell was very small, especially with the skinny bed taking up half of the room, and there was barely any space to move around. A tiny glass hole in the ceiling was the only clock I had to go by. Every time the sun disappeared, I etched a marking on the wall with a loose screw from my bed frame. There were six hundred and forty-seven tally marks and many more to go.

Early on, I noticed a tiny gap in the wall to the cell adjacent to mine. I thought I would be able to chat with someone on the other side to occupy my mind, but that cell remained empty. I did, however, make one friend in the courtyard. His name was Jaaspar, and he was two years older than me. He was much shorter than I was and looked more fit as well. He hadn't committed a crime; at least, that was the story he told me, though I couldn't guarantee his innocence. I could, however, guarantee my own.

Jaaspar had apparently leaked confidential files around his entire department — biomedicine. His team specifically worked on a device that would restore human skin seamlessly in the event of horrendous lacerations beyond ordinary medical aid. From the stories I heard back on Second Earth, the science departments were extremely strict in keeping their projects confidential. Whenever information leaked out, it led to a serious investigation to trace the source. It had already been three revolutions around Mars for Jaaspar. I could barely handle one, let alone three — I was amazed that he'd survived here for so long.

Recreational time was my favourite because I couldn't stand the lack of space in my cell. All thirty-two inmates were designated one hour per day to exercise and stretch in the courtyard. We were a small bunch, and sometimes, if the gazers had a good day, we were given extra time.

The courtyard was a simple gym area in a large room. Its ceiling was a strong glass panel that revealed the orange atmosphere outside. All the equipment was fitted with blue devices that mimicked the gravitational pull of Second Earth. We had similar devices attached to our boots and around our wrists; in fact, the boots were much heavier than normal to keep us all attached to the ground — clearly, they didn't want us to escape, even though there was nowhere to go.

"What was that heat last night, hey?" Jaaspar asked as he reached for the dumbbells.

"I know, right? I was so restless." I attempted to grab a lighter dumbbell but put it back almost immediately. Exercise was not my strong suit. "It's never been that hot during the night, at least for the time I've been here."

"Get used to it. It will get worse," he responded, grunting as he worked his biceps.

One of the newer female inmates barged between us and snatched away two dumbbells neither of us was using. I moved out of her way and sat on the bench as she moved to the other side of the room.

"She's lethal," Jaaspar said as he wiped the sweat from his forehead. "Her name is Jayde. I only remember that because her eyes match her name, and I overheard one of the gazers when they brought her in."

"Jayde," I repeated. "What do you mean she's lethal?"

"I heard she killed three people in her department. I don't think it was an accident. One, sure. Two is suspicious. Three is no coincidence. They've locked her in a special cell away from the others.”

“Far out. That’s a bit serious. Maximum security?”

“It’s not even that. It’s just inconsistent that we are locked in the same place as murderers.”

“Makes no sense. How many revolutions do you have left in here anyway?” I asked curiously, changing the topic of conversation.

“Too many.” He paused.

I waited for him to specify an exact number as the noise grew a bit louder around us with everyone using the equipment. I looked at my fingernails and twiddled my thumbs until he spoke again.

“Twenty-seven,” he finally answered. “Around fifty Earth years left.”

“At least you’ll get out of here before me,” I said, trying to lighten the mood a little.

“You don’t understand. I had my whole life ahead of me back home. By the time I’m done in here, I’ll be old. Seventy ain’t gonna be a good look for me.”

“I won’t even get to see Second Earth again. I’ll die in here,” I said, hoping it would reassure him somewhat.

“I’ve been thinking,” Jaaspar began.

I sat on the edge of my seat and leaned slightly forward. Free thinking, in general, was never a good idea.

“Only because the opportunity will come up very soon. I want to compete in the next Exogames,” he continued, softly. “I need to get out of here sooner, and if I make it through all five rounds, then that’s it. I’ll be free.”

Lines of worry creased my forehead because I couldn't tell if he was being funny or just plain stupid. Jaaspar always found a way to gather new information. First about Jayde, and now about the opportunity to enter the Exogames. It was his superpower.

"I'm not sure that's an entirely intelligent idea, Jaaspar. My father competed in the games many years ago. I never saw him again. It's dangerous stuff, dude. Not many people make it out alive. Think about it carefully."

"I have; every single minute of every single day I've spent in here. I can't do it anymore, Fate. I can't be the only one. You've probably thought about it too," he said.

It was almost like he'd read my mind. I had, in fact, considered entering, multiple times. The heat wasn't the only thing keeping me up at night.

"Many times, as well. But I always come to the conclusion not to enter," I responded.

"Why? If you survive all the games, you get to leave this place early. If both of us won, our lives would return to normal."

Jaaspar spoke a bit too loudly, and we received a few concerning looks from fellow inmates.

"Because they are literally death games. The chances of surviving are so low that it's better just to stay here and serve the rest of my sentence," I answered a bit aggressively.

"Just," he said, quieter, "please just consider it again."

"I'm sorry, Jaaspar, but I've thought about it long and hard. I made the decision a long time ago that I'd never compete in such games."

"If you enter, I will too," he pleaded. "We can play together."

A drop of sweat ran down the bridge of his sharp nose and splashed on the ground. I knew it wasn't the exercise making him sweat; it was his efforts to convince me to join.

"I'm not stopping you from entering the Exogames. I will support whatever decision you choose to make. Just please don't force me," I said, firmly, walking away to the other side of the courtyard.

I notified the gazer that I wanted to go back to my cell, and he allowed it. I needed to be alone, even if it meant going back to my tiny room. I hated when people pushed me into things that wouldn't benefit me. It always happened on Second Earth, and that was part of the reason I had wanted to leave my department. Anyma was the only person who knew about it. Jaaspar was nice, but he wasn't someone I would risk my life for just to play in the Exogames.

The bed clanked, as it usually did when I sat on it. It wasn't uncomfortable, though; the mattress was quite soft and provided enough cushioning from the metal bars. I remained lying down on my bed for most of the afternoon and didn't even leave for dinner. The gazer asked me multiple times to join the rest of the inmates, but I ignored him. Luckily, there was no punishment for not eating dinner because it was a punishment itself, and it gave me time to at least consider what Jaaspar had said. Although, I didn't want to.

I ran the thought through my mind once more. If I survived

the games, then I would get to go home early. Alternatively, I could stay here on Mars and live until the end of my sentence. I could play the games and most likely die, or I could stay on Mars and get old and die. I wasn't really considering it again; I'd already made up my mind many years ago, and nothing was going to change my decision.

The tiny glass hole in the ceiling darkened, and I knew the night had come as quick as a thief, bringing my sentence closer to the end date. I was bored lying down, so I propped my back against the wall and closed my eyes. It was freezing cold against my back — the complete opposite to last night's temperature. My ear scratched the opening of the gap on the wall, and I could have sworn I heard someone. For a full Mars year, the adjacent cell had remained empty. The only new inmate we'd been notified of was Jayde, but she was locked in a special cell with increased safety measures.

"Fate? Fate Artemis? It's me," the voice on the other side whispered.

They knew me by my name as well. I poked my eyes through the gap, not knowing what to expect. Nothing. The other side was too dark to see anything past my nose. Even in my own cell, the light had diminished almost completely.

"Fate?" the voice repeated.

I knew all too well whose voice it was. My eyes lit up, and excitement flooded my body. I immediately stepped off the bed and shook my arms around. I covered my mouth with both hands; then, I frowned slightly.

"Anyma?" I confirmed in a muffled voice.

She squealed in excitement, and I knew, without a doubt, it was my best friend, Anyma, on the other side of the wall.

"What the hell are you doing here?" I asked.

"Fate, it's become unbearable. I had to see you again, or at least talk to you. Two years has been too long."

"Oh no. Why? I mean, how did you even get here?" I asked as hundreds of possibilities flooded my mind.

"The only way I could get here. I had to commit a crime," she said, giggling as if it were funny to break the law. "I stole one of the gazer's helmets. But the Council of High Judges only gave me ten revolutions around Mars," she said, as if losing nearly twenty years of her life was something to be taken lightly.

Mars was the prison where all dangerous criminals were sent: the murderers and anyone else who posed a threat to Second Earth. The prison on Second Earth was for the less threatening criminals: thieves or people who caused minor damage to property. Anyma and Jaaspar should not have been sent to Mars for their crimes, and I believed that my 'crime' shouldn't have made me eligible for a life sentence on Mars either.

"You shouldn't have done that, Anyma."

"Are you not excited to see me? Well, hear my voice again?" Her voice cracked when she spoke.

"No, it's not that. It's just that now we are both stuck here. I'm here until I die, and when you go back to Second Earth after ten revolutions, I won't be there. Especially if... no, never mind."

"If what?" she asked. Her mouth was much closer to the

gap; I heard her lips muffle slightly.

"I think I'm considering entering the next Exogames. I didn't want to think about it again but I think I might have a good chance," I responded recklessly, waiting for her to yell at me.

"What the actual f—"

"Just hear me out, Anyma," I interjected. "I'm stuck here for the rest of my life. All of us have the chance to enter a competition and get our freedom back."

"Only if you win. Your father made it to the final round, and you never saw him again. You're playing with fire, Fate. Everyone who plays with fire gets burned."

"All I have to do is survive, right? The Exogames can't be that hard."

"Just stay here on Mars. You'll live longer."

"The days are all the same here. I can't do it anymore. At the end of the day, the day will be done. Then it just repeats over and over."

"When was the last time you saw the games?"

"I stopped watching after my father's year."

"They would have increased the difficulty by now. They always change the games. You can't be sure you'd make it through all of them. And even if you did, our department might not take you back. I mean, do you really want to see Pallas again? She snitched you out! And Vesta, who probably wanted to see you get a stricter sentence? What about Halley? She couldn't even defend you. She didn't believe that you hadn't sent that message. Staying here is better for you."

"Did they say anything about me when I left?" I asked.

"I changed zones straight after your hearing. I never saw them again. But I imagine it wasn't anything pleasant."

Our department back on Second Earth was split into different zones. We worked in the zone for system software and technology development, but for a long time, Anyma wanted to transfer to one of the other zones. It would have also been easier for me to transfer if I were still there because I had already trained to fly some of the spacecrafts.

"I can't live like this anymore, Anyma," I pleaded as I sat on the bed again and moved closer to the gap in the wall. "I hate it here. One revolution on Mars, I managed to scrape by. But another forty-nine, there's no way."

"I can't let you enter those games, Fate Artemis. I just got here," she demanded as if she had authority over my choices.

"Then join with me. I've met someone else who wants to join. His name is Jaaspar. We can all work together and survive the games."

"I don't know. I really don't want to die. What happened to the Fate that was never going to enter the Exogames? Or even consider entering? What would your father say?"

"My entire department turned their backs on me. Up until this very moment I was adamant I wasn't going to play the games, but the more I think about it, I feel that I have to. And I'm pretty sure my father would encourage me to enter. He was a daredevil; it's pretty much in my blood. I just need to unlock that personality trait for myself."

"Do you know anybody who has won the Exogames?"

"Not directly."

"The games aren't for everyone, Fate Artemis, and there hasn't been a champion in over thirty-five years," she said.

She was right. The Exogames were not for the faint-hearted, and nobody had survived them in such a long time. The last time the games were won was before I was born.

"I know what I am doing," I lied. In fact, I was completely unsure if I was making the right decision. I knew Jaaspar would enter, and if he and I were in the games together, we would have a better chance at survival.

"Just be careful, Fate," she mumbled as she pulled away from the gap. "I'll see you tomorrow."

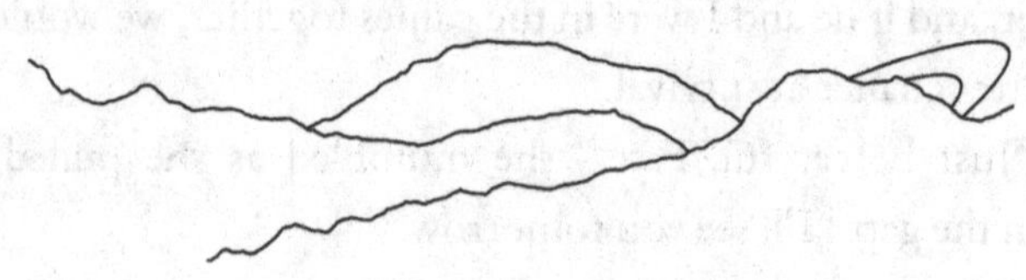

**A** **GAZER RUSHED INTO MY CELL** and pulled me out early in the morning. The sun wasn't as bright as it was on Second Earth, but I preferred it here; it was softer on my eyes, even though I rarely saw it back home.

All the inmates in my corridor lined up in front of their doors. I was the last one to exit. Anyma was already waiting, and the moment she saw me, her arms wrapped themselves around my neck. It felt good to be held like that again, to be noticed.

"I'm entering the games with you," she whispered in my ear.

I wondered what had changed her mind. I wondered what had changed my own.

We followed the gazer to a meeting hall with metal chairs that morphed from the ground just as they did on Second Earth. There was a wall-sized mirror that gave the illusion that the room was much larger than it actually was. It fit all thirty-three inmates, uncomfortably. Half of us sat in the seats, and the rest of us found space on the floor.

A man walked in wearing a tight red suit. He should have unbuttoned his jacket; it looked uncomfortable. He stood at the front of the room and faced us with his tablet in his hand. His assistant — a wiry woman with greying hair — stood to his left and clutched a tablet of her own.

"I'm sure you know why we have gathered you all here today," the man began as he read from a screen.

Jaaspar sat on the other side of the room, away from me, and he didn't look at me once. He was still mad that I had shut him down about entering the games yesterday. I saw it in his eyes.

"The biennial Exogames are in a few weeks, and we would like to extend an opportunity to each and every one of you to join," the man continued. "Five rounds of varying difficulty must be successfully cleared to earn your freedom. If at any point a game is left incomplete or you are unable to continue, you will be immediately terminated."

*Clearly, they haven't got enough participants,* I thought. Usually when an inmate from Mars wanted to join the Exogames, they would let one of the gazers know and be taken back to Second Earth. Two inmates had left Mars to play the games soon after I arrived, but the game makers had never come to recruit anyone from the prison.

"We currently have eight contestants from the prison on Second Earth. If you wish to enter the upcoming Exogames, please stand here and recite your given name. Arachne here will take down your name." He pointed to a space next to his assistant. "I must warn you that this is a verbal contract, and once you have entered, the games must be played."

It didn't take long for people to start standing up and shouting their names. I couldn't figure out why they were so eager to join.

"Jayde Edaj," said the woman Jaaspar had described as lethal.

"Your given name will do just fine," the man said.

His assistant, Arachne, noted her name and welcomed her at the front. Jayde stood very tall with her back straight, and her chest pushed slightly forward. Her piercing stare shot directly at me, but I quickly looked away and covered my mouth with my fist.

One by one, inmates yelled their names.

"Thebe," a thin copper-skinned girl said as she hesitated to walk to the front.

I never spoke to her or any of the other inmates. Jaaspar was my only friend.

"Cobalt."

"Hinata."

Anyma stood up and announced her name, "Anyma." She looked back at me and moved to the front.

Jaaspar called his own name as he looked at me, clearly hoping I would stand up, but I hesitated.

"Kuiper."

"Sol."

There was a long pause before anyone made a noise, and just before Arachne spoke to him, I stood up.

"Fate Artemis," I said.

I had no idea why I said my full name, and something deep inside me hoped that it wouldn't be accepted, but Arachne noted my name and welcomed me at the front. Jaaspar smiled and tried to hide it, but I noticed.

I was the last inmate to stand up. The rest looked away from us as if we had committed even worse crimes than they had. Perhaps they only had a few revolutions left and knew it was wiser to stay locked up than enter a deadly competition and potentially lose their lives.

"Alright, that looks like everybody. Thank you to the eight of you who have chosen to join the next Exogames. We look forward to a terrific event," the man said.

I was sure I had counted nine of us, but I didn't think the man was as intelligent as he looked. The gazers escorted the inmates who hadn't entered out of the room and back to their cells. The rest of us remained with a few gazers, the man and his assistant.

It seemed we had some time before whatever was going to happen to us next. I approached Jaaspar, but Jayde caught my eye before I could say anything.

"We got off on the wrong foot," Jayde said confidently as she stretched her hand out and introduced herself. "The name's Jayde Edaj."

"I'm Fate Artemis." I shook her hand firmly.

Jaaspar still seemed tense from our conversation yesterday. I could see the hesitation in his face before he decided to introduce himself to Jayde.

"Jaaspar Nosna."

I couldn't see where Anyma had run off to, so I would have to introduce her later.

Jayde was much nicer than Jaaspar had made her out to be. At first glance, I also would have thought she killed three people in her department, but once I got to know her, all those assumptions disappeared. She had a small nose ring, and her eyes were bluer than Jaaspar had described them.

"These are gonna be some tough games this round," one of the much older male players said as he invited himself into our conversation. I remembered his name to be Kuiper, like the circumstellar disc in our Solar System.

"Oh yeah? Well, you better toughen up," Jayde said jokingly.

"I just finished speaking to Cobalt. He spoke to that man's assistant, and she told him they are planning a huge event. That's why they had to come here and recruit more of us to join," Kuiper explained.

"I mean, sixteen of us doesn't seem like a large amount for a spectacular Exogames. Some years they've had upwards of fifty contestants. A few years ago, they had over one hundred players," Jayde said.

"I agree. What's so special about the games this year?" Jaaspar asked.

"Don't shoot the messenger," Kuiper laughed, propping up his hands. "But aren't you all a bit nervous we might have to kill each other at some point?"

"Have you not watched any of the previous Exogames, dude?" Jaaspar said with a raised eyebrow. "We don't fight against each other. We just need to survive."

Kuiper gulped and chuckled nervously.

"But at some point, I'm sure we will all turn on each other. These games, they mess with your head. Just stay alert," he warned.

"Watch out, Kuiper. You'd be the first one I'd go for," Jayde said sarcastically.

Her sense of humour was impeccable. I wasn't sure if those types of jokes were appropriate, but I couldn't stop laughing at her comments.

"So, what departments were you all from?" Jaaspar asked, distracting Kuiper from the mess he'd gotten himself into.

"I was in mechanics, level forty-four crew," Jayde said.

"Hey, I was on level forty-three, biomedicine," Jaaspar said excitedly.

"That's where I recognise you from," Kuiper began.

Jaaspar gave him a crooked look as we waited for him to explain.

"I was in biology, level thirty-nine. Our department communicated with yours all the time. We ran documents through to you guys almost every day. I would have seen you around sometimes."

"Most likely. But before I came here, we split up into two separate biomedicine departments so that we wouldn't have to rely on your team anymore," Jaaspar said.

"That was quite a while ago. I think we came here at the same time. I just never introduced myself," Kuiper said.

"What about you, Fate?" Jayde asked.

"I was aerospace. Level eighty," I answered.

"I wanted to transfer to aerospace once, but I wasn't granted the proper clearance," Kuiper said.

Jayde rolled her eyes, and Jaaspar chuckled at her reaction. Kuiper seemed to always have the last word, which didn't sit well with the rest of us.

"It's hard to get a job in aerospace," I explained. "I got the job there because my father originally worked there. And I had to start from a very young age."

"How old were you when you started working?" Jaaspar asked.

"Eleven," I answered.

"Wow, so young," Jayde said.

"I know, but I really enjoyed it."

Arachne called us to follow her to the spaceship for transportation back to Second Earth. From that moment, we were no longer inmates but players in an interplanetary competition of survival — truly a scary and confusing thought.

Each of us was restrained into the seats and put to sleep for a brief time. Space travel had advanced drastically since the end of the world. No fuel was needed to travel at faster-than-light speeds. The spacecraft simply folded the spacetime in front of it and dropped us at the desired location. Our brains would explode if we were awake for the event; it was too powerful.

However, not all spacecrafts worked this way. Some still used traditional fuel, but typically they were smaller vessels travelling shorter distances.

Many scholars theorised the folding event to be a spectacular light show and attempted to travel awake, but their efforts proved unsuccessful. I remembered that many years ago, someone in my department had teamed up with someone from the psychology division and endeavoured to create a device that mimicked the event. I wasn't too sure if they succeeded or if superiors shut down the project. It was most likely the latter. Countless projects were cut from seeing the light of day before they had even begun, more so in my department than any other.

Before we knew it, we had arrived home, back to Second Earth. Our lives were either going to change or end, depending on the outcome of the games — the games I had sworn I would never enter. And now, I was closer to death than I had ever been before.

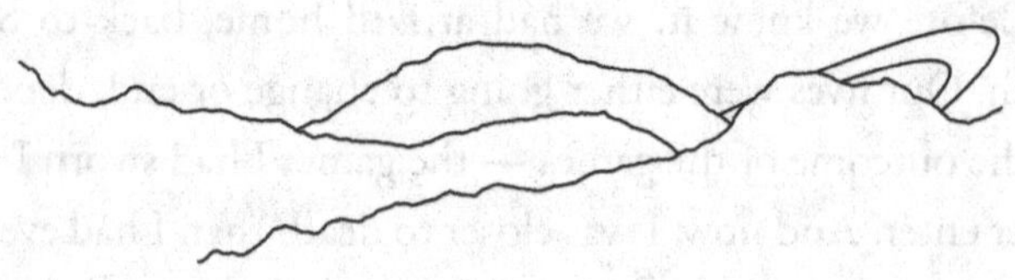

**N**OTHING HAD CHANGED on Second Earth since I'd left. The atmosphere still reeked of dying hope and forgotten mysteries that cowered away in their little corners, afraid to ever step into the light but longing for a moment to be noticed. Jayde and Jaaspar stayed close to me as we marched through a dark and narrow hallway. I assumed the lights weren't working properly in this section, because a bit further ahead, the level was illuminated to the brightness of the sun. This sometimes happened on Second Earth. Sections of particular floors had outages or inconsistent electrical circuit problems that were never going to be fixed.

"Spooky," Jaaspar whispered.

"Scared of the dark, are you?" Jayde asked as she nudged his shoulder.

"I am," I said, a bit embarrassed. "More scared of what I

can't see."

"You have a good point there," Jaaspar said. "We're all scared of things."

"Oh yeah? What are you scared of?" Jayde asked.

"That's a secret."

We took a small flight of stairs to the level above the courthouse on level eighty-one — an all too familiar sector. On Second Earth, any level above ninety-three was restricted for ordinary civilians, including me. They belonged to the game makers of the Exogames — at the discretion of the High Judges.

The gazer leading us through each of the floors paused in front of a black double door and waved his hand over the control panel. It split open into two pieces. He stood to the side and held his arm out, guiding each of us to enter the room.

The lights turned on automatically and revealed a giant board embedded into the wall. It listed everybody's name in the order we had entered the games. The lower half of the board had the names of the players from Mars, with Jayde's at the top of our half and mine at the very bottom. A hologram of Second Earth orbiting its namesake appeared in the centre of the room, and the text 'Exogames 99' spun around it. This year must be the ninety-ninth Exogames. The games didn't start until a few decades after humanity escaped to Second Earth; it took a while to adjust to the new normal back then.

I'd never seen Second Earth from the outside before. None of us had. It looked much smaller than I had imagined; it was approximately half the size of the moon. The lower the levels were on Second Earth, the smaller they became. It was roughly the shape of an upside-down pyramid with abundantly more jagged edges and concave openings.

The door opened once more, and eight strangers walked in, presumably the other players who would be joining us in the games — five women and three men. They varied in age, like those of us from Mars. The oldest one in the group looked to be in her fifties. She tied her hair back behind her ears and left it frizzled and messy. Her wrinkles showed every time she moved a facial muscle, and her skin was much paler than the rest of ours. She was the outlier of the group. The other four young women talked amongst themselves and didn't seem to feel the need to meet the rest of us.

I noticed Thebe, one of the players who joined from Mars, introduce herself to the older woman, but she was quickly shut down. I didn't know if it was because the older woman was nervous or if it was her regular personality, but neither option was good to have in the Exogames. Alliances needed to be formed because the games were far too difficult to complete alone. Thebe awkwardly joined Jaaspar, Jayde, and me to shake off the embarrassment.

"Are you all scared shitless like me?" Thebe asked, not even introducing herself to the rest of us. It might have been easier for her to jump right in at the deep end and skip all the pleasantries.

"I was, but we seem like a pretty cool bunch. I was more scared of the other players joining us than the games themselves," Jayde said, surprisingly. She had initially seemed to be the toughest of all of us.

"I was pretty much the same," Jaaspar added.

"So, how old are you all?" Thebe asked as she fanned air onto her naturally tanned face.

"I'm twenty-two," I answered.

"Same," Jayde said.

"Twenty-four," Jaaspar said as he wobbled from left to right.

"Wow, you guys are much older than me. I'm only seventeen," Thebe said as she tied up hair that was brown at the top and blonde at the bottom.

I widened my eyes and dropped my jaw. She didn't look seventeen. I would have guessed at least twenty-one. Her confidence was much higher than that of most teenagers on Second Earth. For a seventeen-year-old to be sentenced to Mars and then to join the Exogames, she must have committed a terrible crime. I didn't want to be the one to ask her what it was; those types of questions were too invasive.

"You all seem like a solid bunch," one of the male players from the Second Earth prison said as he squeezed into our group. "The name's Neon."

He was a buff kid with styled spiky hair and soft hazel eyes with yellow undertones. I would have guessed he was around twenty years old. But knowing my history of guessing ages, I was probably wrong.

"I'm Fate," I introduced, then went around and stated everyone's names in order of where we stood in a small circle. "Jayde, Jaaspar and Thebe."

"Nice to meet you all. These games are going to be a huge event," Neon said.

"So we've heard," Jayde said.

"That's what Kuiper told us back on Mars." Jaaspar pointed a thumb towards where Kuiper was talking to another prisoner from Second Earth.

"Ninety-nine doesn't sound like a special number to hold an eventful Exogames," I said.

"If you've read about the history of the games, which clearly you haven't," he began as he rolled his eyes, "there was an Exogames before the first. So technically, these games are the hundredth."

"An unofficial Exogames. Thank you for your input," Jayde said to shut him down immediately.

"Let the games begin." Neon smiled intimidatingly.

"Confident much," Jaaspar said.

"Hey, we're all criminals here."

"I think there is a massive difference between criminals and prisoners," I said as I stretched my back straight and stared at him directly in his eyes, not blinking once.

Neon backed away and vanished behind the hologram.

The lights dimmed and the hologram disappeared. All of us bunched into the centre of the room and awaited further instructions from anybody in charge.

"Players of the ninety-ninth Exogames, welcome to your briefing," a deep voice echoed over the loudspeakers in the ceiling. It wasn't robotic like all the other announcements in Second Earth; it was human.

A new hologram appeared, and we spread out like cockroaches fleeing the light. The hologram projected an array of videos of past games in a repeating compilation.

"The sixteen of you have chosen to play a game of life or death," the voice announced.

Again, I counted one more player than the amount stated. Eight from Second Earth and nine from Mars. I checked the leaderboard, and my name was numbered sixteen with nobody underneath me, but I was too preoccupied to figure out who was missing. Nobody was allowed to leave the games once they entered; that was the rule the man in the suit had stated. It was a contract we verbally agreed to.

"The Exogames were created two hundred years ago to give every criminal an opportunity to win their freedom back. It serves as a reminder of your actions in hopes that the survivors are cleansed of their impurities. I am one of the game makers this year. Call me 'Moirai' to shorten things up. Now, the games will test every cell inside your body. A total of five rounds, each varying in difficulty and skill. All will be timed events, some based on speed, and some based on skill."

This information was predetermined, but I understood why he had to explain it. It was probably a legal requirement or a script he had to follow.

"Tonight, we will host a dinner for all of you. I know that the majority of you haven't eaten a good meal in quite a while, so this will be our treat to you before the Exogames begin."

My stomach rumbled at the thought of it, and by the looks on everyone's faces, it was loud enough for them to hear. The food on Mars was terrible, and I hadn't realised how much I missed the food on Second Earth until we arrived back here.

"As many of you know, if you have watched prior Exogames, some players will be given various advantages throughout the games. This is a recent rule implemented ten years ago, and the advantages will be granted at random. The advantages depend on the current game and the number of players remaining. None of you will know the game before it has begun, so sharpen your skills and prepare for one of the best Exogames Second Earth has ever seen. We look forward to seeing you tonight," Moirai concluded.

The lights brightened gradually, and it took a second for my eyes to adjust. A gazer, without a helmet, rounded us all up and moved us into a medical room at the end of the hall.

"All of you need to be examined," she said as she pushed the heavy door forward. It was the only door in Second Earth I ever saw that didn't disappear into the ceiling. "The doctors here will check your vitals and determine if you are all fit for the games."

This wasn't a real medical floor; those were further down on levels fifty-two and fifty-three. I assumed that these doctors were professionally trained for the players in the Exogames. We sat in a random order and didn't speak with each other because it was too uncomfortable. Jaaspar sat nowhere near me, and Jayde was a few seats over. I couldn't find Anyma in the row of players, so I figured she was already being seen by a professional.

"Artemis. Fate Artemis," a doctor called. "You're with me."

I followed the doctor, a thin woman wearing a loose white coat and glasses too big for her face, into a small, enclosed section away from the other players. She sat me down on the bench and asked me to remove my shirt. She proceeded to attach metal circles to my chest, lower back and the sides of my temples. An opaque force field then appeared, blocking my view of the rest of the level and the other players.

"Heart rate looks healthy," she mumbled to herself as she examined the screen on the side. "Breathe deep and hold, then exhale," she commanded.

I did as she asked, breathing in deeply and exhaling slowly through my teeth. I repeated this a few times until she placed her hand out for me to stop.

"Lungs are healthy," she said as she clicked a few buttons on the computer that displayed my vitals. "Alright, Fate," she said as she adjusted the metal circles on my temples. "Close your eyes for me."

The room was sufficiently lit, so closing my eyes didn't make the world completely dark; it just prevented me from seeing. I wished that everything would have gone back to normal when I opened my eyes back up, but it wasn't ever going to happen, and I felt increasingly vulnerable the longer they stayed closed.

"Cognitive." She paused as she clicked her tongue.

I didn't open my eyes because I was scared of not following the rules. However, my curiosity grew heavier in those few seconds as she didn't make any other noise. The cognitive test took much longer than the other vitals, but there was nothing I could have done to speed it up.

"Cognitive... looks good," she said, slowly.

I opened my eyes to the doctor unsticking all the metal circles from my body and placing them back into the little glass jar she had initially pulled them out of. I slipped back into my shirt and jumped up with excitement. I didn't know why I was excited; the Exogames weren't something to be taken lightly. Although, there were inmates with shorter sentences who still joined the games for the thrill of it all.

"Artemis?" the doctor questioned. "That surname sounds familiar."

"It's not a very common last name," I said.

"Have we met before?" she asked.

"I can't say that we have."

I noticed her eyes darting from side to side, trying to link my name to something she must have known. The words were on the tip of her tongue, but she couldn't get them out. She turned to the computer and pulled up my medical history. There wasn't much in there of concern; no broken bones or serious illnesses.

"That's it!" She closed the computer. "Your father was Scorpius Artemis."

"Yeah. Did you know him?"

"I examined his vitals for the Exogames he played. Just like you, everything was in good health."

"He would have been. He really took care of his body when he was alive. He encouraged me to take care of my health too, but I haven't really been focusing on it. I have a few days to get into shape before the games."

"You really should listen to your father. Now more than ever, you will want to take care of your health. The games will test you, not just physically, but," she lowered her voice and leaned forward ever so slightly, "the game makers like to play with everyone's minds."

"So I've heard. It's not just a test of skill or physical ability."

"Hence this pre-examination. I had, in the previous games, a player with poor heart health, and the game makers wouldn't allow him to compete," she said.

"But once someone has entered the games, they aren't allowed to exit. Did they let him go back to prison?" I asked.

"No. You're right, a player can't go back once they have entered the games."

"What did the game makers do to him?"

"They terminated him."

I gulped and gasped at the same time, almost choking on the saliva that had decided my lungs were the best place to settle.

"They escorted him to the airlock and opened it. Poor thing was ejected into outer space like a shooting star. I was there for the whole thing, saw it with my own eyes," she explained.

"Lucky my vitals were all good."

The doctor leaned in again and cautioned as she spoke, almost hesitating before opening her mouth.

"Your cognitive test was inconclusive," she whispered.

"What?" I said a bit too loudly.

"Don't tell anybody about it because they won't let you play the games. You'll be executed before they've even begun."

Not everyone's cognitive test was going to be positive. Some players had mental issues, and although it didn't seem like any of our group had poor mental health, many inmates back on Mars did. If they failed their cognitive tests, they would be terminated from the beginning. Perhaps it was an easy way for the game makers to get rid of prisoners.

"Be careful, Fate Artemis. You don't want to be playing with fire. This is a game of life and death. Play it smart," she warned as she pressed a button that brought down the opaque force field. "Good luck, Fate."

I nodded and proceeded to the other players who'd finished a bit earlier than me. Jayde smiled when she saw that I had also finished and gave me a thumbs up. Everybody else who was waiting hadn't introduced themselves yet, and I wasn't really in the mood to get to know more people. The more people I knew, the more I could lose in the games, and I wasn't prepared for the emotional trauma.

"All good with your pre-examination?" I asked Jayde quietly to not draw attention from the other players or the gazers who stood on either end of where we waited.

"Absolutely. And you?"

"Same. Nothing to worry about," I lied, hoping she wouldn't notice.

"What do you say we explore this level a bit more?" she asked.

I don't know... We could get in trouble." I eyed the gazers nervously.

"As if they're going to punish us. We're already in the games. Isn't that punishment enough?"

I chuckled and thought about it for a moment. The game makers would be able to penalise us if we were caught. But I agreed, realising I didn't care so much about the potential consequences.

"Excuse me." Jayde tapped on the gazer's shoulder. "I need to go to the bathroom," she said, looking at me to do the same.

"I will escort you there," the gazer replied.

"No, you will not!" Jayde exclaimed. "I can find it on my own. I am a woman. How dare you!"

I waited a minute before asking to avoid drawing any suspicion. The gazer crossed his arms and widened his legs to the same spacing as his shoulders.

"I need to go to the bathroom as well," I lied.

"Sorry, bud, but you'll need to wait until the other girl comes back," the gazer said.

"No, you don't understand. I am busting so badly. You're not going to want a mess to clean up," I said, hoping it was convincing enough.

"Alright. Be quick," he said.

I rounded the corner behind the medical room and caught up with Jayde.

"What took you so long?" she asked.

"I was only a minute," I laughed.

We slipped past gazers who were patrolling some control rooms and stopped in front of a hallway without any lights.

"There is no way I'm going through there," I said slowly, taking a step back.

"Come on, live a little. This is exciting," she said.

She was right. After all, I needed to train myself with more fight-or-flight situations. I needed more adrenaline rushes because I didn't want any surprises in the games.

As soon as we stepped into the shadows, a wave of eeriness passed over my entire body. My heart raced, and its beats were deep and heavy. I was pretty sure I could hear Jayde's heartbeat as well, but she was much more skilled in hiding her fear.

A door clanked open just a few metres in front of us, and the lights from inside brightened our view. Jayde and I ducked down and hid in the most shadowed part of the hallway, but there was nothing to hide behind; it must have been hope that helped us become invisible.

"I'm coming back. Leave the door open," someone said as they exited the room and walked into the abyss.

"I want to see what is in there," Jayde whispered.

"No, it's too risky," I warned.

She completely ignored me and ran towards the door. I chased after her and pulled her to the side, slamming against the wall with little noise.

"We are going to get caught," I said.

Jayde covered my mouth with her hand and whispered into my ear, "You are too loud. Shut your mouth."

My body trembled, and I widened my eyes.

We stood on either end of the door and poked our heads in. It wasn't a very large room; there was just enough space for two people to sit comfortably at the desks. My eyes were drawn to the flashing screens, which alternated between various locations and maps of Second Earth. There was a giant panel high up on the wall with all players' names lit up, just like in the briefing room.

"Jayde," I whispered, pointing at our names.

She looked confused, but slowly, I saw the pieces fit together in her mind. This was one of the control rooms for the game makers. I imagined there was a much larger one on another floor, but perhaps this was a designated space for other important parts of the games.

A man pushed a few buttons on the computer he was working at, and on his screen appeared the planet Earth as it remained beneath us.

"What are you two doing here?" The man who'd previously left had returned.

I was one hundred percent sure Jayde and I were both dead. There was no getting out of this, though Jayde was pretty smooth with her words.

"We... got lost," she simply said. "We were looking for the bathroom."

"Move it. Back to medical," he demanded.

I was too stunned to speak or move. My limbs locked into place and my breath became heavy. Jayde grabbed my arm and dragged me out of the hallway.

"Did you see that?" Jayde asked, taking very small pauses between her words.

"The board with our names?"

"Not that, we saw that in the briefing room as well. I'm talking about Earth. Why was he interested in the planet Earth? Nobody has been down there in centuries."

"Do you think it has something to do with the games?" I asked, trying to catch my breath from our half-jog.

"My guess, it does. Everybody's name was on the panel, so

that room definitely has something to do with the games." Jayde looked around to make sure nobody was listening. "Some of us will get advantages. Remember from the briefing?"

"They are given at random," I said.

"In previous Exogames, players wouldn't work together, even with advantages. Players who had been given an advantage were selfish. We have to work together, at least you and me. We know now that they are planning something for Earth; that's our secret. Whether it's for the games or not, we can't repeat it to anyone."

"We have to tell Jaaspar. He trusts me, and I wouldn't be in these games if he hadn't convinced me to join. Definitely, you and I should work together, and we can get Jaaspar as well. We should get everybody in on this. It's the only way most of us, if not all of us, can make it through all five rounds," I said, hoping she would agree with me.

"Of course, I agree. But for now, we keep this between us. If word gets out that we were snooping, our heads could be on the line. That game maker already caught us looking into the room, and we are lucky there weren't any consequences. We can't risk any more until we know for sure."

I crossed my fingers behind my back and agreed. Jayde returned to the medical room first so the gazers wouldn't suspect anything, and I waited outside. This was news I couldn't keep to myself. If Jayde really wanted to work together, she would have to include as many players as possible to give her the greatest advantage. I had to tell the others, but I needed the opportune moment to bring it up. Jayde was right that we needed to wait before we mentioned it to anybody else. She wasn't someone I could trust just yet. My trust had been broken when I was sent to Mars. But if she warmed up to the idea of allowing more players to join our alliance, then perhaps I would have more confidence in her.

"Working together with Jayde, are we?" a voice said from behind me. I didn't need to look to know who it was. I could recognise her voice anywhere.

"Anyma, it's more complicated than it sounds. How long were you standing there?" I asked, turning around to see her appear from the obscured corner.

"I saw you two were caught having a glimpse around here. You mentioned you were working with Jaaspar. Not me? Fate, I joined the Exogames because of you. We are in this together."

"I know. I mentioned that we'd work with all the players."

"It's more important than that, Fate. Every single one of our lives is at stake; get that through your head. You never wanted to join the games, and now you are planning some kind of rebellion?" She was exaggerating, but the disappointment was clear in her tone and all over her face.

"It's hardly a rebellion. It's playing the game smart. The more people we have on our side, the higher chance we all have of surviving the games and getting our lives back," I explained. "You didn't want to join the games either, and if you meant that, you wouldn't be here."

"Just." She exhaled heavily. "Just don't forget about me. I hope you know what you are doing." She shrugged before she went inside to join the others.

I followed shortly after and sat with the rest of the players. Everyone had concluded their pre-examinations, and we awaited further instruction.

Jayde nodded at me without a smile but her eyes had a glint in them, almost as if she knew we were not on the same page about our alliance. But I didn't join the Exogames to make friends. I joined to survive, and return to normality. I definitely wanted her in my alliance, there was no doubt about it, but if she wasn't going to be honest to Jaaspar or the other players, the she needed to find a new team.

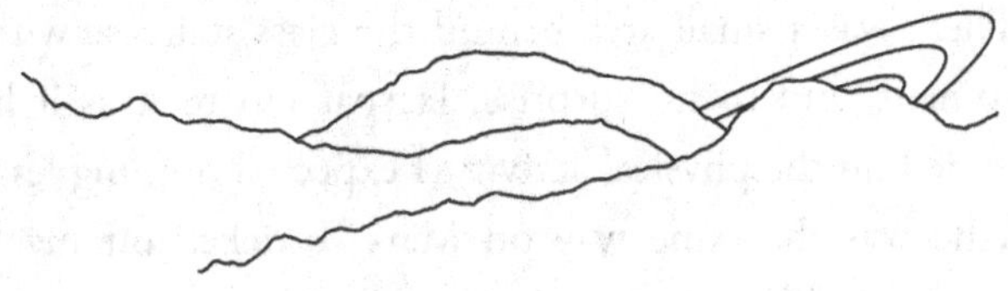

## SEVEN

**I**T WAS STRANGE HOW DIFFERENT my life had become over the last few days. Instead of our regular dorms between levels seventy-one and seventy-seven, we were given gigantic luxurious rooms to spend our days in. There were eight rooms in total, and the seventeen players decided on their roommates. Jaaspar and I chose the first room in the hallway, and it expanded over two floors. A single glass staircase joined the lower level with a smaller mezzanine mostly filled with old paper books nobody would have touched in centuries.

The gazers allowed us to go to our old dorms and collect any important belongings we wanted to have with us. I grabbed as much as I could physically hold because I wasn't sure if I would have gotten a second chance.

"I'm so pumped. This is going to be so fun," Jaaspar said as he tossed his belongings on the couch across from the giant window overlooking planet Earth.

I charged up my dusty tablet after years of a dead battery and unpacked clothing from my bag. Jaaspar and I decided to divide the wardrobe into two sections, but we knew that we would eventually use the wardrobe as if we both owned everything inside it, even if we didn't fit in each other's clothes.

There was a small area behind the glass staircase with gym equipment, and to no surprise, Jaaspar ran to it as if his life depended on the physical activity. I expected nothing less from him; he was the same way on Mars. I kicked off my boots, slumped myself on the couch after moving his bags out of the way, and rested my legs on the fluffy ottoman. The couch was softer than my bed back in my original dorm; this entire room was fantastic. It was primarily an open floor with luxuries fit for a king, an indulgence neither of us deserved. I wondered how many players before us had spent their last days here, and I pondered how many times this room was the mediator between life and death.

My mind raced, thinking about what Jayde and I had discovered earlier and the idea of forming alliances with the other players. Jaaspar would want to know for sure, and I'd definitely known him long enough to share such vital information. I forced my body up from the couch and paced around the room, touching every object I passed: the metal bowl of fake fruit on the dining table, which glimmered in the light; the light strip underneath the kitchen benchtop, which was surprisingly cold; and the hanging pendants above my head, which swung slowly back and forth.

"Fate, are you alright? You seem bothered by something," Jaaspar said between reps of sit-ups.

"I am worried, actually," I responded as I tossed him a clean towel to wipe the sweat from his body. "You might need to sit down for this."

I leaned against the kitchen bench-top with my arms crossed, and he sat on the lowest step of the glass staircase opposite me.

"You're scaring me, Fate. Just spit it out."

"Earlier, Jayde and I explored the level where we had our vitals examined," I said.

Jaaspar leaned further forward, and the glass step creaked slightly.

"We found a control room, and we believe it was a subsection for some of the game makers," I continued as I rubbed my neck, still wondering if this was the right thing to do. I walked to the window opposite the couch and stared at the planet below. "On the screen inside the room were images of Earth, the real planet."

"Do you think it has something to do with the games?" he asked.

"I don't know. I mean, I think it must; otherwise, the game maker wouldn't have had it on the screen."

"But nobody has been to Earth in a really long time. It was destroyed, literally. It's uninhabitable."

"Exactly. That's why we found it strange. Then we got

caught, but I don't think the gazer recognised us. It was too dark to see." I laughed nervously.

"Hopefully, it doesn't backfire on you two. You wouldn't want any disadvantages in the games. They're already going to be difficult as it is."

"So, after that," I said, looking back at him, "Jayde came up with a plan to get as many of us to work together as possible. That way, more of us can get through the games."

"A rebellion?" he asked.

"That's what Anyma said."

"Who?"

"Never mind. But do you think we'd be able to get the numbers?" I asked.

"There's sixteen of us, Fate. There are tens of thousands of gazers, and the population may not be on our side," he responded in a strange tone.

"I'm not talking about a rebellion. Do you really think we'd be able to go against the game makers and High Judges? I'm talking about an alliance between the players so that we survive the games."

"Well, you definitely have me, and I'm sure we can get Thebe on our side. We know Jayde will be with us. What about that Kuiper guy?"

"I'm not sure if he'd be open to joining a team. He seemed pretty set on playing the games by himself, but we can try convincing him," I said. "Neon was keen when he introduced himself. What do you think?"

"No, he was weird. Let's talk to the players who came from

Mars with us and then focus on speaking to the others. It seems like a promising concept, but I'm not convinced that the games are going to be a walk in the park, even if we have the numbers. Sure, we'd have each other's backs, but it just takes one person to hesitate and potentially take the rest with them," Jaaspar said, trying to hide the concern in his voice.

"Even if that happens, both of us can still get through the games."

"And what if an opposing team is formed with more numbers than ours?" he asked with more obvious concern.

"Have a little bit of faith, Jaaspar. Don't be so negative. Tonight is the dinner. We can try to convince everybody to form an alliance. But we have to be subtle about it because I promised Jayde I wouldn't bring it up to anybody yet, and I don't want to be on her bad side."

"Alright, done. We don't know what time this dinner is, so we better take a shower beforehand. You go first," he insisted.

I hadn't taken a shower in days. Back on Mars, water was limited for all of us. It was no secret that there was no water on the planet, and we had to suffer because of it — that was part of our punishment. I had to remember that Mars was my original prison, and the Exogames were still part of my sentence.

The warm water washed over my aching body and soaked into my hair. For a moment, my worries lifted from my shoulders and disappeared down the drain. I scrubbed my dirt-stained skin several times because I still didn't feel clean, and I washed my hair twice over just to be sure it wouldn't be too oily. I must have spent quite a while in the shower because Jaaspar knocked a few times to check if I was alright. I just needed the time to relax my bones and feel the sorrows wash off my body.

I threw the soft cotton towel around my waist and left the shower for Jaaspar to use. By then, my tablet's battery was charged, and I was able to go through the information on it. There wasn't much that I had saved. I rarely took any photos, and half of my inbox was insignificant updates on the projects I was working on back in my aerospace department. Ninety-nine percent of the time, I used my tablet for my work, coding software for the spacecrafts.

I noticed plenty of unread messages I must have skipped past before. I would have been too busy to see them back then. But to my surprise, I saw one from almost a decade ago — from my father. I wished I had seen it earlier, but my tablet had glitched over the years, and it was becoming ancient technology.

My finger swiped across his message, which had a linked video file at the very bottom. I scanned my eyes across the capitalised bold words with shock and read:

## IMPORTANT! OPEN THIS NOW!

It seemed extremely urgent, and my heart was beating quite hard and fast because, somehow, I was only just seeing it. *How important could this message be?* I tried to convince myself that perhaps it was a funny video he sent me ten years ago, but he was never the type to be into humour.

I long pressed on the video file, and it popped open into a

smaller window on a separate page. Immediately, I saw my father running down flights of stairs. The footage was shaky, but I noticed a few gazers chasing after him even in the poorly lit video. The audio cracked when he spoke, and the running and background noise didn't help.

"Fate, listen to me," he shouted as he looked behind him every few seconds. "I've been caught."

The recording must have been moments before his prosecution. I looked at the date it was sent and confirmed that this was two days prior to my father entering the Exogames. He had skipped the bullshit of going to prison and just joined on the spot. If I remembered correctly, his sentence would have equated to five lifetimes in prison. He took the chance at freedom, but clearly, it hadn't been in his favour.

"Fate, they know what I've done," my father continued as he panted down more flights of stairs and eventually through narrow corridors. "They might think you helped me."

My curiosity was piqued when I heard those words come out of his mouth. I wanted to know desperately what my father's crime was. During his hearing, the High Judges hadn't mentioned what he had done; they simply sentenced him without proper reasoning.

"Stay alert, Fate!" he warned. "They think you helped."

I knew I hadn't helped my father commit any crime. I was only twelve years old at the time, and children aren't criminals. I didn't even commit the crime I was later accused of.

"Pay close attention to those around you, Fate. Drop your guard for one second, and the gazers will be on your back."

If I'd opened this video message eight years prior to my sentence, then I could have been more aware of the people around me. I probably would have noticed any suspicious activity in my surroundings, and I could have prevented this whole mess.

"They might ask you questions. Don't say anything without me there!" he said as the camera shook and his words crackled more. "Don't let them interrogate you. They might blame you for my crime or even frame you for another."

A lightbulb flickered in my head like a dying firefly trying to catch its last breath. Nothing about my trial had made any sense: the message from my tablet to Halley; the reason the stop switch was missing from the ship; and the rushed feeling of it all. Stop switches just didn't disappear into thin air, and I was confident that I hadn't typed out that message to Halley. If only they believed me. But it was my word against whoever was in charge — the High Judges, of course.

"Fate, be careful," my father said before the screen dimmed.

Those were not his last words, though. I remembered when I last saw him at his hearing; he told me that he was going to do whatever he could to see me again.

My eyes welled up with tears, and my vision blurred slightly. I tried to blink away the haziness, but that wasn't working how I expected it to. Jaaspar hopped out of the shower and noticed my wretched face pouring out tears all over the couch. I forgot he was still in the room. I forgot about the Exogames, for a moment at least.

"Fate, are you alright?" he asked as he rushed to my side.

I admired his willingness to comfort me, but it wasn't a conversation I felt I was ready to have with him.

"Nothing. I just miss a lot of people," I half-lied. I really did miss a few people, but that wasn't what bothered me.

"I'm sure they miss you as well."

Nobody missed me in reality because all my friends in aerospace had turned their backs on me and pretended I was the enemy. Their betrayal was like a knife penetrating my back, but the knife was blunt, and I was stabbed repeatedly.

A two-tone doorbell rang, and Jaaspar sprinted to answer the door. I had never seen someone so eager to answer a door in my life.

"Nobody is here. Oh, wait," he paused as he leaned over to pick up something.

He walked back towards me with two large boxes in his arms, cradling them as if they were a child. The boxes were almost bigger than he was. They were white with a black lid, decorated with a silver bow, and labelled with our names handwritten on a high-quality card. The box wasn't as heavy as it looked, but maybe it was because we were both nervous and excited to see what was inside.

"What do you think it is?" I said, hesitating before opening mine.

"I'm not entirely sure. Maybe it has to do with the games," he responded as he untied the bow and lifted the lid.

"Obviously, it has something to do with the games; nobody else is allowed on this floor."

I pulled away some of the tissue paper and let it float

elegantly to the floor. There was too much wrapping, although it was beautifully organised. Underneath the paper was a printed note that read:

A SUIT AND TIE FOR AN IMPORTANT OCCASION.

The note inside Jaaspar's box was different from mine. His read:

A SUIT AND TIE FOR AN IMPORTANT ADVANTAGE.

"An advantage?" Jaaspar questioned in a tone that suggested he didn't want to accept it.

"Perhaps you get the first advantage in the games. Congrats, man. That's something to celebrate," I said encouragingly.

"Yeah, I guess. Depends what the game is," he said.

"That's huge to have in the first game. I wonder how many players will have an advantage."

We put the notes aside and lifted out the neatly folded suits. Mine was a dark grey with tiny white lines that weren't noticeable from afar, and Jaaspar's was a very dark blue, almost navy. The ties matched our corresponding suit colour, and we had gold cufflinks to clip the excess material of our buttoned-up shirts.

We tried on our suits to make sure the sizing was correct, and surprisingly, it was spot on. The game makers had thought of everything.

"I don't know how to tie a tie," I said, laughing, hoping Jaaspar was the same.

"Really?" he asked with genuine curiosity.

"I only went to a few events before my father died, and none after. My father used to tie my tie for me. I just never learned to do it myself."

"Here, I'll help you," he insisted as he picked up my tie from the box. "I've done this too many times."

Jaaspar wrapped the fabric around my neck and adjusted the length. He hadn't styled his black hair yet, so it hung in front of his forehead. It was the first time I'd been this close to him. His eyes originally looked brown, but now that I was closer, they were more of a very dark amber and more orange than I initially thought. His light-olive skin tone complimented his eyes and his sharp bone structure. He had a sharp jawline, a sharp nose that was slightly turned up, and his brow ridge was naturally defined.

He tucked the skinnier length in the loop of the larger piece and tightened it around my neck. I assumed we were finished, but it felt as though he was waiting to ask me something or hesitating to get any words out.

"I'm not very confident," he said.

I needed more of an explanation. It was a very vague thing to say, and I wasn't sure I was on the same page as him when he spoke.

"As in, talking to new people? Because I can help you get to know some of the players," I said.

I hated meeting new people because I was an introvert, and I often had to force myself to be more confident.

"Not confident in playing the Exogames," he explained.

"Are you seriously having doubts about entering the games?" I asked, confused and frustrated.

"These games feel rushed, and it's all happening too quickly. I'm not ready to die, Fate."

"Does that scare you?"

"It does if everyone dies alone," he answered, looking down at his shoes. "I don't want to be alone."

"Stop it. You're not going to die. I can promise you that. We have an alliance forming with some of the players. Plus, I entered because you convinced me it was a good idea. There's no backing out now. Even if we wanted to, the game makers wouldn't allow it. If we forfeit our position in the games, they will terminate us. We have to play," I said.

"It's not just that," he began. "Before I was sentenced to Mars... no... I can't."

"Jaaspar, it's alright. You can tell me."

"Before Mars, I had a girlfriend. I loved her with all my heart. But when she found out that I had to stand before the High Judges... she... took her own life."

"Oh, Jaaspar, I'm so sorry."

"She died alone. I haven't been able to get over it. My whole life, I've known death. My girlfriend, my mother, everyone around me dies, except me."

"Do you mind... if I ask how it happened?" I asked softly.

"Overdose."

Jaaspar hadn't mentioned his family before or much of his

past, but it was a small step forward for him to let me into these hidden memories.

The boxes and tissue paper were scattered across the floor in front of the couch. I picked up the scraps and scrunched them into a pile of rubbish, but I felt something hard as I crumpled them. A tiny white pouch fell from the pile and landed heavily on the floor with a thud. We must not have noticed it was there because it was camouflaged by the tissue paper. There was another one pushed against the bottom corner of my box. It was a double surprise.

"Hey, Jaaspar. Look what I found," I said as I tossed him one of the pouches.

"What is it?" he asked nervously.

"Not sure. I guess we will find out."

I pulled open the strings, loosening the opening of the pouch, and inside was a small and shiny piece of metal. Jaaspar received a similar one. There was a tiny etching in the centre, and with proper lighting, it read:

A CLUE FOR THOSE WHO LOOK FOR CLUES WHERE THEY ARE NOT MEANT TO BE FOUND.

"Maybe this is my advantage," Jaaspar said.

"I don't think so because I got one as well," I said, holding our pieces together.

They were pretty similar, both with jagged edges and the same inscription.

"A clue? How is this a clue?" I asked, looking at the piece in the air above my head then towards the ground to come up with any possible answer.

We pondered what it might have meant, but we ended with no reasonable conclusions. The game makers wouldn't have made it easy to figure out the first game before it had even begun. After all, Moirai said that none of the players would know the game beforehand.

"Do you reckon they are testing us?" Jaaspar asked.

"For what, though? Our skills in finding tiny pouches?" I responded with a laugh.

"No. Testing to see who is smart enough to figure out the first game. Maybe that is the advantage. Those tests we did earlier for our heart and cognitive health, perhaps they tested whose brain can figure out this clue," he theorised.

"I understand what you mean, but they wouldn't have just given us these metal pieces. I can only assume that everyone else got one as well. The people who don't find it in the box will be at a disadvantage," I said as I paced up and down the room, dragging my feet across the floor.

"That's what I'm saying."

"But your note said you have an advantage. And the advantages are usually way more significant than a simple clue."

"What if... this is the first game? What if we are playing the first game now," he said, lowering his voice to a hush.

"No, traditionally, they announce the commencement and conclusion of the Exogames. Plus, we still have to attend tonight's dinner. We don't play the games in these fancy formal suits." I shook my head, still hoping the answer would magically appear in my brain.

The more we spoke, the less convinced I was that Jaaspar had watched any previous Exogames. I stopped watching them after my father's year, but I still recalled the general rundown of the event. I had assumed Jaaspar knew what he was doing when he entered, which was what convinced me to join him.

"Maybe it's where the games are. No, that doesn't make any sense. It's a scrap metal piece, not a map," he laughed. "That sounds stupid."

I laughed for a moment with him and looked out the window to the Earth below. The sun was behind us, so the planet was illuminated with sufficient lighting. I stared at my metal piece as I held it with two fingers, then glanced at the planet outside.

My eyes caught the green land masses behind the transparent clouds as they were engulfed with water around the edges.

"No, Jaaspar, you're right! Look," I exclaimed as I held up my piece to the window.

The jagged edges on my metal piece matched perfectly with one of the continents on Earth. Jaaspar held his piece up next to mine, and it matched another landmass: a larger island in the northern hemisphere. His eyes lit up in realisation as he fell back onto the couch and rested his elbows on his knees. His mouth was open but he breathed through his nose, loudly as he tried to fill his lungs with as much air as he could.

"You are right. Jaaspar, you are a genius. These pieces tell us where the first game is," I said in disbelief. "It's on Earth."

# EIGHT

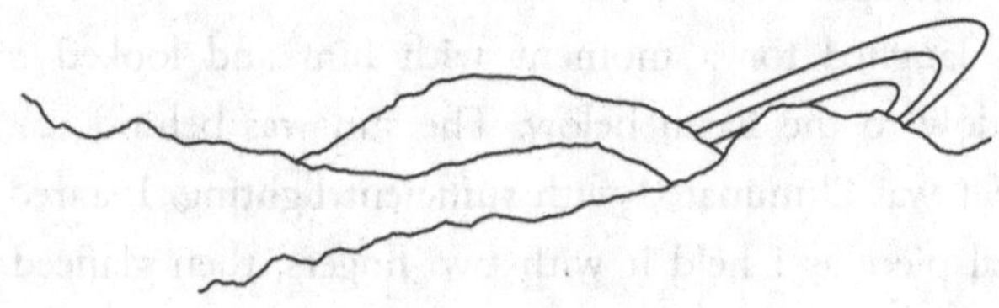

**T**HREE TIMES THE DOORBELL RANG, but Jaaspar and I were too distracted by our excitement to notice the first two times. I opened the door, and a gazer stood directly in the doorway with his arms behind his back and two guns on his holster instead of the one they usually carried.

"Fate, Jaaspar, follow me," he said.

The door automatically shut on our way out, and we followed the gazer to an upper level above our new dorms, level ninety-six. I had never been this high up on Second Earth; I doubted any of the other players had either. These floors were off-limits to the public and were only accessible through special invitation, or in our case, by entering the Exogames.

"Don't mention the location of the first game," Jaaspar whispered into my ear.

I hoped he had a plan because we still needed to build a strong alliance if we were going to make it all the way to the end of the Exogames. I agreed but wanted at least to mention it to Jayde because she was on our side and to Anyma because she had been my best friend since childhood.

The hallway met with a stretched-out red carpet that divided into two separate rooms. The gazer escorted Jaaspar and me into the room on the left, where we met some of the other players. I recognised Neon, who sat on the far end of a giant hollowed-out round table. In the centre was an overflowing arrangement of flowers and four unlit candlesticks. The purpose of the candles was obsolete because there was already sufficient lighting from the light panels on the floor and walls. Eight sets of cutlery and crockery were evenly spaced out around the table.

Kuiper was seated on Neon's righthand side, probably ripping his hair out because Neon was annoying, but it would have seemed rude if he moved seats after he sat down. I also recognised two other players who had joined from Mars with Jaaspar and me. If I remembered correctly, their names were Hinata and Cobalt.

Four empty seats looked lonely as they waited to be filled. There was a single empty chair between Neon and Hinata, but neither Jaaspar nor I were going to sit in that one.

Jaaspar sat directly opposite Neon, where the flower arrangement would block his view. I sat on Jaaspar's righthand side, and I immediately sensed Neon staring at me, even though half of the flowers covered him. My fork was slightly askew, which didn't seem to bother me as much as it did Jaaspar because he realigned it parallel to the spoon and knife.

Cobalt, who sat to my right, nervously trembled as he fidgeted with his cutlery. I could see it from the corner of my eye. I couldn't blame him; I was scared as well. Though, I was not as scared as I had been prior to entering, especially now that Jaaspar and I knew the location of the first game and had started to build an alliance.

Everybody was dressed in suits, which I could only imagine they had received from the game makers like we had. I assumed we had all received the same box, and if that was the case, then perhaps the rest of them had also figured out the clue. I didn't want to be the first to bring it up, but luckily, that was Cobalt's doing.

"Earth," he said simply with his eyes wide open, but he didn't look around the table.

"You've lost the plot, young man," Kuiper said.

"The first game is on Earth," Cobalt elaborated.

Based on his expression, I got the sense that his mind was racing. Jaaspar turned to me, out of arm's reach to nudge me as he usually would, and he shook his head with minuscule movements.

"How do you know that?" Neon asked mockingly.

"The metal piece, inside your box," Hinata answered for Cobalt. He spoke with a light accent.

"I didn't get a metal piece," Kuiper said.

"Neither did I," Jaaspar lied.

"Yeah, me neither," I lied as well.

The door opened again, and two more players walked in with a gazer escorting them. Both had joined from Second Earth, and I hadn't met them yet.

The shorter, chubbier man sat in the empty seat opposite me, blocked by the flower arrangement. The other player sat on Jaaspar's left, accidentally bumping into Hinata as he tried to take his seat. He introduced himself to Jaaspar, and I caught a bit of their conversation. I leaned over and acquainted myself with him because the more people we had in our alliance, the easier it would be to get through the games alive.

"I'm Fate. Fate Artemis."

"Badru," he said.

"I've never heard a name like that before. What does it mean?" I asked curiously.

"It means 'born during a full moon'. My parents were greatly fascinated by lunar events. It's stupid, I know," Badru responded.

"Not at all," Jaaspar said, not very convincingly.

"Did you find a metal piece in your box?" Hinata asked, butting into our conversation.

"No. What metal piece?" Badru asked.

"Never mind."

I was taken aback by what Hinata said because it seemed wrong to disadvantage the other players in a game of life and death. But by the same token, Jaaspar and I kept our knowledge of the first game from the two latecomers as well. And we were probably not the only ones keeping it secret.

All the seats around the table had now been filled. I

wondered where Jayde and Anyma were — and Thebe, whom we'd gotten to know earlier. But only the male players took up the seats in this room. The female players must have had a separate dinner in another room; that was probably why the red carpet split into two paths. I hoped Jayde could convince a few of the girls to join our alliance. But that should have been easy for her, as she was quite persuasive and intelligent.

"Players of the ninety-ninth Exogames," a voice announced from behind Neon. I couldn't see whom it was because of the flower arrangement blocking my view. "Welcome to your last meal," he continued.

I gulped with difficulty as my saliva wouldn't go down my throat easily.

"Only joking. But for some of you, yes, this may be your last dinner. The first game begins in no less than twelve hours."

"I thought the Exogames weren't for a few more weeks," the player behind the flowers said.

"We've brought them forward."

"Who are you?" Neon asked rudely.

"You're a cheeky critter, aren't you? Moirai. They call me Moirai. Game maker of the Exogames. Not head game maker, don't get that wrong, just game maker. Second, in charge, let's say."

I knew his voice sounded familiar. He was the game maker who'd spoken to us in the briefing room. We hadn't seen what he looked like before since he spoke over the speaker system, but now it was clear that his deep voice didn't match his tiny body. Moirai walked around the table as he spoke and tugged at a gold string in his hands.

Eight servants, one for each of us, brought us glasses of champagne. I wasn't a huge fan of alcohol, but it was free of charge, so I decided to drink it. The bubbles tingled and danced in my mouth as the sweet drink coated the inside of my throat. It had a peachy aftertaste, which wasn't as terrible as the last time I drank champagne. Jaaspar took a sip and shivered the moment his lips made contact with the drink. He put his glass back down, looking around the table furtively.

The servants came back and placed our meals in front of us. There were two alternating dishes. I received the olive bread and potato mash, and Jaaspar had the vegetable soup. The bread was soft on my tongue and practically melted like cotton candy. The mix of oregano and olive oil in the little cup beside my plate was warm and soaked into the bread. I left the potato mash because it was a tad too hard. During our meal, game maker Moirai had disappeared, and the rest of us enjoyed our dinner in silence. Not even Neon said a word. All I heard was fizzing champagne, the clinking of knives and forks, and the sounds of everyone swallowing their food.

Slowly but surely, everyone finished their meals and drank all their champagne. Badru called the servant for another glass, but he was ignored, so he snapped his fingers to try again.

"One glass is plenty for all of you," Moirai said as he returned to the table. "You wouldn't want to be drunk through the first game. You will all require a good night's rest because tomorrow's game will test your mind."

"What will the game be?" Hinata asked, trying to obtain

more information.

Moirai pointed his finger at Hinata and said, "Nice try, but you will all find out the instructions a few minutes prior to the commencement of each game."

"Is there a theme to these Exogames?" Kuiper asked as he looked around at all of us. "You know, how the past games all had a theme?"

I stopped watching the Exogames a long time ago, so a lot of what I should have remembered had left my memory. My father's games ruined it for me. The Exogames were meant to be a fun event for everyone on Second Earth. People would take days off work and dress up in fun clothes to watch each of the games as they were played. But over the years, the games had lost their purpose and meaning. They were now the event everyone looked forward to every two years, not so much about refining the criminals on Second Earth.

"I do remember some years back the theme was girls against boys. Is that what you mean?" Jaaspar asked.

"Something like that," Kuiper replied.

"We stopped with the themes many years ago. Now the games are just that, games," Moirai said.

"Can I ask a question?" the player opposite me, who was hidden behind the flowers, said.

"What was your name?"

"Leo."

"Go ahead, Leo," Moirai allowed.

"What is stopping us from leaving the games now? I know we can't exit once we have entered, but theoretically, if someone wanted to leave the games, or rather, escape, could they successfully?"

Moirai applauded very slowly, leaving at least five seconds between claps. He placed his hands on the back of Hinata's chair and stared at Leo with narrowed eyes as he nodded his head.

It wasn't a question that needed to be asked. After Leo's question, the game makers would suspect that he didn't want to play the games anymore or that he was going to attempt to escape. It had happened once — a player attempted to escape the Exogames. He made it out, but it wasn't long before the game makers caught up to him. It was a few years before my father's games, so my recollection was rather vague. I couldn't remember what the game makers did with the player who escaped, but I didn't imagine it was anything pleasant.

"I get that question every time. I'm glad you asked," Moirai said as he walked around the table without stopping behind any of us. "During every Exogames, all players are equipped with a tracking device. It doesn't matter if there are hundreds of you or just sixteen. Everyone will be tracked with a device you all consumed minutes ago."

Jaaspar turned to me with his eyes wide open and his face as white as a sheet. He looked like he'd seen a ghost. My hands trembled as I went to take another sip of my champagne but realised I had drunk it entirely. All eight of us looked at each other in disbelief and confusion, wondering why the game makers didn't just attach a regular tracking device to our bodies as the gazers would.

"Your champagne was filled with nanobots that will link up to our main servers," Moirai continued.

I gagged a bit, but nothing came out of my mouth. I put my champagne glass back on the table and looked away from it. The thought of having tiny robots swimming around in my body was completely terrifying, and never in my twenty-two years alive would I have imagined it actually happening. But it was happening to all eight of us, and it was highly probable that it was happening to the female players in the other dining room as well.

Cobalt pulled his glass up to his face and poked one eye inside to look for the nanobots, but he returned the glass back to the table when he noticed us watching him.

"Don't stress, players. The nanobots won't harm you. Unless you don't play by the rules, of course. Now, on another important—"

Moirai was cut off by Badru, who projectile vomited. His green-brown puke splattered on the floor, in the centre of the table, all over the flower arrangement and on Jaaspar and Hinata, the two players on either side of him. He wasn't the only one who wanted to vomit; I wanted to as well, I felt the bile rise up my oesophagus like hot lava, but Badru was the only one who actually did.

"Never fear, players. The nanobots would have already reached his bloodstream by now. There is no way to get rid of them unless deactivated or filtered out, a facility none of you have access to." Moirai waved his hand to signal for a cleaning team.

The servants who brought us our food rushed to the aid of Badru with small handheld devices. They scanned the floor, and I watched in amazement how their gadgets completely removed the vomit. It evaporated into thin air, and even the horrible smell disappeared with it.

"Back to the second piece of important information," Moirai continued. "As mentioned in the briefing earlier, some players will be given an advantage for particular games. My advice to you all is that whoever has the advantage should use it to help everyone else get through the games."

"At least we know Moirai's thoughts on an alliance," Jaaspar whispered to me.

"All of you would have figured out by now that inside your boxes from tonight were various notes. Players with the advantage for the first game were notified, so please keep it to yourself if you were given an advantage until the first game has begun."

"What's the advantage?" Neon shouted eagerly.

"I cannot reveal that tonight. If you have made any friends, I'm sure the advantage will be revealed to you. I can assure you that you do not have an advantage in the first game if that is what you were wondering."

Neon rolled his eyes and scoffed as he crossed his arms.

"Players with the advantage would have ingested it through their meals, and it will take effect overnight."

I looked at Jaaspar, who stared at his empty bowl. I knew already that Jaaspar had an advantage in the first game, and I was confident there would be more players with this benefit. It was almost a guarantee that both of us would make it through the first game with his advantage. Jaaspar most likely consumed a second set of nanobots from his chicken. He now had twice as many nanobots flowing through his blood as I did. If it were me, I would surely be vomiting all over the table just as Badru did.

"Is there anything else we need to know? Anything we may or may not have ingested?" Kuiper said almost furiously.

"No, that is all. We now just need all of you to wave as this camera comes around. The audience will finally get to meet you," Moirai responded.

A gold metal sphere, big enough to fit in my hand, rose from the middle of the flower arrangement. It hovered above the flowers for a second before it moved around to each of us. To go from discussing the games to announcing ourselves to the audience in the span of a few seconds was slightly concerning. It was as though Moirai was trying to hide something or that he had said too much and wanted to distract us from the truth. But the entirety of Second Earth was filled with secrets to its core, none of which were ever revealed.

"Ladies and gentlemen!" Moirai jovially announced as he stared into the golden sphere.

We all looked around at each other in confusion. None of us knew what to do. Nobody had prepared us for this, for any of it.

"I present to you all, the male players of the ninety-ninth Exogames!" Moirai continued as the gold sphere slowly moved around to each of us. "First, we have Badru!" Moirai exclaimed.

Badru simply smiled and put his thumbs up. He clearly wasn't in the mood to contort his face or swing his hands around with splotches of vomit around his mouth. The camera broadcasted the less-than-spectacular reveal to the people of Second Earth, at least to whoever was interested enough to watch.

"Leo!"

I couldn't see what Leo did, but I assumed it was more entertaining than Badru's introduction.

"Next up, we have Cobalt!"

Cobalt smiled awkwardly and waved at the gold sphere slowly as if he was unsure if he was doing it correctly.

"Hinata!" Moirai pronounced his name completely differently from how I had heard it previously, but it didn't seem to bother Hinata.

"Kuiper," Moirai called him to pay attention as the gold sphere moved to him.

Kuiper jolted awake and smiled with narrow eyes. The camera moved to Neon, who was enthusiastically ready to wave at the camera.

"A little eager there, Neon," Moirai laughed. The rest of us didn't laugh with him. "Next is Neon!"

I was sure Neon wanted more time looking at the camera because he would not stop waving. His smile reached ear to ear as his eyes opened creepily wide.

"Jaaspar!"

The camera hovered in front of Jaaspar momentarily, but he didn't move. There was no smile or even an acknowledgement to the audience.

"Jaaspar," I whispered loudly, but hopefully not loud enough for the audience to hear me. "Jaaspar," I repeated, "smile and wave."

He finally snapped out of his trance and cracked a smile for the camera, although his eyes didn't seem as jolly. It might have been food poisoning that brought him down, or the millions of nanobots that filled his stomach.

"Last, but certainly not least of all, Fate!"

The camera paused in front of my face, and I smiled. The front of the gold sphere had a black lens just big enough for me to see my reflection. There was no hiding my fake smile, and if I noticed it in my reflection, the audience would have as well. I watched it for a few seconds before my smile faded and the camera returned to Moirai.

"Thank you all for a wonderful evening," Moirai said directly into the camera.

Historically, there were events and parties before the first game, and audiences got extremely drunk. My guardian, back when my father entered the games, got a bit too drunk the night before every Exogames. It was quite a mess to go home to, and I am glad I got away from it at an early age.

"Enjoy the rest of the night, and we hope you enjoy the ninety-ninth Exogames!" After Moirai concluded, the camera shot up into a hole in the ceiling. "Players," he turned to the rest of us, "get some rest. You will need lots of it because tomorrow is the beginning of a free life for some of you and the beginning of the end for the rest. Thank you for being a part of the

Exogames this time around, and goodnight."

All the lights shut off except for a thin illuminated path to the exit. Moirai was right; for some of us, this was the beginning of our freedom, but only if we made it through all five games. And for whoever didn't make it, it was the end.

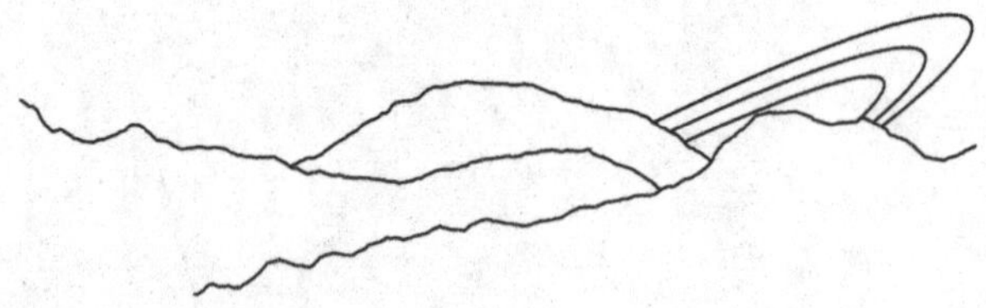

## NINE

**I** **TRIED MY HARDEST TO FALL ASLEEP** so that I would have enough energy for the first game. Every part of my body willed me to sleep except for my brain. I ran through possible scenarios for tomorrow's game. Even though I had absolutely no idea what the game would entail, all possibilities led to death.

Jaaspar must have heard my shallow breaths from the other side of the room because he came over a few times to check if I was alright. Every time he checked on me, I lied and said that I was fine. But I didn't want to be alone on possibly the last night of my life, so when he checked once more, I told him I couldn't sleep.

We moved into the living area where the couch was, and Jaaspar turned on one of the pendant lights so that the room wasn't in complete darkness. He exited through the front door and spoke to one of the gazers who patrolled the hallways.

"Thebe and Jayde are on their way," he said to me when he returned.

The gazers must have been extremely lenient to allow them to visit our room. After all, it was the night before the first game, and we were all on edge.

The door whooshed up, and in came Jayde and Thebe dressed in their plain silk pyjamas — we all looked the same because every player had received a pair. Thebe still had some makeup on her face, most likely from their dinner, and Jayde's hair was messily tied back in a low bun. They shared a room together, just like Jaaspar and me.

"Can't sleep either?" Jayde asked.

"Not just Fate. Me too," Jaaspar said.

I sat on the couch beside Thebe, and Jayde sat on the round ottoman opposite Jaaspar. Jaaspar stretched over the bench and leaned on his forearms as he held his head up with one hand.

"What happened at your dinner?" I asked.

"The eight of us, all the female players, sat around a large table," Jayde began as she adjusted the cushioning underneath herself. "One of the game makers spoke to us about tomorrow's game and the advantage; for whoever has one."

"I have one, an advantage tomorrow," Jaaspar said a little too eagerly.

"We're not supposed to say who has it," Thebe warned, quietly, as if an unknown entity was listening to us.

It wouldn't have surprised me if our conversation was being

recorded. On Second Earth there was no privacy, and we were still not free even in these Exogames.

"I have an advantage as well," Jayde said.

"It sounds like your dinner was pretty similar to ours. We had to smile and wave at the audience," I said, mocking the stupidity of it.

"Us too. It was terrible," Thebe laughed and her small dimples were more noticeable than they had ever been. "Have you got an advantage tomorrow, Fate?"

"Not me."

"Me neither," she responded.

Jayde and Jaaspar were the only two that I knew of with an advantage in the first game. Depending on the advantage, it would allow us all to work together in order to get through the first game. It was either the blessing we needed to calm us down or the curse that would damn the ones without an advantage to a horrible death.

"What are your thoughts on the nanobots they put inside us?" Thebe asked.

"I'm not overly keen on the idea, but I guess if it makes it easier to keep track of us all, then go for it," Jaaspar said.

"You and I now have twice as many as everyone else," Jayde said to Jaaspar.

"It's a bit concerning, hey," Jaaspar said back.

"Did you two also find the clue in your box, the clue for the first game?" Jayde asked.

"We did. A few of the other guys at our dinner also found the clue," I answered as I reached to grab the metal piece from one of our boxes on the floor beside the couch.

"Earth," Thebe whispered. "It's the first time they've taken any of the games back down to Earth. Sure, they play on other planets, but back down there, I'm scared of what we might find."

"We're going to find out tomorrow. Who knows? Maybe we'll all die in the first game," Jayde said.

"Has that happened before?" Jaaspar asked. "Has there been an Exogames where nobody made it past the first game or even the second?"

"The games before my father's year. The furthest the players got was round three. That's when I think they introduced advantages for certain people," I responded.

"That's right," Jayde said as she fixed the hair that had gradually fallen in front of her face. "The only reason the advantages were introduced was so that players would make it to the last game. It's a fairly new rule. Clearly, they want a good show, or else the audience would stop watching."

"I'm glad you two have an advantage tomorrow. I don't feel so nervous now," Thebe said.

"Jaaspar, I don't know if Fate told you, but we are going to work together with as many players as possible to get through to the end," Jayde said.

"Fate mentioned it a few times," Jaaspar said, smiling.

"Thebe is with us too. Did you speak to anybody at the dinner to try and recruit some more players?" Jayde asked.

"Not specifically about joining our alliance, but there are a few players I had in mind that we could work with. Kuiper seemed pretty chill; he spoke with us earlier, if you remember."

"Yeah, Kuiper can definitely work with us," Jaaspar agreed.

"No. Kuiper was strange," Jayde quickly interjected. "He talked about eventually killing off the other players on purpose. I don't want to be murdered at the hands of a psychopath."

"Yeah, you're right. He did say that when we met him on Mars," Jaaspar concurred as he quickly changed his mind.

"Cobalt, I think he'd be good to get on our side. What do you think about Hinata?" I asked Jaaspar.

"Let's see how he does in the first game and then talk to him about working with us. I know I definitely don't want Badru; he vomited all over me," Jaaspar said in disgust.

"Wait, what happened?" Thebe exclaimed with wide eyes as she propped herself forward.

"The player who sat next to Jaaspar puked all over the table, and it landed on Jaaspar."

"Oh, you poor thing," Jayde said satirically and laughed.

"Disgusting," Thebe said, shivering as she made gagging sounds.

"And definitely not Neon. He is too annoying, and he seems like he wants to play solo," Jaaspar added.

"Yes, not him," Jayde and I said in unison.

"When we spoke to him earlier, I got a bad vibe from him," Jayde said.

"Who is Neon?" Thebe asked.

"That guy who always has his hair styled straight up," I described.

"Okay, yes, definitely not him. I spoke to him for a while

after the pre-examination. He bored me to death about his strategies to beat all of us. I don't think he understands that the games are not player against player; they're the players against the game," Thebe said in frustration as she recalled their conversation.

"What about any of the girls?" Jaaspar asked. "Did anyone stick out to you?"

"Sol and Astatine were the two we had a chat with. They're considering it, but I think once they realise they need the numbers, they'll jump on board," Jayde responded.

"I had a really good conversation with Sapphire. We need to get her on our side," Thebe said.

"We can definitely get more numbers. It's just a matter of making sure we can all trust each other and work together," I said.

"I think once the other players realise they need help in the games, they'll come to us. We've planted the seed; now it has to grow on its own," Thebe said.

"Alright, it's getting a bit late now, and we need to conserve as much energy as possible for tomorrow. Earth may not be the paradise it is always described to be," Jaaspar said.

"Well, we know two of us have an advantage tomorrow. I hope it can help us get through the first round — and some other players as well," Jayde said.

"Tomorrow's game will set the bar for the difficulty of the rest of the Exogames," Thebe said as she and Jayde walked towards the door.

"Sleep very well, you two and we will see you tomorrow,

hopefully before the game begins, but if not, then we will survive together," Jayde said as they walked out.

Jaaspar turned to me, half asleep, and smiled nervously to hide his yawn as he placed both his hands on my shoulders.

"Welcome to the ninety-ninth Exogames," he said sarcastically.

# PART II

# THE EXOGAMES

# T E N

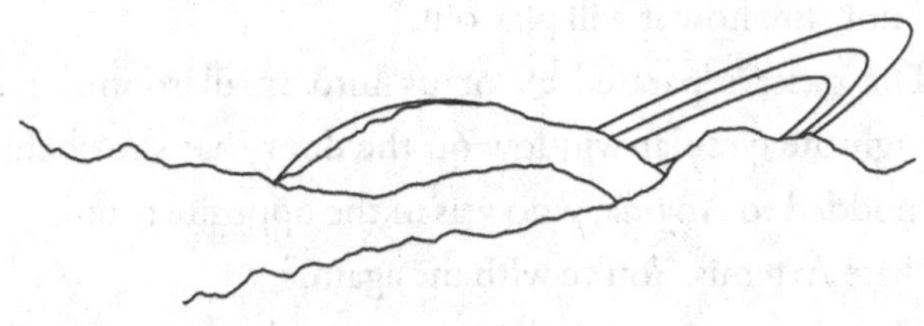

**T**HERE WAS NO SLEEPING LAST NIGHT, simply put. Even after Jayde and Thebe came over and calmed me down, I still struggled to surrender to the darkness that was sleep itself. I wanted and needed to rest, but the thought of dying in the first game kept me tossing and turning.

Jaaspar and I were escorted through the hallway in our pyjamas since we were told to stay in them. My eyelids were heavy, and my back ached as if all the weight of the world were on my shoulders. Jaaspar was the complete opposite. He was wide awake and had the most energy I'd ever seen in him. Eventually, the other players joined us, with Anyma directly behind me.

"Here we go, Fate Artemis," she softly said as she held onto my hand.

"Tag along with Jayde, Jaaspar, Thebe and me. We are all going to get through this game together," I said. "You missed our little meeting last night. Didn't Jaaspar ask the gazer to bring you to our room?"

"No, I fell asleep soon after the dinner. But I'm excited. You guys have a plan."

"Don't be," I whispered as I quickly looked back at her. "I'm not sure how it will play out."

The gazer separated all of us into small rooms. I looked through the circular window on the door that shut behind me and nodded to Anyma, who was in the opposite room.

"Fate Artemis. You're with me again."

There was only one other person in the room with me, the same woman who had pre-examined my vitals.

"Some players take their lives before the games have even begun. It's good to see you've made it through the night alive." She gestured for me to stand on the glowing circle in the centre of the room. It looked the same as the one in the courthouse.

I did as she directed, standing in the centre of the circle. I looked to the ceiling and noticed another illuminated circle directly above my head, the same size as the one beneath my feet. The surrounding lights dimmed, and the two circles flashed once.

"Player eight connected," a robotic voice announced.

Eight was my lucky number, but it was just a coincidence that I was player eight in these Exogames and not an act of God that willed it. The lights turned back on, and the doctor came back into view. I was no longer a real human or even a prisoner.

I was simply a number nobody would care about if I didn't make it out alive.

"Now we have to do something about those clothes you are wearing. You cannot be seen running around Earth with pyjamas on," she said.

She didn't realise that she'd revealed a subtle clue about the first game; two clues, in fact. The first game was on Earth, which I already knew, but it sounded like it would also involve running or physical movement. Although, I hated exercise. I just laughed at her comment and tried to keep my observations subtle.

"No, definitely not," I responded. "What's your name, by the way?" I asked curiously.

"Rubie."

"Just Rubie?"

"Just Rubie," she repeated. "I don't know my parents' last names. I never knew them at all, actually."

"Oh," I said quietly, realising what she meant by it.

"It's okay. I'm past all that." She pressed a button on the control panel. A hidden cupboard in the wall revealed itself, and Rubie pulled out a pile of clothes and placed them on the square metallic table opposite where I stood.

"Change into these; you will be much more comfortable."

I tried to take a step out of the illuminated circle, but something stopped me, a force field of sorts.

"Just wait until your clothes have been incinerated," Rubie said.

"What? Incinerated? With me in them?" I asked in a panic.

The force field surrounding me opacified slowly, thankfully. If I was going to be naked even for a split second, I didn't want anybody to see me. The circle above me brightened intensely, almost like the sun was directly overhead. I covered my eyes with one hand and the top of my head with my other forearm. With a lightning-quick flash, the pyjamas that once were on my body turned to ash. A small vacuum in the floor sucked the charred fabric into the waste system, and the force field faded away.

Rubie wasn't in the room; I assumed she'd exited so I could change. I needed this moment to take captive every negative thought, cast them out of my mind and calm myself down by remembering that both Jayde and Jaaspar had an advantage in this game. I knew I was beginning to panic because my lungs only took in small amounts of air and my legs shuddered when I tried to move. I closed my eyes, took a deep breath in and exhaled slowly through my teeth.

The clothing Rubie left for me wasn't anything extravagant. It was just a simple black shirt and dark-grey cargo pants. Standard black boots waited for me on the floor beside the table. There was also a pair of socks and underwear since my original ones were incinerated along with my pyjamas.

"How do those feel? Too tight?" Rubie asked, giving me a fright. She'd entered the room again without any warning.

"Uh, no, these are perfect, thank you." I tightened the laces on my boots.

The lights on the floor lit up a narrow path to a drop pod at the back of the room. This drop pod looked completely different to any of the other drop pods on Second Earth. It was much larger, enough to fit three people, maybe four if we squashed in like sardines, and it had a solid metal casing as opposed to the regular glass.

"Five minutes until the commencement of the first game," Rubie said as she glanced at her watch. "I have to give you instructions on the game before you land on the ground." She pulled up the instructions on her tablet.

My hands shook as I paced around the room and tried to twiddle my fingers, but the shakiness overpowered my willingness to distract myself. I shook out the nerves and waited for Rubie to read the briefing.

"Game one, Earth puzzle," she read. "Players will be given a twenty-six-hour period to escape planet Earth. To do this, they will need to locate pieces of space bridge portals that have been scattered over the area where the players will land. Three alternating pieces must be found and united to activate a space bridge portal. Once the portal has been activated, only one player can safely cross before it is deactivated. If a second player attempts to cross over through the same portal, both players will expire, as well as any remaining players following the twenty-six-hour period."

I gulped at that last bit. They made it sound so official.

"Portals? As in a gateway from one point to another? When did we invent portals?"

"Second Earth has had them for a while. They are off-limits to the public, hence why you have never seen them before."

"I know we have advanced tech like the ships that fold

spacetime, pretty much travelling faster than light. But portals, that's a game-changer. I have to tell my department about it. They won't believe this," I said excitedly. But the excitement quickly faded when I remembered they had all betrayed me.

"I'm sure they will. If they are watching the games, then they will see the portals in action. It's the first time they have been used in the Exogames."

"I'm a bit confused. What do I have to do?"

"I'll break it down for you. All you have to do is find three pieces, different pieces, of a space bridge portal, alright? Put them together and cross back here to Second Earth. Do not use the same portal as another player, and don't run out of time," she emphasised.

"Okay, you made it sound so much simpler. Why didn't you just explain it like that the first time?" I chuckled.

"I have to do what I have been instructed and read this out to you thoroughly. Every player has to hear the written instructions first," she responded.

"How will I know what the portals look like?"

"You'll know. Just ask your friends."

"Anyma?"

"Who?" she said as she looked at me with raised eyebrows.

"Jaaspar and Jayde," I said in realisation.

Rubie winked before attempting to exit the room.

"What do I do now?"

"Survive," she said as the door shut behind her.

I was moments away from beginning the first round of the Exogames. It was the first time the game makers had hosted one of the games on Earth, and I hoped it wouldn't be a shit show. Nobody knew what was down there. For all we knew, it could be the end of all of us. Perhaps it was the easiest way to terminate all the players at once. Maybe it was punishment because Jayde and I had snooped around after our medical examination, and the other players were about to face the consequences of our actions.

"One minute remaining," a robotic voice announced as the floor lights moved in the direction of the drop pod.

I stepped into the drop pod, and I was automatically strapped in with a hard-shell casing that covered my body. My arms were free to hold onto the handles on my chest, and my head rested comfortably with a considerable amount of cushioning to support it.

"Thirty seconds remaining," the robotic voice said.

The inside was entirely black except for a red emergency button in case the automatic opening malfunctioned.

"Here we go," I whispered to myself, panting as I tried to catch my breath, but my breath was always too quick for me to ensnare it.

"Twenty seconds remaining. Nineteen, eighteen."

The countdown began, and I wasn't prepared. I wanted to go back to Mars and spend the rest of my sentence there, but it was not on the cards anymore. That opportunity was long gone.

"Fourteen, thirteen, twelve."

"God, please let me live through this. I'm not ready to die," I prayed.

"Seven, six, five."

I shut my eyes tightly and waited for the drop pod to move. It should have been only five seconds, but it felt like hours, and the robotic voice continued counting down.

"Three, two, one. Any questions? Too late. Good luck, players."

My drop pod shot out of Second Earth and was free-falling in the direction of the planet beneath my feet. This drop pod was much faster than the ones on Second Earth. My internal organs rose to the top of my head. The only thing that separated me from certain death was only a few layers of metal. The small glass window in front of me was transparent, so I could see outside, but my vision was limited, and my drop pod shook me around as if I were invincible.

The pod linked up with another beside me and then another beside it. Eventually, all the drop pods were linked in a circle, rushing at lightning speeds towards Earth. I knew we had entered the planet's atmosphere when sparks formed underneath the drop pods opposite mine, and the sparks underneath my drop pod crept up to the circular window.

Then I saw something that shook me to my core, something that scared me deeply. It snapped me into reality and made me realise this was all too real, that I was sitting on the fence between life and death, and the Exogames had truly begun. The drop pod directly opposite mine popped open, and the unknown player flew out, burning up in the atmosphere. It could have been one of my friends, and I desperately hoped it wasn't. It could have been me. I held onto the handles so tightly with my sweaty palms, but it made no difference; the tighter I held, the more slippery it became.

Droplets of rain splashed on the glass from the clouds we fell through, and we gradually slowed as to not come to a screeching halt and landed gently in the middle of a dense forest. A thick layer of dust from the ground covered all our drop pods, and the automatic system waited for it to settle before we were allowed outside. I couldn't help but consider the very high possibility that the air was not breathable.

The drop pods opened up, and the players exited in awe as they looked around with dropped jaws and bright eyes. I held my breath for as long as I could because I wasn't going to take the chance at consuming contaminated air. My face turned blue, and I was lightheaded. The other players weren't holding their breath, and they hadn't dropped dead yet, but I was about to if I didn't open my mouth. When I finally inhaled, it was the freshest air I had ever experienced, better than the properly purified oxygen from Second Earth. This natural air was earthy and crisp. It cleared my airways as I sucked it through my nose and let it flow out through my mouth, and for the first time, I felt at home. I felt deep in my heart that Earth was our true home.

The ground was hard underneath my boots but wasn't solid like the metal flooring on Second Earth. It was firm, compact and had life growing through it. Plants, real plants, grew everywhere. I never got to see the plants back on Second Earth; they were reserved to the botanists on level thirty-four. The only time we saw vegetables was when we ate them in the main hall.

Above my head was the sky, a blanket of dark blue with small patches of what looked like cotton. I had never been underneath the clouds; they were always underneath me. I assumed it was towards the end of the afternoon, but I wasn't sure since the daytime was different on Second Earth. A large flock of birds flew by, chirping away. No animals lived on Second Earth; it had been a rule ever since the population escaped the planet. All our meat-based meals were artificially manufactured. Those who had figured this out stopped eating the 'meat'.

I looked behind me, then to both my left and right, but it was all the same, a forest. Twigs and dry leaves crackled under my boots, and the trees rustled in the wind. Grasshoppers churred all around — I recognised the sound because my father had shown me a video of insects once — and lizards scurried underneath the bushes.

I counted sixteen drop pods, but one was burnt charcoal black. I was slightly confused because I had counted seventeen players, eight boys and nine girls, back in the main briefing room. One player must have exited the games early. That, unfortunately, would have been an instant death sentence.

"Jaaspar!" I called with my hand up. "Thank God you didn't die."

"What do you mean?" he asked.

I pointed to the burnt drop pod to my right, and he covered his mouth with one hand then proceeded to inspect it.

"Fate!" Jayde and Thebe called from the direction I pointed.

"You guys made it too," I said as I hugged them both.

"Do you know whose drop pod that was?" Jaaspar asked them.

"No idea," Thebe responded as she attempted to touch it but was pulled back by Jayde who warned her that it was too hot.

Jayde propped herself up on her toes to look around and count the heads of every player who stood in the ring of drop pods.

"Thebe, do you see the girl who sat next to you at the dinner?" she asked.

"Sapphire? Yes, she's over there." Thebe pointed to the short, thin girl with streaks of blue in her mostly bleached hair, who picked up flowers from the edge of her drop pod by herself.

"All the male players are here, so it must be one of the girls," I said, worried that it might have been Anyma, but I caught her staring into the sky.

"Astatine. She's not here," Jayde said.

"I never introduced myself to her," Thebe said with disregard.

"Me neither," Jaaspar and I said together.

"I had a small chat with her at the dinner; she sat next to me. She was the one with dreadlocks," Jayde continued as she moved us to the side, away from everybody who crowded around us to inspect the burnt drop pod.

"Yes, I remember seeing her in the briefing room," I said.

"She was only nineteen and entered the games to try and

give her mother a chance at freedom. Her mother was very weak, she had explained to me, and had quite a long sentence left to serve," Jayde continued.

"Is that allowed?" Jaaspar asked with genuine confusion.

"Apparently, yes. But now I am considering the possibility that the game makers, or even the High Judges, didn't like that she took her mother's place," Jayde said.

"Yeah, I agree. Her drop pod shouldn't have opened like that," I said.

The game makers didn't like what Astatine had done, and they punished her because of it. They could have done the same to Jayde and me. The only reason I could think of as to why we were still alive was that the superiors didn't know we had explored the game makers' room without permission. If they knew, we wouldn't have made it this far either.

All of our drop pods clicked, and gold spheres hovered out, similar to the camera at the previous night's dinner. There was one for each of us. Some hovered high in the air and kept some distance, but mine was at eye level. It was still further away, but the lens followed my movements. The first game was being live-streamed to the audience and the game makers back on Second Earth. We were now at their disposal.

The realisation of our limited time snapped every one of us back into reality, and some players asked around to pair up. Jayde, Jaaspar, Thebe and I had previously decided that it would be best for us to work together, and Anyma was going to tag along with us too. Neon somehow squeezed into our little huddle and joined our conversation.

"What's the plan?" he asked.

Anyma side-eyed me, then looked at Neon. Firstly, it was a 'no' from me. All of us had agreed last night that Neon was not going to join us in the games.

"Why don't you partner up with those two," Jayde suggested as she pointed to Hinata and one of the female players whose name I didn't know.

"What? You guys don't want me to join your group?"

"No, it's not that," I lied as I looked Neon directly in the eyes. "Maybe if we spread everybody around, it will be easier to finish the game."

Surprisingly, he agreed and left our group. I didn't think Hinata was too satisfied to have him either.

"Phew, that was close," Jaaspar said, exhaling loudly.

"Do you two know what your advantage is?" I asked.

"I have no idea," Jaaspar answered.

"Same, I don't know. The instructor, just before we dropped here, only explained what we have to do," Jayde said.

"What was it we need to find? Portals, space bridges?"

"Space bridge portals," Thebe corrected. "We need to find three pieces of a single space bridge portal to activate it, and we cannot use the same portal as someone else, or we die, most likely a horrible death. You know the game makers love that. The portals have all been scattered across this area, and I assume there is enough for one portal per player."

"Sounds pretty straightforward," Jayde said.

"If we each need a portal made up of three pieces, we need to find twelve total," Jaaspar said.

"You mean fifteen," I rectified, but he didn't seem to hear me.

"Do you know what the portals are meant to look like?" Jayde asked as she scratched the tip of her nose.

"I'd imagine they'd be quite large. I don't imagine a portal being activated through a small device," Thebe said.

"How about we start looking around and actually try to find these," I suggested. "We don't know how far the game makers have scattered the portals."

Sapphire was about to leave through a gap between the drop pods, but Thebe called out to her. "Hey, Sapphire, come join our alliance."

"No, thank you," Sapphire responded with a look of concern. "I'm not into joining groups just yet. Give me a few games to adjust to all of this."

"All good," Thebe said. "Good luck."

There was a big enough gap for us to fit underneath the links that connected the drop pods. We crawled through and walked wherever our feet took us, over fallen logs and deeper into the forest.

Mountain ranges shaped the terrain, and each was decorated with more trees. However, a single mountain made of only rock stuck out like a sore thumb. The sun finally sank beneath the horizon, an issue that never arose back home, and the sky darkened completely.

"Shit, this puts us out a few hours," Jaaspar said in frustration. "We can't find any of the portal pieces at night. It's way too dark to hunt the pieces down."

Suddenly, the cameras that followed us shined a light to illuminate our paths, although it didn't make much of a difference for our search.

"Oh... my... goodness," Jayde slowly said as she looked in the distance. "Those must be the pieces."

"What are you looking at?" I asked, confused because the distance was still dark, and trees blocked my view.

I waved my hand in front of her face to get her attention but she was too fixated on what I couldn't see. Thebe clicked her fingers in Jayde's ear to snap her out of the trans but there was no getting her back into our reality.

"Can you not see those?" Jaaspar apprehensively said as he raised his arm to the sky.

Thebe shook her head, and I just looked at him, awaiting a response. Jayde still stared in awe at the sky as if it were obvious what she was looking at, but Thebe and I couldn't see anything.

"What is it?" I asked, terrified of what was concealed from me.

"It's French," Thebe said, randomly. "Sorry, that's something I say when I don't know what is going on. It calms me down."

"I do. I see them," Jayde whispered.

"What is it?" I repeated. "What do you see?"

I needed an answer because the longer we went around in circles, the more my fear settled deeper underneath my skin.

"They're beacons. Everywhere. Lots of beacons," Jaaspar answered.

# ELEVEN

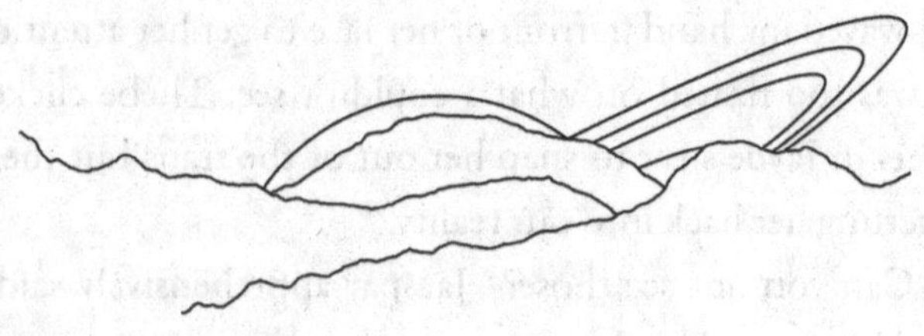

**T**HERE WAS NOTHING IN THE SKY, and not just because it was almost pitch black. But Jayde and Jaaspar saw something that Thebe and I couldn't. They were adamant that a multitude of beacons illuminated the Earth, but Thebe and I were convinced they were hallucinating.

"Jaaspar and I see them," Jayde said, still in awe. "It's just you two who can't."

"We have to go to them," Jaaspar demanded.

"Is it safe?" Thebe said worriedly. "We don't know what they are. For all we know, only you and Jayde can actually see them."

"I think I know why we can't see them," I said aloud, even though I wondered if I should have kept it to myself. But we came into the games together, so it was only right that I communicated everything with my alliance. "Thebe and I don't have an advantage in this game."

Jayde, Jaaspar and Thebe all looked up in realisation, and Anyma glanced at me as if she already knew that vital piece of information.

"Jayde and I have the advantage," Jaaspar said.

I nodded.

"Fate, the beacons probably lead to the space bridge portals," Anyma said, only loud enough for me to hear.

I remembered what Rubie told me just before the drop pods left Second Earth. She said to ask my friends how to complete the game and confirmed that Jaaspar and Jayde would know.

"Those beacons," I began, repeating what Anyma said, "I think they lead to the portals we have to find."

"We have to go to them," Jayde said.

"Wait!" Jaaspar called out as he pointed behind me. "A beacon is moving."

"If those beacons are the portals, and if other players have the advantage, then we aren't the only ones who can see them. Another player must have gotten to it first," Jayde said.

"Let's move," I demanded. "How far is the closest one?"

"It looks like it's just past that tree line," Jayde said.

"I can't see anything, not even the trees," Thebe said.

"The beacons have lit up the entire Earth for us. We can see everything clear as day," Jayde reassured.

"We have to move quickly. One day to find three portal pieces each might not be enough time, especially if other players can see the beacons too," Thebe said.

"There must be plenty of pieces. I'm sure the game makers have scattered them around pretty far," Anyma said.

"Thebe, there might be a way to solve that," Jaaspar began as he combed his fingers through his hair. "I can see three different colours of beacons, red, blue and yellow. Jayde, do you see three different colours?"

"Yes," she answered.

"I'm guessing that each colour beacon leads to a different piece of the portal we need. So, we need to collect each colour to make one portal."

"That doesn't sound too bad if that's also part of your advantage," I said.

"Would it be faster if we split up?" Thebe asked.

"I was thinking the same thing," I responded. "Jayde and Jaaspar, you two can see where the space bridge portals are, so you'll have to lead us to them."

"If we split into two groups, then we have a better chance at making it to the next game. But... I think we should stick together," Anyma said.

"It's easier to split into two groups. It means less work, less walking and fewer pieces to collect," I continued.

"Fate, I'll be with you, and Jaaspar and Thebe can scout together," Jayde suggested.

"You better keep up with me, Jaaspar," Thebe joked.

"I'll join Jaaspar and Thebe," Anyma said to me. "It'll be good to change it up a bit."

"Okay, let's head off in separate directions, so we don't double up on the beacons."

"We'll see you two soon. Good luck," Jaaspar said as his group continued forward while Jayde and I turned back in the direction of the drop pods.

"You're going to have to guide me where to walk because I can't see anything," I said, laughing so that she wouldn't think I was being too harsh.

"Watch out!" she yelled.

I jumped up and screamed in fear at her warning, but she laughed uncontrollably.

"I'm joking, you idiot. Of course I'll tell you where we're walking. We are in this together," she said as she nudged my shoulder.

"You gave me a heart attack, you know," I laughed.

"Alright," she began as she narrowed her eyes and pointed in the distance. "There is a cluster of three beacons, all different colours that way, but we can grab an extra blue one if we go around this way. No, wait, that one is moving; someone else must have gotten to it. We can get this other one over here."

"Yeah, I'm fine to go wherever you say. Just lead the way, and I'll follow."

"Perfect, follow me then."

The ground beneath my boots felt the same as it did when we landed, and the same pine smell tickled the inside of my nose. Jayde occasionally moved branches and leaves out of my way so I wouldn't stumble into them, and she warned me every time we were close to a fallen tree. That's how I knew we were on a different path; there were no fallen trees when we walked away from the drop pods unless I had been too preoccupied with the beauty of Earth to notice.

"How much longer do you reckon until we reach the first beacon?" I asked.

"Another hour maybe. It doesn't look like it's any closer than before. Once we reach the first one, it will be easier to gauge how far the others are."

"We may need to get some rest too," I said, and she snickered softly.

"Let's get to the first beacon so that we've made progress, and then we can find somewhere to camp for a few hours. But we don't want to sleep for too long. Losing time means losing our lives."

"Okay, we can grab the first piece, and then we can rest for a while. My legs are killing me, and I didn't sleep last night at all," I said.

"How could they already be hurting? We landed here not long ago. And didn't you sleep after Thebe and I left last night?"

"They were hurting from before. I must have pulled something earlier. And no, I couldn't sleep. I was panicking about today."

"Right," she said sarcastically before changing the subject. "What do you think happened to Earth? Why didn't humans return sooner?" she asked.

"I don't know," I calmly said as I looked into her eyes, which reflected the lights from the hovering cameras. "The planet is much more sustainable now, but I'm not sure why we didn't come back. I have heard stories, though, about how the Earth was initially destroyed."

"I've heard a few as well. Back home, we had some interesting personalities that came up with theories on the end of the world," she dramatically said as she lowered her voice and laughed.

"You were part of level forty-four, right?"

"Yeah, I was one of the lead mechanics."

"So, how did *you* end up in the Exogames?" I asked cautiously, unsure how she'd react. Jaaspar had told me about her crimes back when we were on Mars.

"It's a long story."

"We have all night. There's time."

"I was wrongly accused. My crime, apparently, was that I murdered three of my fellow coworkers," she began. "But they died at different times, and I was nowhere near them when they were killed. I had alibis and witnesses to prove my innocence, but the High Judges didn't believe me. They still sent me to Mars to serve one hundred and seventy-five revolutions."

"Shit, that's over three hundred Earth years!"

"Yeah, I couldn't believe it either. But when the opportunity arose to enter these Exogames, I jumped at it. I need my freedom back since it was unjustly stolen from me."

"From us. I hope we can all make it out of these games alive. We deserve our freedom."

"What about you?" she asked. "Why were you sent to Mars?"

"It's a shorter story than yours. My name was on the passenger list to journey to the asteroid belt. I never asked for my name to be put there, and I wasn't supposed to be on any ship leaving Second Earth. But the ship exploded soon after take-off."

"How did you survive?"

"I wasn't on the ship," I answered, squinting to see the silhouettes of logs and trees.

"And that makes you a criminal?" she asked in confusion.

"Apparently, it's a crime against Second Earth." I mocked the way Tethys, my interrogator, had said it.

"Reminds me of Jaaspar's crime. Actually, not his crime, but the fact that he also said he was innocent," Jayde said as she demonstrated air quotation marks with her fingers.

"When he and I were on Mars, he told me why he was sent there and that he was wrongly accused. Now we are in this game of life and death, competing for freedom that was already ours," I said.

"Now that's three of us, Jaaspar, you and me, who shouldn't even be here."

"Perhaps this isn't a conversation we should be having out in the open," I said as I pointed to the hovering cameras I had forgotten temporarily.

"We're almost at the first beacon," Jayde said as she began to half-jog in its direction.

I followed her as we disappeared into the foliage. Jayde crouched down next to a small bush that was covered with thick branches and waved her hand over it.

"The beacon is coming from here," she said, trying to grasp it like it was a string.

I crouched beside her, moved away the branches and dug through the bush at its roots. Jayde must have noticed it before I did because she reached into the centre of the leaves and pulled out a trientsphere not too much bigger than her palm. It was the same shade of gold as the hovering cameras and had a latch on both of the flat sides. It was decorated with grid lines that were evenly spaced on the curved side, exactly how lines of latitude and longitude look on the planet Earth. I recognised it from my younger years back in school. Geography was not my strongest subject, and none of us students really cared because we were never supposed to return to Earth. But the more I thought about it, the more it seemed plausible that it was all planned from the beginning.

"One down, five to go," Jayde said.

"Let's find the other ones. No rest tonight," I said through my fatigue.

"Are you sure?" she asked. "What about your legs? Aren't you tired anymore?"

"I am, but we need to find more pieces before the other players. I just pray that Jaaspar can find the pieces too."

"Jaaspar can see the beacons as well, so they'll be able to find the portal pieces much faster than the players who can't see them," she responded. "I hope he makes it out alive," she whispered under her breath.

"What was that?"

"Oh, nothing," Jayde answered hesitantly.

I raised both my eyebrows at her and didn't respond.

"Alright, but you can't tell anyone."

"Okay, my mouth is shut." I was taken aback. I could tell Jayde was about to share something personal with me, and I wasn't prepared for it.

"I think I like Jaaspar," she said, speeding up her words towards the end of her sentence.

"As in... romantically?" I asked.

She nodded, and her cheeks filled with light pink pigmentation. I wasn't sure Jayde and Jaaspar would look good together because he was much shorter than she was, but if Jayde felt that way about him, then it was worth giving it a chance.

"I was in another relationship that didn't last. Don't date anybody from work," she laughed.

"No way. Everyone in my department has... interesting personalities."

"Good. Don't fall into the same trap I did. I kind of wish Jaaspar didn't have the advantage. I wish you had it so that I could partner up with him and search for the portal pieces."

"Wow, thank you for that reassurance. It really gives me a confidence boost," I said sarcastically as we both laughed. "He's going to need someone to love him. He's been through a lot."

The hovering camera's flashlight glinted in her eye, and I froze on the spot. Jayde's secret had been broadcasted to all of Second Earth.

"Oh no," she said in disappointment. "I completely forgot they were there."

"It's alright," I tried to reassure her. "Nobody will tell him." I was lying. Jaaspar was sure to find out the moment we arrived back on Second Earth.

Whoever couldn't see the beacons was at an enormous disadvantage. There was less than one day left to find three matching pieces to make a portal back to Second Earth. Even with the advantage, our time seemed limited.

"Alright, we have to keep moving. The cluster of beacons is that way," she said, pointing to my left. "I can't see any other moving beacons around it. If there are any players around there, then they either have no portal pieces, or they can't see the beacons."

"I hope it's the latter. We need them, desperately."

I shot up from where we were crouched and felt piercing pain in my leg. I didn't say anything because I didn't want Jayde to feel that we had to stop just because of my injury. Jayde got up just as eagerly and walked in the direction we needed to go.

"The ground here is smoother than before." She used the beacon light from the portal piece we found as a flashlight — the beacon light only she could see.

"Perfect. It'll be easier on my feet."

"So, back to our conversation from before," she began.

"Yeah? About Jaaspar?"

"On how we think the Earth was destroyed, or rather, why humans left," she corrected. "What were some of the stories that you've heard?"

"I've been told that it was a doomsday event," I said dramatically, as I waved my hands around. "Apparently, according to the ancient Mayan calendar, the end of the world was supposed to happen way back in the year two thousand and twelve. Massive earthquakes and volcanic eruptions, tsunamis as well. All terrible natural disasters that should have split the Earth in half," I answered as I laughed.

"Clearly, that didn't happen since the Earth is still here," she said, laughing with me.

"I know. What about you, what stories have you heard?" I asked.

"The same. Natural disasters were meant to end the world. But another theory I heard was that there was a frightening war between all the nations here. A nuclear war ended the human population, but the wealthy people that knew what was going down set up Second Earth, and many escaped to it."

"That theory sounds a bit more credible," I said as I accidentally tripped in a small ditch and lost my balance.

Jayde caught me by my shirt, and I almost choked as the collar dug into my throat. We walked in silence for a bit afterwards because it was slightly embarrassing.

"Something must have changed, though. Not much of the population on Second Earth is wealthy," I said, coughing and massaging my throat to release the tension.

"Well, you know the High Judges probably confiscated everyone's money. That's why they're in control."

Through the eeriness of dense brush and towering trees, only the cry-howling of outcast wolves fractured the deafening silence, a sound that made me jump out of my shoes and sent my stomach turning. My insides flipped, and my knees became weak.

"The show begins," Jayde said as she looked around to find where the sounds originated.

"We better start moving faster."

"Run," she whispered loudly.

My legs followed hers into the abyss. I ignored the pain and pushed through my emotions with all my strength — every ounce of it that I could find. Dry leaves cracked under my boots once more, and I knew we had strayed from the path to the cluster of beacons. At least, I assumed so because Jayde had said that the path ahead was smoother.

"Okay, we should be alright now," she said as she attempted to catch her breath.

I struggled to breathe as well. We had gone from a casual stroll to sprinting through bushes and jumping over logs. I wasn't cut out for it. I should have listened to my father's health tips when he was still alive, or at least trained with Jaaspar back on Mars.

"What did you make me run for?" I asked.

"This isn't our territory anymore. The Earth hungers for blood. The wolves were close. Would you rather be their dinner? Because I sure as hell wouldn't," she explained.

Once we both stopped huffing and puffing, we continued at a regular pace towards the cluster of beacons. Or so Jayde said. I trusted her because she had gotten us to the first portal piece. If she wanted me dead, I'm sure she would have killed me by now.

"I have a feeling you want to ask me something, Jayde," I said, recognising her hesitation because it was something I felt all the time.

"What makes you say that?"

"You're never this quiet, and you keep looking at me as if

you're about to say something. Even though it's dark, I can still sense your glance."

"The most likely reason for the Earth's destruction was a nuclear war, which means that this planet must be flooded with radiation right now," she said.

"Nobody has been on Earth in about three hundred years. The radiation would have disappeared by now," I reassured her.

"Sometimes radiation can stay in an area for thousands of years," she said, convincingly, although it was unlikely that the Earth was still radioactive.

"If there were still radiation here, we would surely die."

"I think we're immune."

"How are we immune to radiation?" I asked.

"When we lived on Second Earth, we were exposed to the sun's rays without any atmospheric protection. Humans have been soaking up the sun's radiation for centuries. It's a miracle we haven't died yet."

"If we don't get superpowers now, then I'm going to be very disappointed."

We chuckled at my joke, which I didn't think was very funny, but Jayde had warmed up to me and seemed less intimidating. I think she considered us as more than just acquaintance, or allies in the games. She was softening and warming the frost around her heart, and gradually pulled down her walls.

"Hey, I know before I said we should keep moving, but do you reckon we should stop and rest for an hour?" I asked.

"We're almost there, Fate. I promise once we get those portal pieces, we can stop and rest," she said.

She was tired too. Although I couldn't see that she was physically exhausted, I heard it in her breath. She tried to cover up her heavy panting by stomping her feet louder, but that just made it more obvious.

The wind was colder in this part of the forest. It was a nice breeze that cooled down my overheating body. It made the sweat under my armpits more noticeable and extremely uncomfortable, but I was just grateful to be alive at this point.

"There is another beacon moving closer to the cluster," Jayde said as we paused for a second. "We have to move faster. Quick, Fate, we have to move!"

I limped through my strides and breathed at an uneven pace through the forest. Jayde was much faster than I was, even though she was slightly shorter than me. I imagined Jaaspar was faster than me as well. He was the most athletic of all of us.

The howling of the wolves echoed through the forest once more, much closer than before. Jayde continuously nudged me away from trees that seemed to appear out of nowhere and directed me towards the beacons.

"Here. We're here," she said as she slid to the ground and crash-landed on what sounded like a rotten log and small twigs.

She punched through the log's side and pulled out another portal piece. It was the same shape as the first one, with the exact same etchings over its curved side.

"The other two pieces are just over there," she said as she turned around and pointed ahead.

In a small crevice underneath tree roots was another portal

piece, and the third was just further up and wedged in the crack of a giant boulder.

"Here, you take this one," she said as she handed me the first piece we found. "These three have different colour beacons, so I'm assuming they connect with each other. The one you have is blue; we just need the red and yellow ones to go with it."

"How far are the closest red and yellow beacons?" I asked.

"There," she slowly said as she brought up her hand and pointed to one of the mountains in the distance.

Those mountains looked relatively far when we landed. In the dark, they looked even further away, blending with the black sky.

"That one is red; the closest yellow looks like a twenty-minute walk from here. From yellow to red, maybe an hour or two, depending on how bad your leg feels," Jayde answered.

"What about the wolves?"

"As if I would know. I don't know how to fight off any animals," she said with a bit of a scoff.

Frankly, I didn't either. None of us was cut out for this. But I supposed it was a faster way for the game makers to get rid of us one by one.

"Get some rest; we will need it for that hike," she said.

"What if some of the other players try to get our beacons?" I asked.

"We'll sleep in turns. I'll take the first shift," she said. She tried to start a fire but couldn't manage to ignite any sparks.

"Just leave it. We don't need a fire," I said, slightly shivering through the cold.

"Will you be alright without any heat?"

"Sure. I've slept in plenty of cold places before," I lied.

I hated the cold, but I would have rather suffered freezing to death than watch her struggle at attempting a fire. Life skills wasn't a class taught in school back home. It had been many years ago until it was scrapped because superiors didn't think humans would return to our home planet. They didn't want a repeat of the Titan expedition where we lost contact with the entire crew.

"The beacon that was moving towards us turned away."

"That player probably realised we got here first," I said as I patted the ground and smoothed my hand to brush away any leaves from the dirt.

Jayde looked at all three pieces in her possession and brought them close to each other. This was technology nobody on Second Earth had, not even in aerospace, so it was just as intriguing to me as it was to her. The pieces locked together magnetically with a high-pitched click, and Jayde pulled her head back.

"Woah," she said in awe. "The beacon... it's brown now."

"How does the portal open?" I asked as I rolled flat on my back and rested my head on my palms.

"Not sure. There's no button on it. I can't even pull the pieces apart anymore," she said, struggling to pry them from each other again.

"We'll figure it out; don't stress," I said, nodding to her as my heavy eyelids shut.

"Goodnight, Fate."

# TWELVE

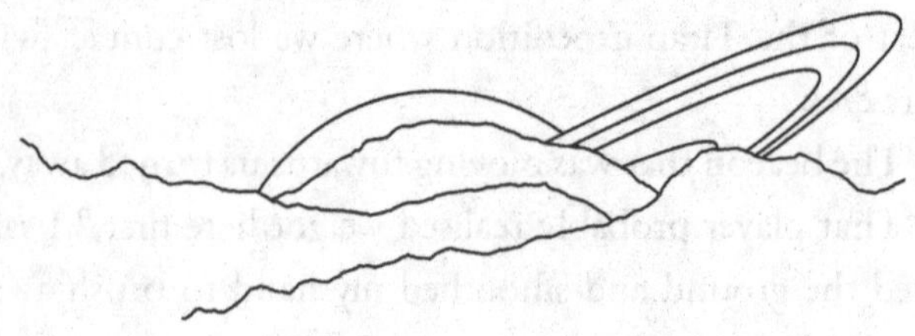

**I** **EXPECTED TO WAKE UP** to Jayde nudging at my shoulders to take her shift so she could rest, but it wasn't her that woke me. It was the huffing of a creature only a few metres from my feet. Its low growl reverberated through the air, and its sharp white fangs sparkled brighter than its piercing white eyes.

I carefully brought my legs closer to my body and pushed myself up with my hands. I saw its eyes follow me as I tiptoed to Jayde, but I didn't want to show any fear that might provoke it. Its fur was black in the darkness, but when the hovering camera shined a light over the wolf, it reflected a white-grey mane.

Jayde was asleep on the ground, too tired to notice. She was as exhausted as I'd presumed, but she was pretty good at hiding it.

"Jayde," I whispered as I crouched beside her and tugged at her arm.

She jolted back into reality and rubbed her eyes.

"What is it?" she said aloud, unbeknownst to her that we were moments away from imminent death.

"Shush," I whispered with my finger on my lips.

It took a second for her to notice the wolf that I hadn't broken eye contact with, not for a moment. She slowly got up, looking as ready to sprint as I was. It was our primal instinct.

"Fate, what are you gonna do?"

"Not me. You need to activate the portal and get us out of here. I don't know what to do."

"But only one of us can go through, remember? It's one portal per player."

*Far out,* I thought with frustration and on the edge of losing control of my emotions. There was no way out of this, at least without one of us ending up dead.

"Alright," I began as I came up with somewhat of a plan on the spot. "You take the portal and get back to Second Earth. I'll figure something out."

"I'm not leaving you here," she begged.

"Jayde, please. It's the only way. That thing looks hungry, and I don't want you being its dinner."

The wolf took a few steps towards us as we maintained the distance and stepped back. From what I'd read years ago, wolves travelled in packs. Either this one was all on its lonesome, or its friends waited eagerly nearby to pounce.

Its growls grew in volume until it barked thunderously loud, booming and echoing. The wolf's eye twitched, and I broke my eye contact with it.

"Run!" I screamed.

The wolf chased us through the entire forest. I didn't care if branches slapped me in the face or if I lost my balance. Whenever we took a sharp turn, the hovering cameras would whizz past our ears before turning back to follow us again.

"I'm going to let it chase me. You go back home," I shouted, hoping she would have listened to me.

"You're crazy! It'll get you; let it follow me," she said as she split away from me, going left as I continued straight ahead.

The huffing wolf stopped following me, but I didn't realise it until I slowed down. Its barks continued to my left as it pursued Jayde. I feared for her life. And as I waited for something to happen, I realised that there were probably more of these dangerous creatures in the forest, and I feared for Jaaspar, Thebe and Anyma, too.

As I stared in the direction Jayde had run, I wondered if she'd made it out alive. The wolf had stopped barking, and I didn't hear anything from Jayde either. For too long, there was silence.

*The wolf got her.* Terrible thoughts crept into my mind, thoughts that I wanted to get rid of almost as immediately as they entered.

Suddenly, an enormous triangular beam of light emerged in the distance and closed just as quickly. In the few seconds that I could see it, I recognised the other side — Second Earth was the same as it had been for the last twenty-two years of my life. I wiped away some of the blood from small scratches on my arms and face, and I sat, with relief, on the hard soil. I rested easily, knowing Jayde had made it through the first round, and I just needed to do the same.

# THIRTEEN

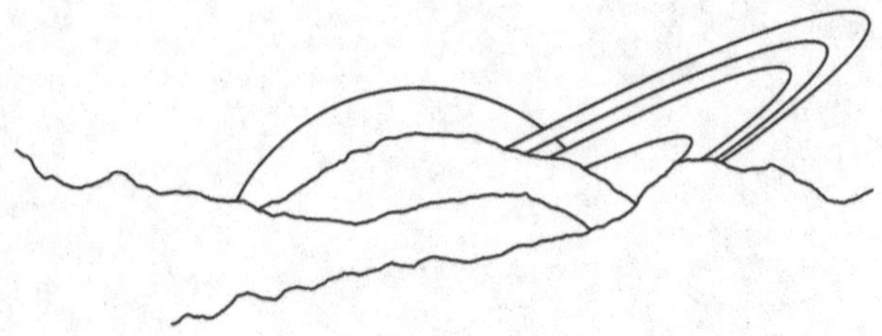

**S**UNLIGHT PEEKED THROUGH tree trunks and slowly rose as it kissed the tips of the leaves. I clutched my single portal piece in my right hand and backtracked as much as I could remember. The mountains were all around me, left, right and centre, so it was almost impossible to remember which Jayde had said the red beacon was on.

I paused for about five minutes and stood in silence, taking in the natural sounds as I composed myself. Birds chirped as the morning wind rustled the dry leaves around my feet, some trapped beneath my boots. They reminded me of myself — the leaves — they reminded me of all of us. All connected until they fall, and when they fall, they become free, until someone comes along and traps them. I felt that Jayde was the most trapped. She suppressed many of her emotions, and even though she never really expressed it to me, I noticed it when we were alone.

I decided to try my luck with one of the mountains closest to me, a shorter one in a group of three and headed in its direction. If I stumbled across spare portal pieces along the way, it'd be a bonus. My guess was that I had less than twelve hours left. It seemed like there was plenty of time, but in reality, I was panicking deep down that I wouldn't make it out alive. This panic struck harder because I had nobody with me who could see the beacons.

Couldn't the game makers have put us on a nice tropical beach somewhere? The one chance we had to visit Earth, we were surrounded by bugs and bush.

Nevertheless, I continued walking through the forest, slapping at mosquitoes that landed on my arms and swatting at flies that decided my face was the best place to rest. Once, back on Second Earth, there was an outbreak of insects that should have been contained on levels thirty-four to thirty-nine. The entirety of Second Earth was swarmed with flies, mosquitos, cockroaches and even locusts. It was a nightmare to live through it. But the biologists were quick to act and managed to exterminate all the bugs. The tedious part was cleaning it all up, but thankfully, only the biology department was ordered to clean the mess. After all, it was their fault.

The wind died down pretty quickly, but leaves were still cracking from within the trees, accompanied by footsteps. At first, I assumed it was another wolf, possibly the same one that had chased Jayde and me, but it wasn't.

"Hello," I called as I leaned against a tree to get a closer look.

The leaves on the ground cracked again, and a shadow quickly disappeared behind another tree.

"Hello. Is anyone there?" I said just to reassure myself that I wasn't seeing or hearing things. "I can see you," I lied, hoping whoever was hiding from me would come into view.

It became more obvious that somebody was there because I recognised one of the hovering cameras around me.

My trick worked. One of the female players revealed herself. She had lightly tanned skin, bright green eyes and straight blonde hair resting over one shoulder. She didn't look any younger than thirty years old. I didn't recognise her from Mars, so she obviously entered the games from the prison on Second Earth.

"My name is Fate. What's yours?" I asked as I crouched down slightly.

"Um, my name?" she muttered under her breath as if she'd forgotten her own name. "Emerald," she answered.

I then noticed what was clutched in her hands like prizes she had won — multiple space bridge portal pieces, a total of three.

"Are you alone?" I asked as my eyes locked onto her portal pieces.

She nodded slowly.

"Where are your friends?" I asked, remembering the group she was with at the briefing.

"We split up." She had the same idea as my alliance, although she didn't seem too impressed that she was no longer with the rest of her group.

"How did you find those?"

She looked up into the sky and then all around us, turning around slowly, then looked at me again.

"I can see them," she said.

"You can see the beacons as well? You have the game's advantage too. You have three pieces; why haven't you gone home yet?"

"I don't have enough," she said as she gradually became more comfortable with my presence.

I raised my eyebrow and tilted my head.

"I have two yellow and one blue. I still need a red one," she explained as she came out from behind the tree and walked towards me. "You have a blue also," she said, staring at the piece in my hand.

Emerald showed me that if we tried to connect two of the same portal pieces together, they would force themselves apart. This prevented the players from cheating the game or at least trying to find an easier way out.

"Yes. I still need the yellow and red pieces to open the portal."

"There's one just here," she said, pointing at a pile of leaves behind me. "Didn't you see it?"

Emerald dug through the pile of leaves and into the dirt and pulled out her final portal piece, a red one that was noticeably dirtier than her others.

"I can't see the beacons."

"I thought you also had the advantage," she said with concern as she backed away.

"My friends could see the beacons. Jaaspar and Jayde. You

would have seen them before the games."

"I met Jayde at the dinner but don't know who Jaaspar is," she said. "Where are they?"

"We split up to find the portal pieces faster, just like your group did. I tagged along with Jayde, but we were separated. It's a long story, but she crossed over to Second Earth not long ago. At least, I hope she did; I'm not too sure exactly. I need to find the other pieces before the time runs out. Can you help me? Please?"

"I work alone. Always have and always will. I don't want anybody owing me any favours, and I don't want to owe any favours to anybody else," Emerald said as she clicked her three pieces together. "I know Sapphire is helping all the other players find the beacons. She can see them too."

"Wait, before you go!" I called a bit too loudly. "Can you tell me where I can find another red and yellow portal piece?"

"Take this yellow one," she said kindly as she tossed me her spare one. "It doesn't count as a favour, by the way."

"It's all good; I wasn't expecting it anyway."

"Where were you headed?"

"Into the mountains," I answered.

"There's nothing there. The closest red beacon is quite a distance. Just keep walking that way and check carefully everywhere." Emerald physically turned my body and pointed straight ahead into the thick forest. Fog still blanketed the ground. "The game makers have hidden them pretty well. Check under rocks, inside trees and any part of the ground that looks like it has been tampered with."

"Alright. I'll make it. Thank you for this."

Emerald grasped the complete portal in her hand, which was now in the shape of a sphere, and threw it out in front of her. The sphere split into three separate pieces, which hovered in the air and were connected by thick lasers. The large triangular shape became opaque and gradually cleared itself up. Second Earth was on the other side, along with two gazers waiting to welcome Emerald. The warmth from the portal's lasers radiated onto my skin. She stepped in and paused before turning around to me.

"Can I ask something?" I said to the gazer who stared at me with his hand on his gun.

"What is it?" he said with his other hand stretched out to ensure I wouldn't step foot inside.

"My friend, Jayde. Did she make it?" I asked as my heart pumped faster.

The gazer didn't answer at first, but I assumed he was just being cautious that I wouldn't enter the portal at the same time as Emerald, and I didn't want to put her life at risk either.

"Jayde?"

"Uh-huh," I responded.

"She made it through," he said.

I nodded and thanked him.

"Fate, good luck," Emerald said as the portal closed and the pieces imploded into themselves.

The game makers probably programmed the pieces to self-destruct so players wouldn't reuse them. I wished that wasn't a rule. I could have made it across with Emerald or even earlier when Jayde made it through. But that was the game.

Emerald's instructions were pretty clear; I just needed to keep walking in the same direction to find the last portal piece. I hoped Sapphire wasn't looking for the same one or anyone else who could see the beacons, even Jaaspar. As much as I wanted him and the others to finish the first game, my life was more important at this moment.

I didn't blame Emerald for leaving me here. It might have been easier to give me the portal, considering she could find the red beacon faster, but I completely understood her decision not to help me. That said, I wouldn't have been able to do the same if I were in her position. I would have made sure that I helped as many players as possible. I just wouldn't have been able to leave this game knowing some players wouldn't make it out alive.

I scanned the ground thoroughly, checked underneath every rock and cracked open obvious gaps in tree trunks to find the last piece. I kept one piece of the portal in each of the pockets in my cargo pants. They bulged out quite a bit and were very heavy, so I had to keep pulling my pants up every so often.

"Fate!" I heard someone scream mutedly through the forest, accompanied by the heavy stomping of feet and whooshing of air.

My heart was beating extremely fast. I propped myself up onto my toes to try to see who'd called me. Perhaps Jayde. No, Jayde already made it through. Maybe it was Jaaspar.

"Fate!" they screamed again, more obviously a female voice.

That definitely ruled out Jaaspar because his voice was much deeper. I narrowed my eyes to see the silhouette running towards me and stepped back to not become a crash-landing zone. My body relaxed once I saw who it was. Anyma. But she should have been with Jaaspar and Thebe, collecting their portal pieces nowhere near where I was.

"Fate, I lost them," she said between breaths.

I wasn't one to jump to conclusions, but the way she said it made it sound like Jaaspar and Thebe were dead.

"What... what happened?" I asked, almost hyperventilating in worry.

"One minute they were with me, and the next, they were gone. I don't know where they went. What about you? Where's Jayde?" she asked.

"She made it back to Second Earth."

"Without you?"

"We were being chased by a wolf. I told her to go without me," I answered.

"How many more pieces do you need?"

"One. You?"

"Three," she said, embarrassed.

"Did Thebe and Jaaspar go back to Second Earth?" I asked, frustrated that they'd left Anyma.

"I'm not sure. They just disappeared."

"Did any of you have any portal pieces before they disappeared?"

"I don't know," she answered.

None of what Anyma was saying made any sense; she couldn't have lost Jaaspar and Thebe if they all stuck together as they should have. And the fact that she was unaware if they'd found any portal pieces was confusing. If Jayde and I had found enough to get one of us back to Second Earth, they should have found some portal pieces too.

"Okay... okay. We can find a way through this."

"Neither of us can see the beacons, Fate. There's no way out of this game," she said softly, resigned.

"We have to try. We have to."

"How, when we have no indication of where the pieces are hidden?"

"There's another player who can see the beacons. Sapphire. If she's still on Earth, we might be able to get her help."

"Fate, there is less than half a day to get off this planet. Don't you see? There's no way we can both make it out."

I didn't want to believe it, but what she said was true. It was impossible for both of us to make it out alive. I only had two pieces, and Anyma had none. I had no clue where Sapphire was or if she would even help us. I didn't know if Emerald had lied about where the red beacon was or if I'd gone in the right direction. These games forced the players to lose their trust — and not just with other players, but with themselves.

"I know where the last piece is to complete my portal," I said with no confidence at all.

"Then let's not waste any more time," she said as she gestured for me to lead the way.

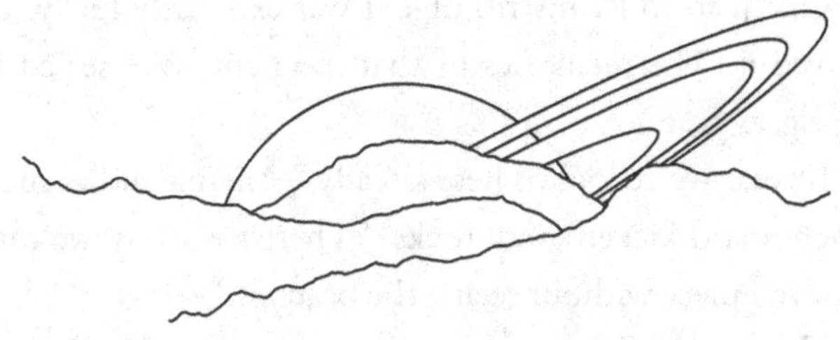

## FOURTEEN

THE AFTERNOON SUN INCHED CLOSER to the horizon, teasing the Earth as it willed itself to hide away from us. Anyma helped me look for the portal piece, but we were still out of luck.

I was going to give her the completed portal once we found the last piece. I didn't tell her because I hated conflict, and I didn't want her to convince me to go without her.

Anyma's eyes scoured the ground, using the limited sunlight to try to find the final piece. She searched low while I tried to see if there was anything shiny in the trees. The game makers could have hidden the pieces anywhere. Jayde and I had found them in all sorts of weird places, so it was pretty much guaranteed that the next portal piece would be concealed very well. If the piece was somewhere up in the trees, I didn't want to be the one to climb up and get it. I had a fear of climbing, not so much a fear of heights, just climbing.

Years ago, I had climbed up the side railing of one of the flights of stairs on Second Earth. The sweat on my hands made me slip off the bars, and I fell a few metres down onto a pile of unopened crates. I crashed into them and sliced open the side of my waist just under my rib cage. I was extremely lucky to have survived it. The memories of that moment were sealed in the long zigzag scar.

"I swear we've looked here already," Anyma said as she lifted branches and kicked away rocks. "There's no way we can find the portal piece without seeing the beacons."

"Have faith, Anyma. Emerald sent me in this direction. I have no reason not to trust her. We have to work together, not just you and me, but all of us," I said as a gleam of light caught my eye.

I assumed it was the hovering camera and tried to smack it away without looking, but the camera was closer to the ground. The flashlight that came from it reflected off another shiny object camouflaged in a spread of dry yellow leaves and branches.

I knew exactly what it was before I picked it up, but I didn't want to jinx it. Anyma and I walked over to it slowly, trying not to crunch the leaves too much. I crouched down carefully, as only the wind and I were moving. Not even the leaves on the trees made any noise. I splayed my fingers out into a fan and wrapped them around the golden metallic piece in the centre of the pile of leaves. I pulled out the other two portal pieces, which were already magnetically attached. I felt the third piece tug towards the other two and swiftly lock into the gap to complete the sphere.

"We've done it," Anyma said.

"I know. We found it," I said between breaths, still in disbelief as the sun finally sank beneath the horizon.

The grid lines all over the completed portal glowed and slowly dimmed as if it were breathing.

"Here," I said as I held the portal out for her.

My eyes welled up momentarily, but I blinked the blurriness away. Of course, I was ecstatic that one of us was going to make it out of here alive, but at the same time, I wasn't ready for the Grim Reaper to snatch me away. Anyma stared at the portal for a moment and shook her head.

"No," she whispered. "You collected those pieces. It's yours. We can find three other pieces for me."

"In less than an hour? I doubt it. Take it. Please," I begged.

Anyma turned the other way and marched off. I followed her footsteps into the dark, using the glowing portal light and the illumination from the camera as a guide.

"Anyma, hold up," I called.

"Take the portal home. I'll find three pieces and make it back," she answered.

"You're lying."

"Am not," she said in a very high pitch. "I know what I'm doing."

"You're not thinking properly. Come back. We need to find the other pieces together," I said as I caught up to her.

"You don't get it, Fate," she said as she swung around and faced me. "I'm dead already. You have the portal, and I have no pieces."

"Any—"

"Just... let me not think about dying right now," she said sadly.

I nodded and tried to hold in any tears that wanted to break free. We continued walking and made it to an open field with barely any trees. The cloudless navy-coloured sky was sprinkled with millions of tiny sparkling spotlights. The stars were much nicer to look at from the surface of the planet. I only ever saw them from my dorm back on Second Earth, and from there, they were only giant balls of burning gas freely roaming outer space.

"Look up," I whispered, trying to remove any negative thoughts from my mind.

"Wow," she breathed a sigh of relief. "It looks so much better than from Second Earth."

The stars twinkled and moved closer towards us as if they were falling from the sky. Suddenly, thousands of lights flashed around us and on the ground near our feet, rustling and buzzing in the trees.

"Fireflies," I said.

I had never seen them in real life. I never dreamed of seeing one, let alone an entire swarm. Their wings buzzed softly as they flew in circles around us and glowed in sync with the lights on the portal.

"Wow," Anyma said as she held up her hands and caught

one.

If there were no time limit to this game, I would have sacrificed my life on Second Earth to spend the rest of my days here on this planet.

The fireflies flew into the sky above and disappeared towards the stars. A noise emerged from the hovering camera.

"Five minutes remaining until the end of the first game," the robotic voice announced.

I heard Anyma turn to face me, and although I didn't see the worry or stress on her face, I imagined it was eating her up inside.

"That's the only warning? Not even ten minutes? Fate, what do I do?" she quivered.

I looked around as if I would be able to come up with a solution on the spot.

"Fate," she repeated.

"I don't know," I answered. "If you keep moving, it'll take your mind off of things. It'll take your mind off the game."

"What are you saying?" a voice asked from the shadows. "Who are you talking to?"

I couldn't see his face, but I recognised his voice from dinner the other night.

"Badru, what do you want?"

"That portal," he answered.

"This is mine. You will have to find your own."

"Give it to me," he demanded as he inched ever so slowly towards us.

"Anyma, run," I commanded quietly.

Anyma and I turned and ran in the same direction, not knowing if we would crash into any trees or slip in the mud. Badru's panting was loud as he chased us, but we were slightly faster.

"Fate Artemis!" he yelled. "Give me that portal."

"Activate the portal!" Anyma screamed.

"What?" I shouted, knowing exactly what she'd said.

"Now!"

I had no idea how to open the portal, so I slowed down for a second to glance at the sphere as quickly as I possibly could. If only I could remember how Emerald had opened her portal. But my mind was flooded with adrenaline. Badru was close; I heard his breaths behind me. After finding no words or instructions on the portal, I continued sprinting and caught up to Anyma again. Badru was still too slow to catch us. He heaved and groaned with every stride as he struggled to get closer to us.

"I can't open it," I said, worried that neither of us would make it out alive.

"I don't know, Fate."

"Twenty seconds remaining," the robotic voice announced from the camera.

"Argh," I yelled in frustration. "What the hell am I supposed to do with this... this stupid ball?"

"I've got it. Fate, what do you do with a ball?" she asked.

"Tell me," I said with too many answers in mind.

"Throw it."

I brought my arm back behind my head and hurled the completed portal far in front of me. It exploded into its three separate pieces, and thick white lasers connected each of them. The warmth from the portal radiated onto our skin.

"Ten, nine," the countdown began.

"Jump through with me," I said.

"It's only one player per portal," Anyma reminded me.

"Fuck it. Both of us are going through."

The lasers blended into a thin opaque sheet, which cleared to reveal the inside of Second Earth. Two gazers pointed their guns and stared sharply at us.

"Both of us can make it," I said with hope. "Run!"

"Four, three." The countdown was almost over.

Anyma and I dived through the portal and landed on the other side. I fell awkwardly on my back, which bruised up soon after.

"We made it," I sighed with relief.

"One." The countdown ended, and the gazers each fired a shot at Badru.

Badru yelled out to me with his arm outstretched as I watched him horrifically explode. Splotches of his blood landed at my feet just before the lasers to the portal turned off, and the planet disappeared from sight. I screamed and pushed myself away from the portal. I shakily turned to Anyma with my eyes wide open and heavy breaths coming from my mouth. We broke one of the rules to the first game, and I prayed neither of us would explode because of it.

# FIFTEEN

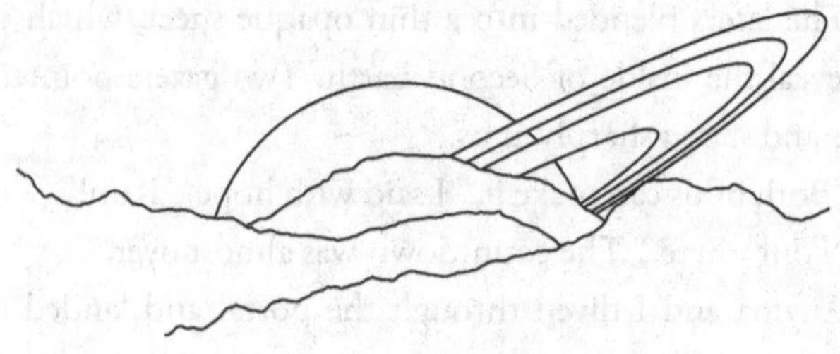

**F**LUORESCENT LIGHTS MOVED in the direction of the open door to our left. The hovering camera shut off its single, useless light and whizzed through the door first. Anyma went through before me without any hesitation. I could feel she wanted to get away from Badru's blood. I just stayed on the floor for a moment and thought about how lucky we were to have made it through the first game. The next game was sure to be much more difficult, and I wasn't entirely confident in my skills.

A gazer came through the door and stood in front of me momentarily. His boots smeared Badru's blood, but I didn't think he noticed — or if he did, he didn't care. My eyes would never be able to un-see what I'd just witnessed. A human being had exploded in front of me, popped like a balloon. My hands trembled, and my legs didn't seem to want to move.

"Fate Artemis, your presence is required," he said as he directed with his hands for me to stand up.

I followed him through the door into a large holding bay and was relieved to see Jaaspar, Thebe and Jayde unharmed. Jayde and Thebe ran to me first and threw their arms around me. Jaaspar rubbed his hands through my already messy hair and squeezed me between his arms as well.

"I was worried you wouldn't make it," Jayde said, nearly tearing up. "I'm so sorry I left you. After I got here, I realised I shouldn't have activated the portal. It was so stupid of me."

"I have Emerald to thank. She led me to the last portal piece. We nearly died out there," I said as I nervously laughed.

"Who is Emerald?" Jaaspar asked.

I looked around the room and spotted her with Cobalt and Neon.

"That one over there, with blonde hair and green eyes," I said as I pointed.

She caught me pointing at her and smiled, acknowledging that I made it through with her help.

"How long ago did you two get here?" I asked.

"A few hours ago," Jaaspar answered. "We struggled to get to some of the beacons. Once we found enough for one portal, I sent Thebe through, and I looked for the rest of the pieces alone."

Thebe smiled and nudged Jaaspar. "He had heat stroke," she said worriedly. "He's alright now, but you should have seen him. He couldn't stand up straight."

"The gazers probably didn't care. Typical."

"They actually rushed to his attention," Thebe responded. "I know. I was really surprised."

"That's a first. The gazers never give a shit about us. When did everyone else get here?"

"Jayde came through just before Jaaspar," Thebe said. "I was so excited to see you, Fate, but you didn't show up. You have no idea how much we were all stressing about you. Jayde told us about the run-in you had with the wolf."

"I thought it got you, the wolf. I thought you were dead." Jayde hugged me once more. "Sorry," she said as she let go of me. "It's such a relief to see you alive, to see all of us alive."

"Drinks?" one of the servants asked as she came around with a tray of champagne propped on one hand and her available arm behind her back.

We all grabbed one, even Thebe, who was only seventeen. There was no legal drinking age on Second Earth. The majority of the population was pretty responsible when it came to drinking, except a select few who always took it too far at parties — especially the parties during the Exogames.

"Hey, you!" Kuiper shouted from the other end of the room as he stormed over to Cobalt, Neon and Emerald with flared nostrils.

The entire room went silent, and all eyes were on Kuiper as he threw his empty glass at Cobalt and let it shatter on the ground.

"Whoa, why is he so angry?" Jaaspar whispered.

"I thought you two said he was chill," Thebe said.

"He was," I responded. "No idea what's gotten into him."

Neon disappeared away from the tension timidly, but Emerald stayed to protect Cobalt.

"Kuiper, you're drunk," Emerald said as she held out her arm. "Think about what you are doing."

"I am thinking clearly!" he mocked loudly. "This idiot left my team and me for dead," he spat his words out, pointing at Cobalt and shaking his arm around.

"Kuiper has been here for a while, and he's had quite a few drinks," Jayde said.

"Cobalt could see the beacons too," Thebe explained. "He told me when he made it back."

"I'm sorry... I... I panicked," Cobalt pleaded.

"Watch out in the next game, Cobalt. You're a dead man," Kuiper warned.

His words didn't sound like a bluff. After all, he had been the one talking about murdering the other players during the games. It was only a matter of time before it actually happened.

The room livened up afterwards, but we were all still a bit on edge after Kuiper's scene. Never in a million years did we imagine Kuiper would throw his glass at someone and yell at the top of his lungs. The games changed people, and Kuiper was the first victim.

"What did Kuiper mean, that Cobalt left his team?" Jayde asked, more so directed towards Thebe because she spoke to him earlier.

"Cobalt had teamed up with Kuiper and a few others to try and find some of the portal pieces," Thebe explained. "Cobalt came back alone, and the rest of the players he was with hadn't come through yet. I can only assume that he left the others to search for the portals without any direction on where to find them."

"Damn, that's tough," Jaaspar said. "What happened to the others that were left behind?"

"I assume they will slowly die off unless they find a way to survive on Earth," Jayde said with no confidence at all. "I don't remember if the rules said anything about it."

"The players exploded," I said, strangely calm. It was easier to talk about if I detached from my emotions.

Jaaspar and Thebe gasped, and Jayde shook her head in disbelief.

"I saw Badru explode just before my portal closed."

"Explode? As in blow up, blood everywhere?" Jayde asked.

"Yes."

"That's... very concerning," Jaaspar said slowly. "Whatever goes through the game makers' heads is not right."

"Yeah, that's a bit extreme," Thebe said. "Even for the Exogames, there's no need for the theatrics."

Moirai entered the room and tapped his gold ring on his champagne glass to get our undivided attention. The entire room hushed, and we all watched him step onto a pedestal at the front, not too far off the ground. He was too short and I wouldn't have been able to see him if he didn't stand on the raised platform.

"Congratulations, players, on making it through the first game," he announced without needing to project his voice too far. "This one was a close game. Unfortunately, four players were unsuccessful. May we take a moment of silence to remember them."

The only players I knew hadn't made it back were Badru and Leo, the male player who sat opposite me at the dinner. I didn't get to know him too well, nor had I met the two missing female players. Although, we had figured out previously that Astatine was the player who died as we entered Earth's atmosphere. Kuiper spent the entire moment of silence giving Cobalt a death stare from the side, and although I was in a similar situation where I was left behind, I couldn't imagine the anger that boiled up deep inside his heart.

"Thank you," Moirai said as he stretched a gold string in his hands to the point where it looked as though it was about to snap. "Now, you are all lucky, and not just because you made it past this round, but because there is a small break until the next game. You should all have familiarised yourselves with the rules by now. As the games progress, the difficulty level will increase. The third game will be played immediately following game two."

Hinata fainted when he heard those words. I would have too, but I managed to avoid the embarrassment. I was already struggling to keep myself upright. There was no way I would have been able to keep myself awake through the next two games. I guessed this was another way for the game makers to get rid of us.

"Get some rest now," Moirai recommended. "The next games will be tough. However, it is also important to note that, unlike the first game, no players in the second game will have an advantage. The next advantage will be in the third game. Some players will receive those nanobots shortly." He paused and touched his earpiece. "Never mind. The nanobots have already been consumed by players chosen through a random lottery. The second game will begin tomorrow, and you will be briefed on the task beforehand. Good luck, and goodnight."

Everyone dispersed across the holding bay, and some were quick to exit the room.

"I'm going back to our room," Jaaspar said. "Are you two visiting for a bit like last time?" he asked Jayde and Thebe.

"I think we're just going to rest up as much as we can. It's the appropriate thing to do, especially since we have back-to-back games coming up," Jayde said, ever the intelligent one.

"I'm going to the pool to relax. I'm completely drained," I said.

"There's a pool on this level?" Jayde asked with excitement.

"I saw the door to it before we dropped to Earth. It's on the opposite end of our dorms. You'll see it; your room is closest to it," I responded.

"I must not have paid attention to anything going on around here."

"That's where I'll be if anyone wants to join," I said.

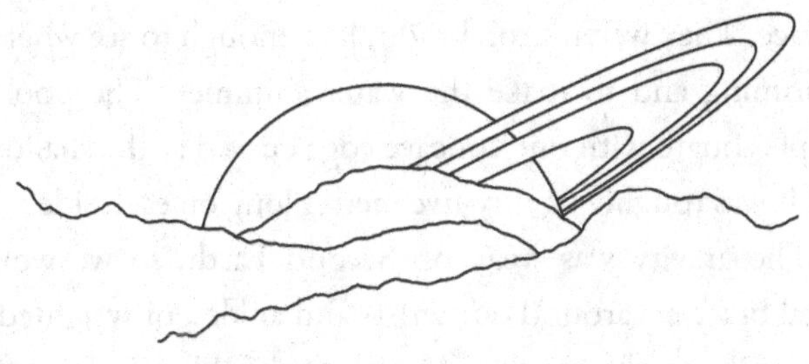

## SIXTEEN

**T**HE WATER WAS REFRESHINGLY COLD against my sweaty skin. I always entered pools from the deep end first. It was my way of jumping in without any hesitation — physical or emotional. I always used this analogy when stuck in a situation. Since childhood, I never entered the pool from the stairs. That was the coward's way in, and I refused to call myself a coward.

Not every floor on Second Earth had a pool room. My department, aerospace on level eighty, had a pool. So did two of the dorm levels — I think seventy-one and seventy-four. My dorm didn't, but I was lucky that my department did. Sometimes we took our half-hour meal breaks in the pool room to take our minds off our projects, and sometimes our meal breaks turned into three-hour-long breaks. Supervisor Hoba didn't care; he joined us most of the time. He was pretty relaxed about us taking longer breaks as long as we finished our projects by the due date. Those were the good old days.

Nobody else was in the pool. Nobody was even in the room. I had it all to myself. White-blue lights lined the bottom of the pool and crawled up the side walls but never reached the water's surface. They weren't too bright, just enough to see where I was swimming and to make the water shimmer. The pool was a simple square with one concave edge curved at the shallow end, and it was roughly twenty-five metres long on each side.

The gravity was weak on Second Earth, so we wore thin metal bracelets around our wrists and ankles, or weighted boots to keep us on the ground. A weak forcefield over the surface of the pool prevented the water from floating all around Second Earth. Humans could penetrate it easily, but it was strong enough that the water couldn't. Everything else on Second Earth had differing strengths of magnetism which was pulled from the ground to keep them as close to standard gravity as it possibly could.

Anyma walked in shortly after I swam a few laps, and she sat on the edge with her legs inside the pool.

"Remember when we were kids, Fate? We played so many games. Your father never liked it when all of us played in the pool together," she said as the memories flooded back.

"It was you, me, Halley and Vesta. That was so long ago. Yeah, my dad warned us so many times not to go to the deep end."

"He looked out for all of us. You didn't want any of us to

drown, did you?" she laughed.

"God, no."

"Okay, just checking. Fate, let's play a game," she said.

"Sure, what were you thinking?"

"Um, what were some of the really good ones we always played?"

"Marco Polo, shark, volleyball. There's so many."

"For volleyball, we need a whole team, and we would almost drown playing shark," she said.

"Marco Polo it is," I said as I closed my eyes, assuming the role of the chaser.

Anyma splashed into the pool and tried to make as little noise as possible when swimming around. I trod water and tried to hear her movements.

"Marco," I called.

There was a moment of silence, but I could still hear the swooshing of water behind me. My sense of hearing heightened to replace the vision I'd lost.

"Polo," she replied, in front of me this time.

I dived to reach her, but she slipped away too quickly.

"Don't make this too easy for me, Anyma."

"Not at all, Fate. You know I always win this game."

I dived again in the direction of her voice, but once more, she was too quick.

"Marco." My hands moved with the small waves our splashing created, and my body bobbed up and down in the water. I could hear her breathing near me, so I trod water in her direction. I felt her immediately begin holding her breath.

"Polo," she huffed out the word.

I sank to the bottom of the pool and leaped up to catch her. And I did.

"Got you," I laughed as I wiped away the water from my eyes.

The water was too deep for us to stand, so she clutched her arms around my neck to keep herself afloat, and I swam forward. We made it to the wall, and we both took off our weighted bracelets and left them on the edge of the pool. There was no more weight in our bodies as we rose to the ceiling and suspended mid-air for a while. It was rare for people to take off their bracelets, myself included. But whenever I did, it felt like there was no more responsibility holding me down.

Anyma and I hovered around until we became bored of it all, and we kicked ourselves back towards the pool from the ceiling. The moment our bracelets were over our wrists and ankles again, the gravity returned to normal. I leaned against the side of the pool while she sat on the edge and kicked the water around without splashing.

"I can't believe it's our last night, again," she whispered, sounding disappointed.

"Last? We are going to get through the next two games and the ones after those as well. Anyma, don't think negatively. I know this is scary times."

"We barely got through the first game. The next one is going to be harder, and the next one after that will be even more difficult."

"We're lucky the gazer let us go, considering we broke the

rules. I hope nothing terrible happens to him," I said as I rubbed my lower back from the slight pain. "We are so lucky Jaaspar and Jayde had the advantage to help us."

"Nobody has an advantage in the next game. Fate, don't you see? There's no way we are going to survive this."

"Why do you always doubt so much?" I asked with frustration.

"I doubt because you doubt everything too."

"Anyma—"

"I miss our childhood. I was hoping tonight I'd get some of it back," Anyma said as she pressed her lips against my forehead and wrapped the towel around her body.

"I miss our childhood too—"

"Goodnight, Fate. I'll see you tomorrow," she said, not letting me finish my sentence as she exited through the door on the opposite side of the pool.

I swam around with my head underwater from end-to-end of the pool. Every time I broke the surface, the rushing water over my head carried my past life away with it. Everything important to me before was now gone — my department, my old friends and my dreams, which remained in their truest form, dreams.

I sank to the very bottom of the pool and sat on the floor with my feet crossed. The air slowly escaped my lungs and bubbled to the surface, but not so fast that I would lose my breath. It was so quiet that my thoughts screamed at me. A part of me really regretted entering the games, but I felt the tugging ambition to finish them. I had to; there was no way out. Before my consciousness slipped away, I pushed myself up and breathed in the clean Second Earth air after I broke the surface.

The door opened again just as I was about to exit the pool, and in came Jaaspar, holding a stack of towels, and Jayde, who was laughing with Thebe. They plonked their belongings on the daybed closest to them, and each looked at me with bright eyes.

"Fate, you aren't getting out, are you?" Jaaspar said when he noticed me wrapping a towel around my body and the droplets of water floating in the air around me.

"I'm just going to sit out here for a bit," I answered. "I'll jump back in soon," I lied because I had enough of the water and just wanted to sleep.

"Yeah, you better," Jayde said cheekily, still laughing with Thebe.

I took the towel off and just sat on the edge of the pool as I watched the three of them swim around. I splashed some water on them occasionally as a joke, and they did the same to me.

"I'm so sorry," Jayde said to Jaaspar after she accidentally kicked him in the face when pushing off the wall.

"Don't worry about it," he responded, holding onto his forehead, which soon bruised up.

I honestly found the situation hilarious. I shouldn't have laughed at Jaaspar's injury, but I couldn't contain myself. Jayde and Thebe moved to one end of the pool to have their own private conversation while Jaaspar sat on the edge with me.

"I can't believe Jayde left you on Earth," Jaaspar said in a non-threatening way.

"I told her to go without me when the wolf was chasing us."

"She was kicking herself about it before. You have no idea how bad she feels."

"It's all good. We're still a strong alliance."

"Thebe and I were lucky not to have run into any wild animals. I have no idea what we would have done."

"Anyma couldn't find you two. Did you guys suddenly disappear?" I asked.

"Is that some kind of joke?" he responded with genuine curiosity.

I just let bygones be bygones. It wasn't worth arguing about it. Besides, we all made it out alive.

"Can I tell you a secret, Fate?"

"Yeah." I nodded.

"Don't laugh at me, but... I'm actually scared of the water."

"Really?" I asked with interest.

"My mother drowned when I was twelve," he continued. "I vaguely remember how it happened, but ever since that moment, I have been absolutely terrified of water."

"How scared do you usually get?"

"I'm alright swimming with other people, don't get me wrong. It's just when I have to go completely under the water that I start to panic. That's why I never go to the deep end. Even before, I stayed here where my feet could still touch the bottom."

"That's so tough, man. I'm so sorry."

"It's alright. I haven't told many people. Not even those two know," he said, looking in the direction of Jayde and Thebe.

"I'm honoured you felt comfortable enough to tell me."

"She had big dreams for me, my mother. She always told me about the land somewhere among the stars." It seemed he was repeating the phrase the same way his mother would have said it.

"I like that," I said. "Land among the stars. Sometimes I want to join the stars. My father had something similar he used to say to me."

"Oh yeah? What was it?"

"He said, 'Don't fight the mountains; move them,'" I answered, imitating my father's tone and cadence.

"What inspirational parents we had," he said as he gently nudged me and chuckled.

"I guess our alliance plan didn't entirely work out."

Jaaspar looked at me with raised eyebrows as if I had said something totally out of line.

"Of course, all of us are our own alliance. I mean the other players," I corrected.

"Okay, you had me worried there for a second." He exhaled in relief.

"I know Sapphire helped many players in the first game. She could see the beacons too. Emerald told me."

"Have you tried getting either of them to join us?"

"I'm sure Sapphire would be open to it. Emerald, not so much. She said that she always works alone because she doesn't want anybody owing her any favours."

"Right," he said as he rolled his eyes.

"Can you imagine we were thinking of getting Kuiper to

join us? After the shit he pulled on Cobalt back there, there's no way we can let him in now."

"I kind of want Cobalt to join us. To protect him, in a way. I feel like Kuiper is going to try to do something terrible in tomorrow's game."

"I know what you mean. We have to keep our eyes on them tomorrow to try and make sure nothing goes wrong."

"Back-to-back games tomorrow. I'm not sure I'm ready," Jaaspar said.

"We have to rest up anyways. Recharge. It's getting late, too, and the gazers are probably wondering where we all are."

"Nah. We've got the nanobot trackers in our bloodstream. They know where we are," he said too confidently.

"There's something you should know," I began as I stopped him from calling the girls over.

"What is it?" he asked worriedly.

"Before you find out from any of the other players, or the game makers or any of the audience members," I continued without really considering if it was a good idea to tell him, "Jayde and I were talking about you in the first game."

I immediately regretted bringing it up because it was Jayde's secret to tell, not mine.

"I hope it was nothing bad," he mocked.

"Of course not," I laughed. "We said how lucky we were to have you and Thebe in our alliance." I quickly tried to cover my blunder.

"Thebe and I spoke about you and Jayde as well. We said the same. We're lucky to have both of you in our alliance as well."

He smiled and nodded his head slowly.

"Hey, you two," I called to Thebe and Jayde, who looked like they were just about finished with their conversation. "The two of us are headed back to our dorm. You should do the same; it's getting late."

"We're coming out now," Thebe said.

All four of us walked back to our rooms and wished each other a good night's rest. We needed it after the difficulty of the first game. And there was no telling how difficult the next game would be. We just knew that it wouldn't compare to the first. The gazer patrolling the hallway didn't mind that we were super late for our curfew. I figured he just wanted to get paid and leave.

The door to our room automatically unlocked when it detected our presence. Jaaspar and I both dropped our piles of clothes and screeched to a halt when we noticed a gazer standing in front of the couch, staring through the window into outer space. She was slightly shorter than most gazers on Second Earth but stood with her shoulders back, and head held high. Jaaspar and I were completely embarrassed when she noticed us. We just stood frozen, shocked, and shirtless.

"Well done for making it through the first game," she congratulated. "This is for you two," she said as she handed me a black envelope.

"What is it?" Jaaspar asked.

"A clue for the next game," she answered.

"I thought nobody was getting an advantage in game two," I said with confusion.

"Nobody gets an advantage. Everybody gets a clue," she responded before walking out.

We waited for her to be out of earshot and for the door to shut before speaking.

"How did she get in here?" Jaaspar whispered in case she was waiting by the door to listen to our conversation.

"I have no idea, but that was a bit concerning."

"Alright, go ahead. Open it," Jaaspar said eagerly.

I tore the blank wax seal off the black envelope and saw a single white card. I pulled it out slowly and left the envelope on the kitchen benchtop.

"It's blank," I said as I checked both sides to make sure I wasn't going crazy.

"Is this some kind of joke they're trying to pull?" Jaaspar said angrily.

The card was warm, and I assumed it was just my body heat, but it wasn't. In less than a minute, the card reached boiling point. My fingers almost blistered up because of the intense heat. I flung the card from my hands and watched it fall like a stone onto the floor.

"What? What is it?" Jaaspar asked.

"It's... hot," I answered in confusion.

Jaaspar curiously kneeled to touch it. He pulled his fingers away the moment they made contact with the card.

"It's a thermosheet. Chemically engineered paper designed to heat up when touched. I know a guy who helped design it."

"What does it have to do with the game? Because I'm no good at origami." I chuckled nervously.

Jaaspar paced up and down and paused every time he had a half-decent thought but resumed pacing when he realised it wasn't a good one.

"The envelope delivers messages, right?" he said.

I thought he was on to something.

"The clue is obviously not written on the card," he continued, pausing every few words. "What if... the clue... is the card. What if the next game has something to do with heat?"

"Like fire? No way. I hate when it's hot. I hate sweating."

"The game makers aren't going to design a game that works in your favour, or any of ours. They want us to play a game that entertains," he said as he scooped up the card with the envelope, so he didn't burn himself again. "Remember a few years ago there was a game where the players had to retrieve something from the centre of the sun?"

"I haven't watched the Exogames in a while," I responded and remembered that I wasn't sure Jaaspar had seen them in a while either, but shrugged it off so that he could continue his point.

"Well, half the players died, and there were a lot of players that year. Their suits malfunctioned, and they would have evaporated instantly. That was a quick game. I hope they don't make us play that one tomorrow."

"If we are going to burn to death in the second game, I need to be prepared."

"If we are going to burn tomorrow, then it's going to be one hell of a game."

"Not for us," I exclaimed. "It will be a hell of a game for the audience and game makers. You're right; these games are not in our favour, and knowing how the game makers like to design them, we are surely dead men. The first game was a warm-up. The next one is where shit gets real."

"Then we better not die. They'll need someone to tell the story of the ninety-ninth Exogames. And dead men tell no tales," Jaaspar said with seriousness in his tone.

# SEVENTEEN

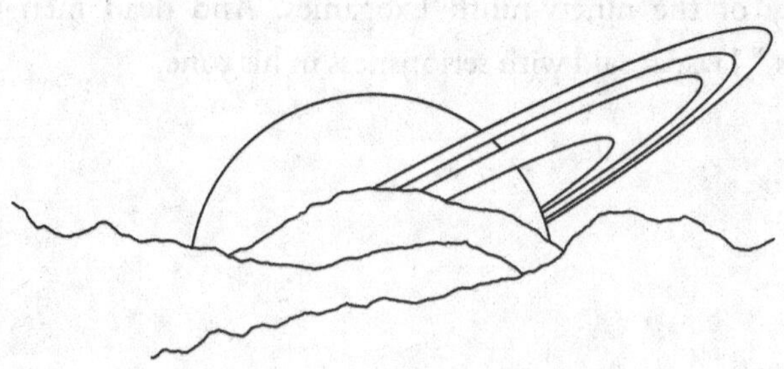

**W**E WERE ESCORTED THROUGH the hallway just as we had been before the first game. Although last time I was half asleep, I had sensed the exhilaration from the other players. But this time was different. None of us were excited to continue the Exogames. There was no telling how prepared we were for this next game, let alone two back-to-back. I was even more worried about the lives of my friends than I was about my own.

Instead of taking us to the small rooms like before, the gazer ushering us had left us in another holding bay, or so we were told. I immediately recognised where we stood. The black walls were different from every other room on Second Earth. There was only one place these walls made an appearance — the spaceships intended for voyages around our solar system.

I immediately concluded that the second game was not going to be played on Second Earth or even the real planet Earth. It made sense, though; the Exogames were never played on Second Earth or in the same location twice.

We quickly became restless, so everyone decided to take a seat in the white metal chairs lined with a light strip around the edges. There were two rows of chairs on either end of the ship. I, of course, sat between Jaaspar and Jayde, with Thebe on the other side of Jaaspar. Anyma sat in a chair on the opposite side of the ship because all the chairs on my side had been taken up.

"Did you girls get the clue last night as well?" I whispered to Jayde.

"Yes," she whispered back. "The gazer standing in our room nearly gave me a heart attack."

"Same with us," I said, laughing.

Jaaspar heard part of the conversation and laughed with us. Then he turned to Thebe and spoke with her.

"What do you think it means?" I asked.

"Not sure. Our card was blank."

"Ours as well. And we almost burnt ourselves."

"From what?" Jayde asked with concern.

"The card," I said slowly. "Did you touch it?"

"Thebe did. I didn't grab it."

I turned to Thebe, leaning over Jaaspar.

"Thebe, the clue from last night, was the card hot?" I asked. She shook her head.

"It was saturated. It disintegrated through my fingers. I assumed that's why there was no writing on it. The water must have washed it out."

"Strange. Ours was hot, almost at boiling point," I said.

Jaaspar agreed, and I turned back to Jayde. My mind was filled with clouds of confusion, storming like thunder and lightning inside my head.

"Your clue was wet; ours was hot."

"What do you think it means?" Jayde asked.

"I'm not sure. Maybe the next game involves boiling water. I have no idea."

"The next two games are back-to-back. What if each clue is part of a specific game?"

"That makes sense. But what if someone else got a completely different clue?" I asked.

Jayde leaned over to the player on the other side of her and snapped her fingers at them. Without even looking at the player, I knew exactly who it was. Jayde would have never snapped her fingers like that to anybody else.

"Your clue, what was it?" she asked.

"I'm not telling you," Neon responded aggressively.

Jayde tilted her head down and stared at him without blinking. Neon leaned further back, almost becoming one with his chair, and hesitated as he made a strange face.

"It was a wet card with nothing on it," he answered.

I smiled at him politely when he looked at me and I nodded my head down with minuscule movements before looking away. I didn't want to get stuck in an awkward conversation with him or else he would have gone on about his theories about the Exogames which I didn't care about.

"There you go, Fate," Jayde said. "Half of us would have received the wet card, and the other half, the hot card."

"Prepare for the heat, I guess."

"What if the water clue is the next game?"

"Then prepare to swim," I said, realising the implication after I said it. Jaaspar was afraid of water, terrified of being submerged in it. I hoped, for his sake, that if the game involved swimming, we would at least have our heads above the surface.

The door reopened, and Rubie walked in, the doctor who'd recorded my vitals and given me the instructions for the first game. She recognised me and smirked, then stood in the centre between the two rows of chairs. Gazers came in as well and dropped new attire, still sealed in plastic, at our feet. Then they exited the ship, and the door shut.

"Players, again, congratulations on making it past the first game," she said as she moved between speaking to each side of the ship. "As you all must have heard many times, the difficulty of these next games will be increased."

"No shit," Jayde whispered loud enough for only me to hear.

Rubie pulled out her tablet and read the instructions from the screen.

"Game two, a race on Venus," she said.

"I guess your clue is this next game. My clue has to be the game after," Jayde whispered to me.

I swore quietly. Venus was the hottest planet in our solar system, with burning sulphur and lava on its rocky surface. It was a fiery furnace, and we were all going to burn to death.

There was no doubt about it.

"The suits at your feet will protect you from Venus' heat and atmosphere," Rubie continued. "But not for long. Thirty minutes is all you will have to make your way from the drop-off zone to Maat Mons, Venus' largest volcano. There you will find the open portal to the third game, where I will be waiting to give you further instructions. Halfway across, you will find hoverboards, one for each of you to ride the remaining distance to the portal. Make it there alive before the thirty-minute timer ends and before the portal closes. Good luck," she said as she turned off her tablet.

Cobalt raised his hand to ask a question, and Rubie nodded to allow him to speak, although nobody really needed permission. We were all adults, except for Thebe, who was only seventeen years old, and we were mature enough to interrupt in order to raise any concerns.

"May I exit to change into the suit?" Cobalt asked.

"The game will begin shortly. Change here now before take-off, or else take your chances on Venus. It's up to you," she responded.

Immediately, all the players, including myself, ripped open our plastic packaging and took out our suits. They were black and made of a synthetic material I had never seen before. The suit was seamed together with red stitching and was rather flexible. Nobody cared that we were naked for a split second; we just didn't want to burn up as soon as the doors opened to the fiery planet.

"Is there a helmet we need to wear?" Neon asked.

"Push the white button between your collarbones, and a force field will activate to protect your head for the duration of the second game."

"What about footwear?" Kuiper asked.

"Did you check your satchel properly?"

"Never mind, I found them."

Rubie rolled her eyes; we all did. The boots were the same as they were in the first game. When the tops of the boots made contact with the bottom of the suit, they sealed together tightly, and no matter how hard I tried to disconnect the two materials, they wouldn't budge.

We were all strapped into our seats with a large restraint over our shoulders. The moment the restraint was secured over my body, familiar emotions came over me, emotions that reminded me of the journey to Mars. It happened exactly like this. One moment, I was enjoying myself on Second Earth, and the next, I was being transported through the solar system on a spacecraft that didn't feel real.

"Here we go," Jaaspar said with excitement, but I could tell he wasn't really in the mood to play another game. "Who's ready to die?" he asked sarcastically.

The overhead lights turned off, and only a blue light strip from underneath our seats illuminated the ship.

"Good luck, players. See you on the other side, whoever makes it out alive," Rubie said as she exited.

The ship whirred and made all sorts of strange noises before it folded spacetime to take us to Venus. But that was all we remembered. The human brain wasn't designed to survive the event, so we were put to sleep. A strange-smelling gas filled the entire ship, and in no less than ten seconds, my eyelids shut, and the world around me faded away as if it didn't exist in the first place.

# EIGHTEEN

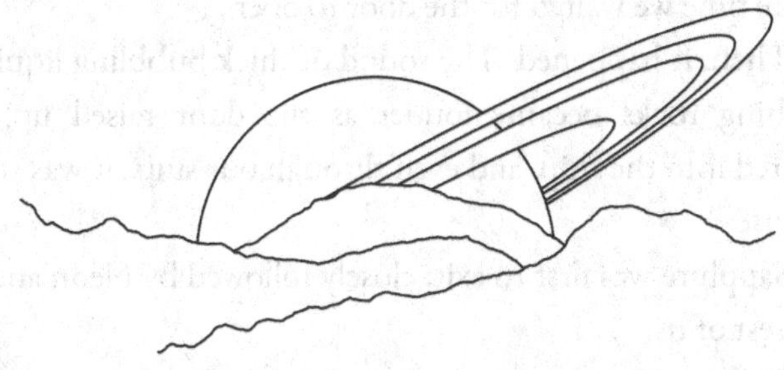

**T**HEBE WAS THE FIRST TO WAKE. I knew this because I was the second player to open my eyes. Then, slowly but surely, everyone else began waking up in their seats and looking around in confusion, wondering if we had landed on Venus. I turned to Jaaspar and smiled nervously, fear in my eyes, but he was still half asleep. A million possibilities ran through my mind over and over. *What if the heat kills us instantly? What if I don't make it to the end of this game? Or my friends, what if they die? What if I forget to activate my helmet?*

I pressed the white button between my collarbones and saw the force field shimmer over my head. Everybody else did the same one by one, and a small blue light on the button confirmed that they were activated.

A robotic announcement was made through the speakers

above our heads. "Door opening in one minute."

A small hole opened in the floor, and out came the hovering spherical cameras, one for each of us. The restraints around our bodies unlocked, and we were free to stretch our muscles. Kuiper, with his menacing and sharp eyes, stared at Cobalt the entire time we waited for the door to open.

Then, it happened. The sound of thick bubbling liquid and crashing rocks became louder as the door raised up. Heat poured into the ship, and even through our suits, it was still too intense.

Sapphire was first to exit, closely followed by Neon and then the rest of us.

Red.

That was all I saw.

Red.

But it wasn't red like on Mars. It was a type of red that glowed a bright scarlet in a spectacular light show. The smoke in the air was thick, but it didn't block my vision of the uneven terrain ahead. The sky was a melancholic dark grey. The volcano ahead — Maat Mons — actively burned thick sulphur and spat out molten rock. The lava overflowed from the peak and very slowly trickled down. It looked so beautiful that I almost wanted to touch it. The cameras hovered above each of our heads as we moved towards the volcano.

The gravity on Venus was weaker than it was on Earth, but the weighted boots made it feel the same. The gravity regulation methods on Second Earth were very similar, which was why we were required to wear special bracelets around our ankles and wrists.

"How do we find the exit?" Sapphire asked over the winds that slowly picked up.

"There!" Emerald shouted as she pointed in front of us.

A thin green beam of light shot out of the top of the volcano and disappeared into the sky. No wonder Jayde was in awe back on Earth. The beacons would have been immaculate; the one that I could see was more than extraordinary.

Everyone concurred that it led to the portal, just as the beacons had in the first game. We all jogged towards the volcano together but distinctly split into two groups. Jayde, Jaaspar, Thebe and I huddled around Cobalt to protect him from Kuiper. Emerald and Sapphire helped as well. The other players stayed a few metres to the right of us, seeming more concerned about the heat than about Cobalt.

It hadn't been more than two minutes before the ground rumbled slowly like the beginnings of a growl from the belly of the planet. We paused, and we waited.

"This isn't going to be as easy as it looks," Thebe said over the hot winds.

Emerald stepped forward slightly, pressing harder onto the ground with her feet. She must have pushed too hard because small cracks formed everywhere she stepped.

"It's alright—" She was propelled hundreds of metres into the air, and she landed with a splat onto the hard terrain.

Sapphire painfully screamed as she watched in horror. Boiling blood bubbled slowly out of Emerald's charred body. I breathed unevenly and fast, and my hands trembled uncontrollably. Jaaspar shook my shoulders to snap me back into reality, and Jayde snapped her fingers in my face.

The ground in front of us cracked as the entire planet growled once more. I finally saw what had killed Emerald only moments ago. It wasn't a creature or a monster, although, I preferred it to be. It was nature itself. A booming eruption of hot orange lava exploded from the ground into a pillar hundreds of metres into the sky, then crashed back down. Suddenly, more eruptions broke through the cracks in a random arrangement, and the lava splashed everywhere in a pool of thick orange slosh.

"RUN!" Jayde screamed at the top of her lungs.

I sprinted into the expanse without a care of who was behind me. Out of the corner of my eye, I saw Cobalt racing just ahead of me with Kuiper close behind him. The Exogames didn't feel like a way to cleanse ourselves of the impurities our crimes had caused; they felt like a way to cleanse Second Earth of its prisoners. There was no way any of us would make it out alive and be sane afterwards.

"Fate, watch out!" Jaaspar called out as he nudged me out of the way of a lava geyser that would have most certainly killed me.

"Thanks," I said as we continued running and dodging the lava.

The geysers erupted in a spread-out manner and always twice in the same spot.

"Don't look back. Just keep moving," Jaaspar instructed.

But I did what he'd told me not to do. I looked back. There

was only one person who wasn't running through the expanse. Thebe. She stood motionless at the beginning of the race as if she were frozen in time. The bright orange and red lava, which was exploding in front of her, didn't seem to faze her at all.

"Thebe!" I screamed.

She didn't hear me from where I stood. After all, she was quite far behind and the explosions were deafening. I sprinted back to her, trying not to step in the pools of lava or into a geyser.

"Thebe," I repeated when I finally reached her.

Still, there was no response. Her pupils were dilated, and even though she was looking directly at me, it was as if I were invisible. I clutched her hand in mine and dragged her into the expanse. Only then did she regain her mobility and realise the sudden danger we were all in.

The pools of lava started merging and left almost no visible terrain. There were small patches of rocky dirt, which Thebe and I utilised to jump across to larger areas of the ground. The geysers on our end had slowed down, but if we stopped for too long, the lava would completely cover the ground and take us both.

"Try to keep up, Thebe!" I panted between words, trying to catch up to the other players.

"How much longer until we get to the hoverboards?" she asked, sidestepping into me a few times to dodge the lava.

"I'm not sure. But as soon as we get there, we'll be on the home stretch," I said without any way of knowing if it were true.

The two of us were not too far from the rest of the players. I recognised Sapphire up ahead, leaping over large rocks and boulders. The hovering cameras flew in front of us with their lenses pointed towards the volcano. A lava geyser exploded inches from my face and crashed down close to Thebe.

"Watch out!" I screamed as I brought my arms close to my body and jumped out of the splash zone. "Did you see that?" I asked.

"It's French to me," she joked to comfort herself, but it wasn't a great time to make jokes. She realised I was serious. "No, what is it?"

"The hovering camera moved out of the way a few seconds before the geyser exploded."

She looked at me with raised eyebrows and tilted her head forward slightly. Thebe wasn't as intelligent in difficult situations.

"The cameras know when the lava is about to erupt," I continued. "We can follow the cameras and make it to the hoverboards."

She brushed past me and jogged closer to the volcano.

"Careful, Thebe," I warned as I pulled her away from another geyser explosion. "Look at your hovering camera. It will move away from the lava," I explained slowly and simply.

"Alright, yes, now that makes sense," she said as her eyes widened.

We raced through the expanse and followed the cameras left and right, zigzagging past every geyser and weaving around each other. We jumped over boulders and puddles of boiling, red-hot lava to avoid the splashes which bounced up far off the ground. We almost tripped on the convex openings the geysers had formed as they broke through the terrain but regained our balance quickly.

The two of us caught up to the rest of the players, who were slowly trying to get through the mess of lava. Jaaspar and Jayde were partnered together just as Thebe and I were. Cobalt was with Sapphire, using the same technique of following the hovering cameras. Kuiper was close behind them with his eyes locked on Cobalt.

"You're a dead man!" Kuiper screamed as he stretched his arms out.

"Oh no," Thebe said to me, "he's going to kill him."

A pillar of lava erupted from the ground, and at that exact moment, Kuiper, with every ounce of revenge in him, placed his hands on Cobalt and threw him into the geyser. Cobalt disappeared into the lava; he didn't even scream as he died. Kuiper had kept his promise of ending Cobalt's life in this game and I wondered how many more of us he was going to kill as the games progressed.

"Oh, God," I whispered to myself. "Shit just got real."

Sapphire screamed in horror and shouted profanities at Kuiper.

"Do you want to be next?" Kuiper warned her with ill intent and seriousness.

She shook her head, and Kuiper continued through the expanse.

Kuiper had spoken to us about murdering some of the

players during the games, and the more I thought about it, the more it seemed like it was his plan all along. He just needed a target, and Cobalt was unfortunate enough to fall into his trap.

"Fifteen minutes remaining," the robotic voice announced through the cameras.

"We have to get to the hoverboards," Thebe said.

Once the geyser that had killed Cobalt crashed back down, the hoverboards were in view. They floated just off the ground at the bottom of Maat Mons in an evenly spread-out row. Neon was first to claim one, closely followed by Hinata. Sapphire managed to pick herself up and jumped on the next hoverboard with Jayde and Jaaspar behind her.

As Thebe and I raced to the remaining hoverboards, we overtook the other players who hadn't figured out a safe way through the geysers yet.

The oval-shaped hoverboards were plain sheets of a gold metal, much like the surfboards people used on planet Earth hundreds of years ago. I jumped onto one of the remaining boards, and my feet magnetically clicked into place. It was wobbly at first and difficult to keep balanced, but I stretched my hands out on either side of my body to stabilise. Thebe did the same, but she found it easier to control than I did.

Kuiper jumped on the hoverboard next to mine and scrunched his face when he looked at Thebe and me. He leaned forward on his hoverboard and zoomed up the volcano. I leaned forward as well and felt the hot air whizz past my body.

From a distance, I saw Jaaspar struggling to keep himself balanced, and he fell onto Jayde's hoverboard. He only held onto the edge with a few fingers and raised his legs up to not get hit by any of the geysers, but he seemed unaware that the hoverboards couldn't hold the weight of two people. Jayde lifted Jaaspar with one arm back onto his own hoverboard, which was still flying beside hers, and I exhaled in relief.

"Hey!" I called at Kuiper, hoping to get his attention.

He didn't stop or acknowledge my call.

"Kuiper!" I screamed as I pulled up beside him.

"What?" he asked aggressively and rolled his eyes.

"Why did you kill Cobalt?" I had to fight over the rumbling volcano and crashing rocks for Kuiper to hear me.

"I warned him after he left my team and me in the first game. He deserved it."

"So do all of us. We're all criminals."

"Not me. I was framed; I can promise you that," he responded as he began moving away from me.

"Wait, what do you mean you were framed?" I asked, trying to catch up to him again.

I made the mistake of placing my hands on Kuiper to get his attention again. He retaliated by grasping my shoulders tightly in his fists, and with a hard nudge, he knocked me off my hoverboard. I rolled down the side of the volcano, slowing as the ground evened out. I must have hit my head unknowingly because my vision was slightly blurred. I knew I was bruised up badly because every muscle in my body ached as if it were being torn off my bones.

Thebe rode down to where I had landed and picked me up. I was too heavy for her, and she grunted as she helped me back on my feet. My hoverboard had landed further down the volcano from where I was, and it was almost impossible to reach.

"Ten minutes remaining," the announcement was made.

"Fate, we still have time," Thebe said.

I knew Thebe was just trying to convince herself that I would make it out of this game alive, but as the clock ticked closer to the finishing time, the portal looked further away.

The ground rumbled and shook much harder than the previous quakes. It felt as though somebody had taken the planet in their hands and was shaking it around like a maraca. The rocks around us fell, and the smoke from the top of the volcano thickened. Thebe fell off her hoverboard and landed on her back.

"Run." Thebe tried to scream but her vocal cords made no noise and only air came out of her mouth like a loud whisper.

"Run, Fate. Fate Artemis, run!" Anyma screamed at the top of her lungs as she rode down to encourage me to start moving.

I let my feet take me across the even plain, sprinting faster than I had ever run before in my life. I needed to get my hoverboard to make it to the portal at the top of the volcano. But it was too difficult for me to reach.

"Jump!" Anyma instructed as she followed me.

"What? Are you crazy?" I yelled.

"Just do it, Fate! Jump!" she repeated.

I closed my eyes, which I shouldn't have done while running, and trusted Anyma's words. I let my body fly through the air off the side of a volcano, not knowing where I would land. Thankfully, my feet attached to the hoverboard magnetically to prevent me from splattering all over the side of the volcano.

The expanse where the geysers had erupted was no longer covered by pillars of hot, thick lava. It had been replaced by a lake that burned with fire and sulphur. Emerald and Cobalt, who were both killed by a geyser, were now swimming at the very bottom of that lake of fire. It was a second death for them.

My eyes locked onto the beacon above, and the quaking strengthened. Kuiper was nearly at the top of the volcano, along with most of the other players. Hinata rode directly beside him, determined to get to the portal. At that moment, the ground beneath them exploded with heavy ash, and a monstrous wave of lava devoured both of them. The wave was mostly red as lava bubbled out, with patches of blue molten sulphur that mixed into a deep violet.

The entire half of Maat Mons had erupted with ash and giant boulders, which Anyma and I tried to dodge. The lava wave quickly consumed anything in its path as it rolled down the volcano. Thebe wasn't in front of us, so I turned my head to make sure she was close behind.

She wasn't.

"Thebe!" I called.

She was still on the ground where I had fallen previously, and she was tugging at her leg. From where I was, she looked like a tiny speck on the ground, and the lava was quickly approaching her. I leaned as far forward on my hoverboard as I possibly could without falling off and raced towards her.

I was fast. Very fast. I was speeding down the side of the volcano in the opposite direction of the exit. But the lava wave was faster.

"Thebe, what's wrong? What is it?" I couldn't understand what kept her from resuming her pace towards the portal.

"It's French." She was trying to distract herself from her quickly approaching death. It was something she did to comfort herself. "It's my leg," she answered.

The closer I was to her, the clearer I could see that her foot was stuck in a small hole in the ground and didn't look like it would budge. I stretched out my arm and splayed out my fingers to grab her. Her glossy eyes stared deep into my soul, her mouth quivered, and her body trembled as she called for me to save her. I swallowed hard, knowing that I wasn't going to be fast enough to catch her. Thebe closed her eyes and before she could take hold of my hand, the lava swallowed her whole and took her under. Her hovering camera zoomed up into the portal, and I knew for certain that she was gone.

"No!" I cried as my throat tightened and tears ran down my face. The temperature was so hot that they dried up as quickly as they fell.

"One minute remaining," the voice announced from my camera.

One minute was not enough. I needed more time to dodge the lava, rocks and anything else the volcano decided to spit out.

My shallow breaths eventually eased, but my eyes were filled with tears, and my vision was blurry. I leaned forward and hoped that none of the projectile rocks would hit me.

"Thirty, twenty-nine," the countdown began.

Boulders crashed near me and splashed hot lava high into the air. I swung my hoverboard around and blinked the blurriness away so that I could find a safe way to the top. But to be honest, there was never a safe way from the beginning. The game makers planned this round carefully.

I swallowed the built-up saliva in my mouth and screamed as I let the hoverboard take me to the portal. The countdown disappeared in the crashes and rumbling explosions. If I made it through to the next game, it would be for Thebe. If I didn't, then Thebe sacrificed her life for nothing, and I wasn't going to let that happen.

The portal was within reach, but I couldn't see through to the other side. It remained opaque for one of two reasons. Either the game makers didn't want any of us to know the location of the third game before it began, or it was some sort of shield so that no lava or debris would be able to get to the other side. Both reasons made sense, but there was no point in trying to figure out which was the correct one.

The beacon turned off from the top down, and the lasers that lined the portal flickered. I only had mere seconds to make it across, and even though the portal was directly in front of me, I still wasn't going to reach it. So, there was only one thing left to do.

I leaned as far forward as possible that it felt like I was going to fall into the raging lava below, and swung both of my arms forward, releasing my legs from the hoverboard and allowing my body to fly through the portal just in time before it closed behind me. For a moment, I wasn't sure if I had made it across or if I was dead, but when I saw Rubie's face, I was certain that I was still in the games and hadn't died, at least not yet.

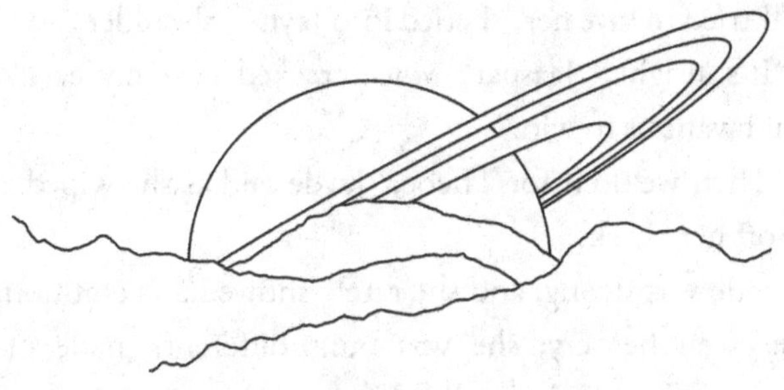

**J**AYDE **WAS THE SECOND PERSON I SAW** after I recognised Rubie. The portal had taken us to another ship, but something inside me felt as though we were far from Second Earth and even farther from Venus.

The players that had made it through the previous game waited in a small holding bay. Sapphire stood with Neon and two female players I didn't know the names of, and Jayde was with Jaaspar. Anyma sat by herself on the floor with her arms wrapped around her knees and her head buried in them.

Jayde glanced around at everyone, quickly identifying each player. Jaaspar stared at me, but I didn't want to meet his eyes. I didn't want to face the music. There was no easy way to tell them that our alliance was falling apart; that Thebe had died.

"Thebe?" Jayde asked me quietly.

I shook my head and creased my mouth as wrinkles lined my forehead. My throat tightened, and tears began to stream down my face. Jayde threw her arms around my slim body and squeezed tightly. Jaaspar joined in for the group hug, but it only made it harder to take in deep breaths.

"I tried to save her," I cried into Jayde's shoulder.

"It's alright," Jaaspar's voice cracked near my ear. "Thebe would want us to win."

"Then we do it for Thebe," Jayde said as she wiped a single tear off her cheek.

Jayde was strong, and she rarely showed any emotion. I had never seen her cry; she was built different, made of stone perhaps. Thebe's death didn't trigger any more tears or cries from Jayde, but I could see her fighting to keep her composure.

"We do it for Thebe," I repeated as we let go of each other, and I wiped the tears from my cheeks.

"I see Kuiper got what he deserved," Sapphire said.

I nodded.

"He killed Cobalt," she continued.

"I know. I saw," I said.

"Karma's a bitch," Jaaspar said.

"No," Jayde said seriously. "Karma is my best friend." She was trying to lighten the mood, but our grief was too heavy.

"Kuiper didn't have to kill Cobalt," Jaaspar began. Everyone's attention was on him. "We can all make it out of these games alive; nobody has to die from here on out. If we all work together, we can all win the Exogames."

"That's a wonderful speech," a female player said

sarcastically as she clapped.

"Sol, he's right," Sapphire said.

"Alright, time is up for quick reunions." Rubie took back control of the room.

She stood, like before, in the centre of the holding bay and congratulated us on making it through the second game. She held a plain mesh bag open in front of her.

"As Moirai mentioned prior to the commencement of the second game, some players will receive an advantage in the third game. However, one player will receive a disadvantage."

My heart sank straight to the very bottom of my stomach. Nobody had said anything about a disadvantage in the Exogames, and now wasn't the best time to find out about it. We had all just been through literal hell and back to win our freedom. A disadvantage was never on the cards.

"The rules for this game are simple," Rubie continued, this time not reading the instructions from her tablet. "Game three, light the way. Players, your suits are not only designed for the heat; they are also designed for the cold. Swim through the depths of Enceladus, one of Saturn's moons, and try to find your way out of the maze. But be warned, the maze is dark, and your suits will not be waterproof forever. Three players consumed nanobots following the first game and have now been equipped with a source of light. Use your players wisely," she concluded.

"How much time do we get to complete this task?" Sol asked.

"That is all up to you," she answered. "The suits will begin to dissolve once the game has begun. My advice? Swim quickly."

I really didn't want to know the answer to Sol's question. The more Rubie spoke, the more difficult this next game seemed, and it hadn't even begun yet.

"Is this game underwater?" Jaaspar asked nervously.

*Oh no.* Jaaspar was terrified of being submerged in water. It was an absolute truth that was never going to change.

"Can't breathe, won't be able to breathe, can't breathe," he muttered uncontrollably under his breath and his hands shuddered.

"Each of you will take an aqua shield from this bag and fasten it to your suit. One of them is faulty. The rest will allow you to breathe underwater," Rubie said as she looked directly at me to choose first.

I took a step forward but hesitated to walk all the way to her. She rotated the bag towards me and nodded for me to reach in. Jayde nudged me gently from behind to hurry the process, but it just made me more nervous. I reached my hand into the bag, not knowing what I would touch, and pulled out a finger-sized metal latch that fitted perfectly over the suit's white button between my collarbones.

Rubie leaned closer to me and whispered into my ear so quietly that nobody else could hear her, "Two rights, two lefts, straight ahead, then right again."

Jaaspar was next, followed by Jayde and the rest of the players. Sapphire and the last female player I didn't know the name of were last to take their aqua shields.

"Good luck, players," Rubie announced as she exited to another room through the airtight door hidden in the corner.

The ceiling opened slowly, and heavy water rushed in and filled the entire holding bay to the brim. It was freezing cold, nothing like the warm shower water in our luxury player dorms back on Second Earth.

I covered my face with my arms to stop the water from splashing into my eyes, but the aqua shield had activated, creating a force field around my head to keep the water out and the oxygen in. When I opened my eyes, I wasn't sure if they were actually open because all that surrounded me was darkness. It was pitch black left, right and centre.

"Can anyone hear me?" I heard a voice ask, but I wasn't sure where it came from.

"Loud and clear," someone else said.

"Who said that?" I asked, thinking I was going crazy.

"It was me. Sapphire," she answered.

"Testing, testing, one, two," I said aloud.

"We can hear you, Fate," Sapphire responded.

It took a second for me to realise that our suits were equipped with radios to communicate with each other. At least the game makers didn't want us to lose each other in the dark. They had thought of everything, but the cruel part about it was that we would hear each other's deaths.

"Jaaspar, are you okay?" The whole time Rubie was explaining the rules, I thought about him. He would have been too distracted by his panicked thoughts to pay any attention to her.

"No," he said simply as he hyperventilated loudly.

"Breath. Breathe slowly," I commanded, and I performed breathing exercises with him.

"So, who has the advantage?" Jayde asked.

Three yellow lights gradually emerged from the darkness like tiny glowing orbs that lit up the surrounding water. The lights spread out and formed the shapes of three humans.

"What's happening to me?" Neon shrieked.

"You must have the advantage in this game," I said excitedly. It was the first time I was pleased with what Neon said.

"Me too," Sol and Sapphire said in unison.

"This is the second advantage you've had, Sapphire," Neon scoffed.

"Hey, I didn't ask for any advantage, but I'll take it. I got a whole bunch of players out of the first game. I can be useful in this one, too," she responded.

Their entire bodies glowed as if they had consumed a small slice of the sun which was now burning deep under their skin — harmlessly, of course, and blindingly bright.

Sapphire led the way out of the holding bay. It was part of a small spaceship I had never seen before. Perhaps it was a submarine of sorts; my department had never dealt with submersible ships.

The water was colder outside the holding bay, and I shivered uncontrollably for a moment. It was pitch black beneath us, but above us was what looked like a stone ceiling that seamlessly connected to rock walls on the sides. The hovering cameras followed our every movement, without any flashlights this time.

"Who has the faulty aqua shield?" Jaaspar asked as he trod towards me. His eyes glinted with worry.

"I don't know. Maybe the game makers wanted us to think one of them was faulty to have us on edge," I answered as I grabbed his hand in case he had the disadvantage.

"Guys," Jayde said slowly.

Neon, who had been glowing previously, flickered like a broken light bulb — on, off, on, off. His gasps for air were heard through the speaker as gushing water filled his throat, and his screams bubbled out. We watched, horrified, as his body sank below the point where his light could reach us.

"Oh, God," I said as I gulped. "One of the aqua shields was indeed faulty."

"Shit, now there's only two of us with the advantage. Only two of us can lead the way through," Sol said, seeming annoyed that she had more responsibility on her shoulders.

When we realised that below us was an endless abyss waiting to swallow us, we trod the water as if our lives depended on it; because they did.

"Look at this place. How are we going to find a way out?" the only player whose name I didn't know asked.

"No idea, Ocean," Jayde answered.

"It seems impossible," Anyma said.

"I might know a way," Jaaspar began, then paused for too long.

"Tell us," Sol demanded, without understanding that he needed a minute to calm down.

"I read about this once," he continued. "There is a way to

get out of a maze, but it won't always work."

"We can always try," I encouraged.

"If you keep your hand on the wall, either right or left, it will lead you to the exit," he concluded.

"That could take hours or even days. We don't know how big this maze is," Ocean complained. "We don't have time. Our suits are dissolving as we speak."

"It's worth trying," Jayde said. "We don't know how long we have to complete this game, so we might as well start figuring a way out. If nobody else has any solutions, we're going with Jaaspar's idea."

We lined up against the wall on our left side with Sol at the front and Sapphire at the back to spread out the light. The wall was cold, and I felt it through the suit.

"What is the maze made from?" Ocean asked.

"I think it's just stone," I said.

Sapphire looked at the wall closely. "Ice," she answered. "It's made of ice."

"That makes more sense," I responded. "That's right, Enceladus is covered entirely in ice."

Forty years ago, my department had studied all the moons of Saturn. They researched the most viable moons to resettle the human population because they were unsure if planet Earth would be sustainable again. That was around the time we sent an expedition crew to Titan and lost everybody on board. Never again did Second Earth attempt another expedition. It was too risky to begin with.

The ice shook slightly, and we could hear a low rumble, but

it was nowhere near as vigorous as Venus' quakes and I hoped it wouldn't be as detrimental either; but we were already made aware that the games were more difficult the further we progressed. Venus would have been nothing compared to Enceladus.

"What was that?" Jayde asked.

"Is water the only thing your down here, Fate?" Jaaspar worriedly asked as he held onto Jayde.

"I'm not sure," I answered, not knowing why he asked me in the first place.

"I don't want to face any monsters. Not now, not ever," Sol announced as she began leading us through the maze.

We turned at every left bend, never taking the path on our right, unsure if we were any closer to the exit. It felt like we were moving further away from it. At this point, my legs ached and almost detached themselves from my body from all the swimming. I was sure we all felt it. But none of us wanted to end up like Neon — in the deep dark depths of Enceladus. His body was certainly compressed from the pressure so far down, shrivelling like a thin piece of spaghetti.

The maze rumbled again, and crashing noises grew louder.

"Watch out!" Sol yelled.

We pushed away from the wall as an enormous chunk of ice crashed between us. The light from in front of me went out as Sol disappeared on the other side of the new wall.

Sapphire, who was now the only one providing light, called us to join together. Jaaspar, Jayde, Sapphire and I were the only ones left. Ocean, Sol and Anyma were either dead or trapped on the other side.

"Sol," Sapphire called.

There was a moment of silence, complete silence. Nobody breathed until we knew what had happened.

"Are they dead?" Jaaspar asked.

"We're alright, guys," Sol panted. "We're alright."

"Same here," I said in relief.

"We all have to get out of this maze," Anyma said.

"There's no way out," I responded.

"Jaaspar's method won't work anymore," Sapphire said. "The maze just changed on us."

"There has to be another way we can get out of this maze," Jaaspar said as his breaths became increasingly irregular.

"We have to split up," I suggested.

The others gasped.

"No, it's alright." I tried to calm them down. "You have a light on the other side. Luckily, nobody was trapped without light. We're basically already split up. If we follow the paths, I'm sure we can find the way out."

"I'm not sure it's a gamble I'm willing to take," Sol said.

"I agree. We don't know how far the exit is or if we'll even be going the right way," Ocean sounded as though she was beginning to panic as well.

"Have any of you got a better solution?" Jaaspar asked.

He gave them a few seconds to answer, but they were speechless.

"Exactly," Jaaspar said with enough confidence to mask his inner fear. "We use Fate's method of finding a way out. You can choose to do whatever you want, but we're not going to die here."

I nodded to Jaaspar and smiled. He smiled back, and it was the first time he actually smiled with his teeth. Jayde chuckled with Sapphire because nobody else had stood up to Sol like that.

Sapphire explained to us that she and Sol were cousins and that at family gatherings, Sol would act as if she owned the place. In reality, Sapphire was two years older than her cousin.

"She's only twenty-three and acts as if she's the older one," Sapphire scoffed.

"Hey, I heard that," Sol said.

Even though my group was moving farther away from theirs, our radios still connected through the thick walls of ice and freezing cold water.

Sapphire led us lower, sinking below the rest of us, and I assumed it was because her muscles could no longer tread the water efficiently, but it was because she saw something the rest of us didn't.

"There's a path we can walk on," she said. "Hey, Sol, look for a physical path to walk on. It might lead you to the exit."

"Yeah, we found one a few minutes ago," she responded.

"Thank you for telling us, greatly appreciated," Sapphire said sarcastically.

My legs collapsed when I made contact with the ground, and I just sat on the cold ice floor for a moment to regain my strength. Jayde sat beside me while Sapphire and Jaaspar leaned against the wall.

The new path was a cave system entirely made of ice. It was big enough for all of us to fit, but we were squished together a bit too much. We travelled in one direct line with Sapphire at the front to guide the way. Jayde stayed at the back, and Jaaspar and I were in the middle.

The maze rumbled and crashed constantly, and the water whooshed around us with every noise. Whenever there was a crashing sound, a small current pulled us forward, and there was no warning when it came.

"I guess there are no monsters," Jaaspar said, laughing.

"OCEAN!" Sol shrieked at the top of her lungs, catching us off guard.

None of us could do anything because they were nowhere near us. Sol's deafening screams filled our ears, and I felt goosebumps rising on my skin.

"Sol, calm down," Jaaspar said. "What happened?"

"It's Ocean," she answered, panting between words. "She's trapped. An ice wall split us up."

"Ocean?" Jaaspar asked. "Can you hear us?"

"It's dark," she whispered. "And cold."

"I can't see a way to get to you," Sol said before she let out a scream of frustration.

"Go without me. I enjoyed playing the Exogames with you, with you all," Ocean said.

"Sol, you'll have to keep moving," Jaaspar said. "We don't know how much time is left, and we don't know where the exit is."

"Fate, it's only Sol and me on this side, and I don't know

where to go," Anyma said.

"Where do we go from here?" Jayde asked.

"Just keep moving, and eventually, we should find a way out," I answered.

Sapphire continued leading us through the maze, but the path was one direct line, continuously straight. There were no turns, left or right. Eventually, the grey ice walls transitioned to a pristine light blue, although, the soft amber glow from Sapphire's body tinted the colour slightly. Further ahead, we reached a fork in the path. There was one opening on the left and another on the right. Our hovering cameras looked down both paths, which didn't help in choosing the correct one.

"Which way do you think we should go?" Sapphire asked.

Something deep inside of me tugged towards the path on the right.

"I think we should go left," Jayde suggested.

"Me too," Jaaspar agreed.

Just before Sapphire could enter the path on the left, I shouted a bit too aggressively for her to stop.

"Wait!" I said as Jaaspar and Sapphire looked at me with haughty eyes. "I think the path on the right is the correct one."

"How do you know for sure?" Sapphire asked with genuine interest, but her delivery was slightly harsh, and she definitely realised because she tried to pull back her words as they came out of her mouth.

"I can't be certain. It's a feeling I can't really explain. Just... trust me. I feel that it's the right path," I answered.

"Alright then. There's no way of knowing for sure, but hey,

anything is possible," Jaaspar said.

The water in the new path was ever so slightly warmer.

"What do you think the exit looks like?" Sapphire asked.

"I'm assuming it'll be the same as the exits in the previous two games," Jayde said. "Another space bridge portal to take us out of here."

The portals generated quite a bit of heat. So if the water was warming up, it was a sign that we were getting closer to reaching the end. My instincts fired up pretty well, but they were usually incorrect. This time though, I was certain I was right.

We stumbled on another fork, this time with three paths to choose from.

"Now, look." Sapphire waved her arm. "Which one do we go through?"

I tapped my chest with my finger as I tried to think of which direction to follow; the answer formed in my brain like a beam of light wanting to poke through the cracks.

"The one on the right," I said eagerly.

Sapphire guided us through the path on the right, and thankfully, my intuition was correct again. The water was warmer than before. I realised why I knew which paths to take. When we chose our aqua shields, Rubie had whispered something in my ear. I think it was the path out of the maze. But I didn't want to tell the others in case there would be detrimental consequences for Rubie.

"Swim faster," I encouraged everyone. "I know the way out of here."

"How do you know that?" Sapphire asked.

"The warmer paths will lead us to the portal," I told them. "Sol, if you can hear me, find the paths where the water is warmer. The portal generates heat."

"Thanks, Fate. I'll find the way out. I hope you're right," she responded between breaths.

The maze growled again, and a much larger current pulled us backwards. A thick wall of ice crashed down and cut off the path behind us just after Jayde had pushed me out of its way.

"Phew, that was close," I said in relief.

Jaaspar placed his palm on the new ice wall and felt all around it for some kind of opening. "Jayde!" he screamed in a panic and his entire body trembled as if he was having a seizure, but he was still in control of his muscles.

"Jayde! Oh no," I said in shock as I rushed to the wall, struggling to get there. "No, no!"

"Jayde, we are going to get you out," Jaaspar said.

I knew he was lying. It was impossible to find a way out of the maze in complete darkness.

"There's no way out," Jayde whispered in disappointment. "I'm blocked on both sides."

"We have to try," Jaaspar responded as his voice cracked.

"Good luck, you two. I know you can make it out of here alive and win the Exogames. I know it," Jayde said.

"You'll die here, Jayde," I cried.

"I know. There's no other choice. This is what I signed up for. I knew the consequences."

"Jayde, please," Jaaspar begged. "We have to try to get you out. You'll die alone," he sobbed.

"I'm going to deactivate my aqua shield now," Jayde said quietly. "Please go. Get out of here. I'm grateful to have met you both, honestly. Thank you."

"No, Jayde, please," I said, choking between sobs.

Jayde's silent cries were muffled by the rushing water that filled her lungs as she deactivated her aqua shield. My throat tightened, and tears flooded my eyes. Jaaspar sobbed uncontrollably. Sapphire pulled both of us away from the ice wall. I tried to resist her tugs, but I was too weak. It should have been me on the other side of that wall. Jayde had pushed me out of the way. I was meant to die, not her.

"Pull yourselves together," Sapphire said. "We have to keep swimming."

I knew we had to make it out of this maze, for Jayde at least. My heart was ripped out of my chest, and Jaaspar's soul was most likely torn in half. Jayde never had the opportunity to express her feelings towards Jaaspar, and I knew she wanted to.

We came across another two forks in the path, and each time, we took the left opening where the water was warmer. My disoriented brain occasionally mixed up which way we were going, and I wasn't even sure if the temperature was warmer or colder than before.

"Fate, which way now?" Sapphire asked.

"What?" I responded because I wasn't paying attention to her words. I was too disoriented to concentrate on the game.

"The path. Which path do we take?"

"Um." I tried to recall Rubie's words. We had taken two rights and two lefts. "The middle one, straight ahead."

"Fate, I hope you're correct."

I hoped I was correct as well. Otherwise, the game makers would lose more players, and the Exogames would end here with us unless Sol and Anyma made it out safely. We hadn't heard from the others in a while, so Sapphire checked in to make sure they were alright.

"Sol, how are you tracking along?" she asked.

"Following Fate's instructions to take the warmer paths. I hope it's getting me closer to the portal," Sol answered.

"Alright, keep us updated if you get stuck."

"Hey, Fate and Jaaspar," Sol said softly. "I'm sorry about Jayde. She really cared for you two."

"Thanks, Sol," Jaaspar said.

"Jaaspar, there's something you should know," I said as I grabbed his arm.

I paused and considered if Jayde would have wanted me to tell him, but she was no longer here, and I felt that Jaaspar needed to know.

"Back in game one, when Jayde and I were talking about you," I continued as he paid closer attention to my words, "Jayde told me how she felt about you."

"What do you mean?" His voice quivered.

"She cared about you, Jaaspar. She wanted to be more than friends with you." I let him soak in my words.

"I liked her too," he whispered, almost unable to get the words out.

That was the sad thing about love; sometimes, it hurt more to keep it a secret. Now Jayde was dead, and she would never know Jaaspar felt the same way about her.

We stopped in front of a much larger fork in our path, the largest we had come across. Five different openings waited for us to choose a path. The last direction Rubie had told me was the path on the right. But there were two options to choose from.

"This one's hard," I said.

I shook my head to refocus my thoughts. *Middle right or furthest right?* There was only one other way to find out.

"Sapphire, we take the path on the furthest right, and if there is no temperature change, then it's the middle right," I said.

She agreed that it was the best possible plan to find a way out quickly, so we took the path on the far right and swam for a few minutes. There was no change in temperature, but before we could turn back around, a giant ice wall crashed down and blocked our path back to the main fork. Thankfully, nobody was trapped this time.

"Oh no, what do we do now?" Sapphire said with a mix of frustration and fear.

"I guess we keep swimming forward and hope there will be a way out from here," I said.

We followed the path all the way around until it spat us out into the open space to choose another path. It was as if the maze had given us a second chance. We took the path on the middle right this time, and as predicted, the water was warmer. Sapphire wasn't the only source of light anymore. The walls glowed a bright white, and the further along we swam, the brighter it glowed.

"We're at the homestretch," Jaaspar said in excitement.

We exited the path into a large opening where the triangular portal rotated slowly in the centre of the abyss. There were multiple openings in the walls, which suggested that there were multiple paths to take from where we began the game. On the opposite side of the portal, an amber glow emerged from an opening. It was Sol who swam out to us, with Anyma following close behind.

"You made it," Sapphire said. "I'm so happy to see you alive."

"Let's get out of this nightmare right now," Sol said as she made her way towards the portal.

"Fate, I'm so glad you made it," Anyma said.

"There should have been more players here," I responded.

We swam through the portal and landed safely on the other side, where Second Earth greeted us, almost as equals. Our suits dried up quickly, and Moirai entered the holding bay with his hands behind his back and head held high. I didn't know what his natural posture looked like, but I was sure this wasn't it.

I looked over to Jaaspar, who shrugged his shoulders and gave me a look of bewilderment. Moirai cleared his throat three times and shook his head at all of us. None of us wanted to get up because by the look on Moirai's face, we would have faced severe consequences if we moved; consequences I was certain we were about to face regardless of our actions.

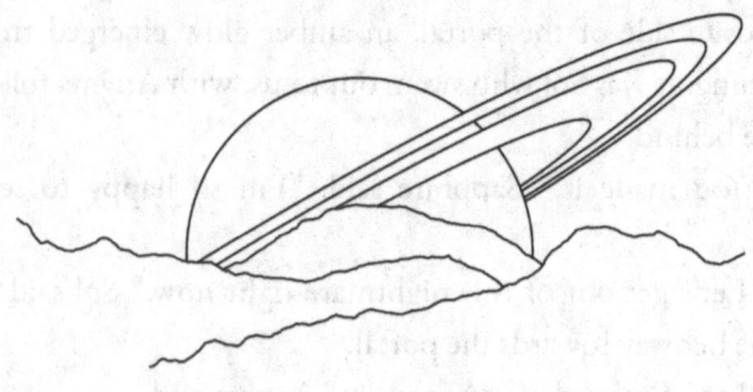

## TWENTY

**M**OIRAI SILENTLY USHERED US to a holding bay with a holographic viewing screen and a single metal chair for each of us. He shut the door and locked us inside. The last things I saw on his face were lowered eyebrows and growing suspicion. I didn't want to be anywhere near Moirai, he looked far too dangerous to be in control of the Exogames.

Jaaspar and I sat on the seats first, followed by the rest of the players. There were only five of us left in the Exogames: Anyma, Jaaspar, Sol, Sapphire, and me. The glow emanating from Sapphire and Sol faded quickly, and their bodies returned to their original pigmentation. Heaters turned on above us because we had been stuck in the freezing water for so long, but that was probably the only generosity the game makers showed us.

"What's going on?" Sapphire asked nervously. "They never locked us in after the other games."

"Silence, please," a non-robotic male voice announced through the ceiling speakers.

"Oh no, what is happening?" Sol whispered, panic-stricken.

Since we were not permitted to speak to each other, all I could do was twiddle my fingers and continuously restyle my hair. I counted the light strips on the floor — sixteen — and stared at the single faulty one that flickered every few seconds. After a while, I lost interest, and began to think about how we were here without Jayde or Thebe. But before I could reminisce too much, the door shot up, and in walked Moirai with Rubie by his side. She kept her head down, and her back was hunched over slightly, probably pulled down by her cuffed hands in front of her.

"Firstly, players, congratulations on making it to the fourth round of the Exogames," Moirai said in a tone that suggested he didn't care.

Sol clapped but quickly withdrew her applause when Moirai's intimidating eyes locked onto her.

"But one of you, or more, will not proceed to the next round. Mark my words," he continued.

My heart sank, and my breathing grew heavy. I glanced at Jaaspar beside me and saw his expression darken. When I looked back at Moirai, he was glaring at me. I dropped my head down and stared at my boots, which were scuffed from the two previous games.

"Exactly forty-seven minutes. Forty-seven minutes was the

time it took you all to complete the third game. We thought by making your suits dissolve in the water, you would all die. When this game was played many years ago, before any of you were born, it took over four hours for the players to complete it. How is it that you lot finished so quickly?" he asked as he continuously fiddled with his usual gold string in his fingers.

Nobody answered his question, but it was even more concerning that Moirai revealed his true intentions on ensuring none of us progressed through the Exogames.

"You see, the one thing we attach to our announcers, like Rubie here, without their notice, is a microphone."

My heart sank further below my stomach, further than where it had fallen before. *Fuck, he knows Rubie told me the way out.* I hoped I was wrong for my sake and for hers. But unfortunately, my thoughts were correct.

"It seems that Rubie here," he touched her face with two fingers threateningly, "had provided the directions out of the maze to a player. The player in question... is one of you. This advantage will not be tolerated."

"You don't know who was given the directions?" Sol asked.

"We will investigate further. In the meantime, nobody leaves this room."

A spare chair morphed from the ground, and Rubie filled its space. Rubie didn't look at me, nor did I look at her. Even a sliver of acknowledgement could have been taken the wrong way. Nobody knew who Moirai was looking for, except for Rubie and me.

The game makers took cheating very seriously. About twelve

years ago, a player's identical twin brother played the games instead of the criminal. When the game makers found this out, they executed both of them without hesitation.

"Player Sol," a robotic voice spoke over the loudspeaker. "Please follow the path to the interrogation room."

Sol rose from her chair and made her way to the interrogation room using the moving lights on the ground as a guide. The viewing screen turned on and broadcast Sol's movements. She entered a room that looked identical to the one Tethys had interrogated me in prior to my sentencing. Moirai sat opposite her and asked questions relating to the previous game.

"How did you get out of the maze so quickly?" he asked, skipping the pleasantries.

"We followed the warmer paths to the portal," she answered.

"What do you mean 'the warmer paths'?"

"The water was warmer as we swam closer to the portal."

"How did you know that the warmer water would lead you to the portal?"

"Fate had said that the portal generated heat, and obviously, the closer we were to it, the warmer the water was."

"Fate Artemis, correct?"

Sol nodded and pursed her lips.

"It is my understanding that you were all split up. Did everybody use the same technique?"

"I assume so. I was alone, and Fate was with the others, so yes, I suppose we all used the same technique."

I was confused because Anyma had been with Sol the entire

time. Perhaps she was changing her story to protect me. But she hardly knew me, so I couldn't understand why she felt the need to do so.

Moirai interrogated Sol about the third game for another thirty minutes before he said something that confused not only me, but the rest of us watching. He threw a spanner in the works and there was no telling anybody's true reaction. Moirai was actively changing the rules of the Exogames, and a part of me hoped that the High Judges would do something about it.

"Now, Sol, would you like to continue the Exogames or forfeit your position and return to prison?" he asked.

"I'm not sure I understand," she responded slowly.

None of us understood. The rules were crystal clear that once a player had entered the Exogames, there was no way of withdrawing their position. It was a verbal contract, and if broken, imminent death would be the only thing left for the player. My stomach churned and growled at me, and not because I was hungry, but because something inside of me didn't believe Moirai's words. The game makers had lied to us before — about the commencement date of the games and about the tracking system they had secretly put inside of us. If they could lie about all of that, then they could lie about giving us the opportunity to leave the games early.

"I'll continue the Exogames," Sol said before she was able to return to the rest of us.

"Player Sapphire, please follow the path to the interrogation room," the robotic voice announced.

Sapphire's eyes darted across the room when she heard her

name, but it was as if she were glued to her chair.

"Player Sapphire, please follow the path to the interrogation room," the voice repeated.

Sol nudged at Sapphire to get up before things got worse for her. She followed the lights to the interrogation room, and her interview was broadcasted back to us.

"Sol is your cousin, correct?" Moirai asked.

"Yes. My younger cousin," she emphasised.

"Why did you enter the Exogames?"

"The only reason I entered was to get my freedom back."

The angle of the camera didn't allow us to see what Moirai was doing, but it looked like he was scrolling on his tablet.

"Please tell the audience what your crime was," he insisted.

"The players already know what my crime was."

That was a lie because I had no idea what she had done to end up in prison, let alone the Exogames.

"But the rest of Second Earth doesn't," Moirai said.

"Hang on a moment. Is this being live streamed to all of Second Earth?" she asked loudly.

"Precisely."

Sapphire rolled her eyes and slouched in her chair. She stared directly into the camera with sharp eyes before speaking.

"Sol and I were sent to prison. Mind you, we were sent to different prisons. She was sent to Mars while I stayed here on Second Earth. What was our crime, you ask? Well, ask Moirai here and the Council of High Judges. I'm sure they'd love to tell you their version of events."

Sapphire's frustration was something I never thought I'd see.

After all, she was a sweet girl and always saw the positives in every conversation. But something had clearly ticked her off.

Moirai signalled to somebody out of view to cut off the video feed, and the holographic viewing screen became a stream of uninterrupted static. Sol gasped, and I covered my mouth with my palm. Sapphire was a dead woman. Clearly what she had said wasn't taken lightly by Moirai, and he had total control over the Exogames, and therefore, our lives.

Time passed slowly as we sat together in silence, but after a while, the viewing screen turned back on. We were relieved to see that Sapphire was unharmed, and Moirai was still interviewing her.

"Last question. Would you like to continue the Exogames or forfeit your—"

"Clearly, I want my freedom back. What a stupid fucking question," she interjected angrily. "I'm continuing the Exogames."

Sapphire stormed back into the holding bay and slumped into her chair. The heat of her anger warmed the entire room. Her cheeks were filled with red dots, and sweat covered her forehead. Her muscles were tensed, her veins were poking out of her neck and for a moment, I thought she was going to physically attack someone.

"Player Jaaspar, please follow the path to the interrogation room."

Jaaspar didn't hesitate to leave the room. He immediately removed himself once his name was called.

"You've made quite a few friends in these Exogames,"

Moirai began.

Jaaspar didn't respond. He simply sat in the chair and stared at Moirai with a blank face.

"Thebe, Jayde, Fate," Moirai continued. "It's unfortunate two of them haven't made it as far as you. Why do you think that is?"

"Thebe and Jayde were good friends. I've never had friends like them before," he said softly but didn't answer the question.

"It's my understanding that you tried to get all the players to work together, to form an alliance. Tell me more about that."

"It was Jayde and Fate's idea from the beginning. Thebe and I thought it was a good idea too. We concluded that if we all worked together, we'd be able to win the Exogames. We'd be able to give everyone a chance to win," Jaaspar answered.

"Do you think it worked?"

"I don't know. You tell me. Clearly, there aren't a whole lot of players left for the last two games, are there?" Jaaspar said sarcastically as he waved his arms around then slammed them on the table.

"I want to talk about your future, Jaaspar," Moirai said.

"Forgive me for interrupting, but I don't think any of us are in the mood for these types of questions. Nobody cheated in the previous game. This is a waste of time, and what future do I have if I don't make it through the next game?"

"Then I want to talk about your past," Moirai said more seriously. "It is our understanding that your mother killed herself. Is that correct?"

"My mother didn't kill herself. She drowned when I was

young," he answered quietly.

"In our reports, we have someone of relation to you who took their own life."

"My girlfriend. She killed herself before my court hearing."

"Young love, so tragic," Moirai said without any consideration of Jaaspar's emotional state. "It's too bad Jayde died. She liked you. Really liked you."

"Jayde's gone, and there is nobody left for me," Jaaspar said as his voice cracked and his eyes welled up with tears.

"Right then, the final question—"

"Don't bother asking. I'm here to play. That's what I signed up for," he answered with so much seriousness in his tone that the melancholy in his voice disappeared, and he left the room without being dismissed.

Before Jaaspar returned to the holding bay, my name was called to the interrogation room. I crossed paths with Jaaspar in the hallway, but there were gazers lined up the walls, so I was petrified to even look at him.

"Fate Artemis," Moirai said, almost apathetic as I entered the room.

I sat in the chair without touching the backrest and placed my hands together on the table.

"Legacies are a running theme in these Exogames. Sol and Sapphire are blood related. A few others were related to previous players, and your father, Scorpius, played ten years ago."

"I don't want to talk about my father," I said.

"Because he didn't win?"

"Because he entered the Exogames. He was never supposed to enter. I was never supposed to enter."

"And I was never meant to be a game maker. Yet, here we are," Moirai said as he swiped on his tablet. "You know he made it to the very last game."

"Obviously, he didn't make it out, so that is a meaningless comment."

"He clearly entered the games so he wouldn't have to serve the punishment for his crime. I can see here that your mother passed away when you were young, and you have no siblings. You have much in common with Jaaspar. Were you close with your father?"

"Yes."

"He clearly tried to cut his sentence short by playing the games. Unfortunately, he was unsuccessful and did not make it out alive."

"We've established that he died. Can we move on please?" I said in annoyance.

"Thankfully, we don't broadcast the final game, so you wouldn't have witnessed his death. That usually scars a person. It certainly would have scarred his son."

"Thankfully?" I growled. "The last moments I saw of him were on a screen, fighting for his life in the fourth game."

"Ah, yes," Moirai said as he scrolled further on his tablet. "The fourth game your father played was a showstopper. Sacrificing his ally to get to the shuttle in time was quite the move."

"That's not what happened," I said, even though I didn't

remember that part in detail.

"Take a look," he said as he flipped the tablet to show me the video footage of the exact moment.

"Are we done here?" I asked without looking at the footage.

"Not quite," Moirai said. "Your department was responsible for many mistakes, mistakes like the expedition to Titan thirty-five years ago. Do you think they made a mistake having you work for them?"

"Firstly, I wasn't alive when the Titan expedition took place, and secondly, their mistakes are not a reflection on my character," I answered.

"Will you continue the Exogames or return to prison to serve the remainder of your sentence?"

I wanted to think about it a bit longer. I should have come up with an answer while I was waiting in the holding bay because time moved even more slowly in here. My sentence was lifelong, so I was guaranteed to die in prison if I went back. In the Exogames, there was a chance of surviving and regaining my freedom. Of course, my chances were extremely slim, but there was still a chance. I didn't want to die a potentially slow and painful death in the games, but I also didn't want to return to Mars.

"I'll play," I answered with too many doubts to my answer.

I returned to the holding bay to join the others, only to find that Rubie was no longer there. When I sat back down in my seat, Jaaspar was uncontrollably tapping his feet. His eyes were wide, but there were still dark circles around them, and his head turned as he glanced across the room.

"Dude, calm down," I whispered to him. "Are you alright?"

"Quiet in the holding bay," a regular male voice demanded over the loudspeaker.

Jaaspar inched closer to me and covered the side of his mouth before he attempted to whisper something into my ear, but whoever was watching us through hidden cameras commanded him to stop.

"Jaaspar, please move to the empty chair behind Sapphire," he said over the ceiling speakers.

I chuckled softly, but quickly stopped because I didn't want to get into any more trouble. Moirai entered the holding bay again with his tablet propped under his arm and stood underneath the door frame to allow the sensors to recognise that he was in the way. I kind of wished the door would close on him and squash his miniature body.

"Thank you all for your interviews," he began.

They were more like interrogations. They were even announced as interrogations when our names were called.

"You will all be escorted back to your dorms on level ninety-five to rest before the fourth game. For transparency, Rubie will be taken to the prison on Mars to serve out a life sentence. Thank you all for your cooperation."

Everyone was interrogated by Moirai. Everyone except Anyma. *What if she took the blame?* Perhaps she already spoke to Moirai prior to the other interrogations, but even if she did, the game makers didn't punish her.

I stood at the back of the line, behind Anyma, as the gazer walked us back to our rooms.

"Why didn't you have an interview?" I whispered into her ear.

"What are you talking about, Fate?" she answered as she snapped her head back.

"Moirai didn't speak with you."

"Stop it," Sol, who was standing in front of Anyma, said aggressively.

I rolled my eyes at her and scoffed.

As we rounded the corner, my arm was immediately clutched by something, or rather someone, and I was tugged to the side, out of view of anyone walking by. The lighting was sufficient for me to see who pulled me there. It was Halley — my colleague from the aerospace department.

"Thank God you're still alive," she said as she threw her arms over my shoulders and didn't let go for a while.

"What are you doing up here?" I whispered so nobody could hear us.

"Fate, I don't know how much time I have, but I must tell you what I've discovered," she began as she pulled out her afticuvos and gave me half.

The surrounding noises muted automatically. There was no more whirring or clacking from machinery behind the walls in Second Earth. The noises disappeared except for the sounds of our breathing.

"After watching you complete the second game — well done, by the way — I couldn't imagine how difficult all of this was for you. I went back to all our messages," she continued.

"Aw, how sweet," I said genuinely but a bit confused.

"Not really. You are the only person named 'Fate' that I know."

"Yeah?"

"Why the hell would you sign the bottom of the message with your full name?"

"I never do," I said as I looked around the side to see if anyone was there before I remembered the afticuvos was activated. "I sometimes don't even sign with my name at all."

"Exactly right. So, I went through every single one of our messages, and the only one signed with your full name is the most recent one. That suggests two things to me. Either you were out of your mind when you wrote that message, or somebody else sent it from your tablet," she said.

"You already know I don't remember writing that message."

"And I believe you, Fate. Now I do."

"But nobody else does. Except for some of the players. You know, some of the other players think they were framed as well, and I believe them. These games don't make sense."

"The same thing probably happened to you. If you didn't write that message, then somebody else did, but for what reason? Who wants you dead, and why?" she asked, not expecting me to answer.

"Not just me. Who wants all the players dead? If we are all innocent, then why were we taken to prison and given an opportunity to play in the Exogames?"

"I don't know, Fate, but I'm going to sleuth my way to the bottom of this. I promise."

"Don't promise me. I have faith you'll figure it out. But

don't promise me anything," I pleaded.

Halley looked at me with one eyebrow raised and propped her head forward.

"I've made promises to people too," I continued. "I promised my friends that we would make it out of the games alive. And now two of them are dead."

"I'm sorry, Fate. Alright. I'll find out the truth for you, I pr —" She paused. "I'll do my best."

I handed back her afticuvos after one last hug, and she disappeared through a narrow passageway hidden between two walls. A gazer rounded the corner and noticed me through the helmet that covered the top half of his face.

"What are you doing here, player?" he asked as he reached for his gun but never pulled it out.

"I... um," I hesitated. "I got lost," I lied and hoped he would let go of his gun.

"Back to your dorm," he demanded as he grasped my arms behind my back. "I will escort you there."

The gazer's kept kicking the back of my ankles as he pushed me to my dorm. It was as if he was doing it on purpose and it became increasingly uncomfortable. It seemed far too long before we reached my room, but I was most likely just being impatient, and eventually we made it. Jaaspar waited up for me before he went to sleep; he couldn't face the dark anymore, and I didn't blame him because the dark was what took Thebe and Jayde from us.

I really hoped Halley would be able to uncover the truth. I was ecstatic she finally believed that I wasn't the one who sent her that message. It only took her a few years. The dark grey fog that clouded the halls of Second Earth and concealed its mysteries was beginning to clear. But the closer the truth was, the more entangled those mysteries became, and I didn't want to be the one to drown in them.

# TWENTY ONE

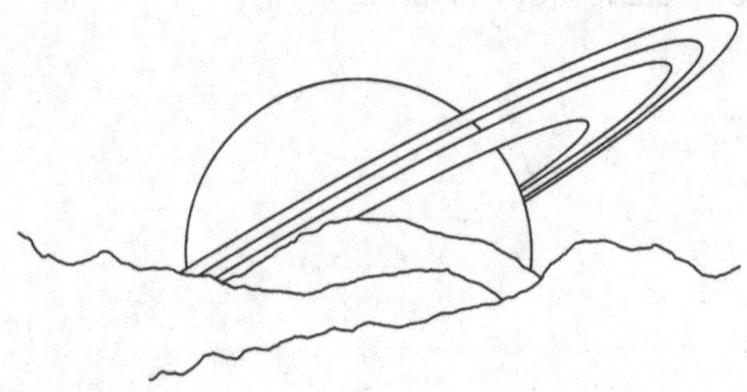

**G**AME FOUR WAS DIFFERENT, and not just because we had lost so many players, but because we didn't take a spaceship to the next location. We used a space bridge portal to seamlessly travel from Second Earth.

We were taken to a large ship orbiting Jupiter. The planet was unimaginably massive compared to how Earth looked below our old home. Vibrant tapestries of crimson and orange clouds spun in a giant ball below us. It looked like a watercolour painting in motion, and my face fogged up the glass just as it had the day before my court hearing.

Jaaspar hadn't spoken to me at all. His eyes were circled with dark and heavy bags, and his face drooped as the corners of his lips were pulled downwards.

Moirai was the one to give us the rundown of the game this

time because Rubie had been taken to prison.

"Players," he began as we sat ourselves in strange acrylic seats, "Jupiter's eye, better known as the great red spot, is a terrible storm. You will all be racing through it."

*Another race? We barely made it through the race on Venus.*

"Each of you are seated in a shuttle, which you will need to pilot from the outer edge of the storm to the portal in the centre."

In the aerospace department, I had trained in simulations to pilot various shuttles for about a month. Even though nobody had an advantage in this game, I definitely had the upper hand. It was unlikely the other players had any experience with piloting, and I feared it would be the reason they won't survive.

"There are automatic communication devices for you to speak to each other because it is guaranteed that some of you, if not all of you, will have your very last moments soon," Moirai said.

I gulped. It was concerning that they wanted us to hear each other's last moments because again, he confirmed that we were all going to die. Sol raised her hand, but Moirai ignored her, so she shook her hand harder to grab his attention. After a moment, Moirai rolled his eyes and called on her to speak.

"So, in this game, what do we have to do again?" she asked impatiently.

"If you listened to what I just said and waited until I was finished, you would know," he said mockingly.

Luckily, I didn't ask the same question as Sol, even though also I had no idea what to do. My emotional energy depleted and my attention span was lower because of the exhaustion the games provided. They simply drained the life out of us.

"You will all begin at the very edge of Jupiter's red spot and race to the centre where the portal is waiting to take you back to Second Earth," Moirai continued. "There won't be a time limit, but if you want to survive the storm, you'll need to fly your ships as fast as possible."

Something felt wrong. Terribly wrong. When I had done the training simulations, I learned that not every shuttle can clock top speeds. It was generally common knowledge in my department, and Moirai would have known it as well. If the shuttle exceeded its maximum speed, the internal motors would fry themselves, and it would either explode or fall to the ground.

"No time limit, so we could just fly around forever on Jupiter?" Sol asked in a way that implied she didn't want an answer.

"The fuel in your shuttles will not last forever. By all means, go ahead and fly around forever, but eventually you will fall to the very core of Jupiter and be squashed to death."

Sol glanced at her cousin and looked back at Moirai with a scrunched nose.

"Good luck, players. The game begins in, three, two, one," he said slowly.

A large multi-layered glass casing emerged from the ground beside me and covered my head. A control panel with a single cyclic stick emerged with flashing lights. Finally, a steel shell wrapped around portions of the glass on the sides of my body. I assumed our shuttles were equipped with a device to prevent Jupiter's radiation from penetrating them unless the game makers wanted to kill us off all at the same time. Honestly, I wouldn't been surprised after how difficult and deadly the previous three games were.

Moirai took a step back to avoid being crushed by the airtight door. The floor broke away beneath us, and our shuttles were each held by giant claws that rotated to face the gas planet below. It looked even prettier now, whether it was due to my adrenaline or simply being closer to Jupiter.

"Here we go," Anyma said with a bit too much excitement.

"I'm not ready for this," Sapphire said nervously as we were dropped below.

The shuttles automatically accelerated to the edge of the planet to prevent us from taking control and flying away. The tips of our shuttles caught fire as we entered Jupiter's atmosphere. I thought they were going to explode because the fire was directly in front of our noses, closer than it was when we broke Earth's atmosphere in the first game.

It was the first time I'd ever touched the controls of a real shuttle, but there was no excitement. I was too preoccupied with staying alive to celebrate this moment.

The hovering camera appeared from the centre console and remained in my shuttle. It was annoying to have it hovering beside my ear, but we were all in the same boat, and it soon became unnoticeable. Once our shuttles broke through Jupiter's atmosphere, I knew it would be a quick game, or at least, I hoped.

We were lined up on the very edge of Jupiter's red spot, and our shuttles waited for us to take control of the cyclic sticks. The creamy clouds were filled with what I assumed was water because the front glass was covered in droplets. Only metres in front of us, the swirling red clouds began spinning much faster than where we currently were. The darkness of outer space disappeared as we were entirely consumed by the gasses around us.

"Okay, let's go," I said as I grabbed hold of the cyclic stick firmly and pushed it forward.

Jaaspar's voice crackled through the communication system. "Be careful. The hydrogen gas can be pretty dangerous."

That was what it was. Hydrogen. My shuttle shot forward with a slight jerk, and I was sent flying into the storm. I was engulfed in a colourful whirlpool with liquid hydrogen splashing all over the windshield. It was difficult to see anything in front of me, but if I remained on a straight course, I would reach the portal. I couldn't see any of the other shuttles; they had all disappeared into the storm.

The G-forces were extremely strong, and my head became fixed to the back of my seat. I had no G-force training in my department because I hadn't yet reached that level, and because of it, I wasn't sure how long I would be able to survive the game.

"Is everyone doing okay?" I asked out of concern.

"This storm is terrible. I can't even control my shuttle," Sapphire yelled in frustration as she tried to stabilise.

"It's not that hard," Sol said rudely, although her attitude may not have been intentional.

"I'm alright," Anyma said. I felt her nerves through the speaker. She had the same nerves as I did.

"We just need to get to the centre of the storm," Jaaspar said, taking quick breaths between his words. "How far is it?"

"Don't know," Sol said with the same attitude.

"Fate, you worked in aerospace back on Second Earth. How fast can these shuttles go?" Jaaspar asked.

"There's no definitive answer. I'm not sure what type of shuttles these are. But try not to go too fast because the engine can overheat and explode," I answered a bit too loudly.

The winds picked up significantly and knocked my shuttle from side to side. The clouds darkened into a deeper crimson with patches of orange, like cotton candy that hadn't been coloured correctly.

"Sack it, I'm clocking full speed," Sol said and laughed almost wickedly as her shuttle whizzed past mine, nearly crashing into me, and disappeared into the clouds ahead. "I'm on fire!" she cheered excitedly.

"You've gone too fast, Sol. Your shuttle is going to—"

My sentence was cut short by the flatlining sound immediately after Sol's shuttle exploded into a million and one pieces. I flew through the debris, which cleared up pretty quickly. There was no fire; her shuttle had simply popped like an overly inflated balloon.

"She's dead," Sapphire said carelessly.

"She didn't want to listen to my advice. That was her own fault," I responded. "Be careful. The shuttles won't go full speed."

The clouds darkened even further into a maroon with touches of bright pink, which swirled and mixed into each other. The liquid hydrogen splashed against my shuttle from all angles, and the wind tossed me around without a care. I had no idea if I was heading in the right direction. For all I knew, I could have been flying away from the portal.

Thankfully, a flash of light illuminated the entire planet. The clouds grew more vibrant, and I knew where the portal was. I saw two shuttles on either side of me but couldn't see a third.

"Did you guys see that?" Anyma asked.

"What was that?" Jaaspar asked.

A part of me hoped Thebe would joke about it being 'French', but I soon remembered that she was dead.

"The portal, I'm pretty sure," I answered, with more doubt as the flashes grew stronger.

"No," Sapphire said very slowly. "That wasn't the portal." She was an intelligent young woman and realised what it was before the rest of us even questioned it.

Another electrifying flash lit up the entire planet, and it couldn't be clearer what it actually was. The portal was never within reach. As Jupiter's eye darkened further, the flashes became increasingly abundant. Suddenly, a blue bolt of lightning shot down from above me and scratched the side of my shuttle. I pulled the cyclic stick so hard to dodge the strike that I thought it was going to break.

"Lightning!" I shrieked. "Don't get hit!"

Jaaspar screamed every time the lightning flashed. The storm was dark, almost pitch black, and I didn't want to know what secret monsters were hiding inside. The only source of light was the flashes of lightning, and they only lasted a few seconds at a time. The other players' shuttles were around me, but they moved with every flash and then disappeared into the darkness.

"There's too much rain and wind and lightning." Jaaspar panicked as his breath became shallow.

I swerved my shuttle away from lightning strikes that came from every direction — the worst part was trying to keep an eye on the strikes from behind me. The deeper into the storm we were, the more lightning there was. It was impossible to get through alive.

The shuttle on my right dodged the lightning strikes pretty well; however, the shuttle on my left was struggling to get through them.

"Slow and steady wins the race, guys. We can do this." I tried to encourage the other players so they wouldn't panic and make a wrong move, but I wasn't sure they cared enough about my advice.

"This isn't a race, Fate. We just have to make it out alive," Jaaspar said with frustration.

I understood where he was coming from. I was terrified as well. My heart felt like it was going to pop out of my chest every time a lightning bolt crashed near me, and my hand was beginning to sweat, which made the cyclic stick very slippery.

The sky flashed twice, and a strong bolt of lightning zapped the shuttle on my left. It didn't explode, but the rear sparked up and smoke poured out of it.

"I've been hit," Jaaspar screeched. "Oh no, what do I do?"

"Jaaspar!" I panicked as I tried to think of a solution.

I had no idea what to do. The only thing Jaaspar could do was get to the portal in time. But we had no idea how far it was.

"I think... I think this is the end for me," he said.

"Don't talk like that," Sapphire said.

"You'll make it out with us," Anyma tried to encourage him.

"Jaaspar, keep dodging the lightning, and you'll get to the portal," I said, hoping that the portal was only metres away.

"Fate?" he said too calmly to hide the fear deep in his voice.

"Please don't," I said as my eyes watered and my voice croaked. "Please promise me you'll make it to the portal."

Jaaspar was good at lying, at least I assumed he was. The whole time I knew Jaaspar I never suspected he was lying. But the promise I requested of him was not achievable. Jaaspar wanted to die; I knew it even before the first game. There was a reason Jaaspar had dark patches around his eyes. He didn't sleep the night before, he couldn't, because nightmares of Jayde's death ate up his soul and drowned out his light. Throughout the night, he screamed Jayde's name as he relived the same moment repeatedly in his sleep. I had the same nightmares too, but about myself.

"Don't fight the mountains, Fate, move them. Just as your father used to say," he said.

"Jaaspar don't."

"Fate, there is no saving me. My shuttle is too far gone."

I didn't want to believe it but what he said was right.

"Land somewhere among the stars for me," I whispered.

"I want you to join me in the stars one day," he said moments before he was struck with another thick bolt of lightning. His shuttle exploded into an enormous fire in front of me and I knew for sure that he wouldn't have survived it.

The shrill flatlining sound rang through the communication system briefly before it cut off completely.

"Jaaspar!" I wailed as tears flooded my face. "No!" I cried.

"Focus, Fate," Sapphire said pretty loudly through the communication system, but I didn't pay any attention to her voice. "You must concentrate to get to the portal."

"Jaaspar's dead," I said as I sniffled so hard that my eardrums popped. "He's dead." I tried to breathe, but my throat wouldn't allow any air to pass through.

I couldn't let down my guard. If I slipped up, it would be over for me as well. Stronger winds made it increasingly difficult to stabilise my shuttle. More clouds obscured my vision along with the hydrogen rain, which didn't allow me to see where the lightning strikes came from. I couldn't dodge anything anymore. I just had to hope for the best.

"Fate," Anyma said with pain in her voice. "Fate, I'm so sorry about Jaaspar."

A shuttle whizzed past mine as I manoeuvred away from the flashing clouds, missing me by mere millimetres.

"Someone is going too fast," I said, not knowing who it was.

"The lightning is chasing me!" Sapphire screamed.

"Slow down!"

Lightning bolts snapped in front of me and blocked my

path through. I spun my shuttle upside down to fit through a tiny gap between two bolts and looped over another one that nearly hit me. It was pitch black. Lightning and thunder didn't even illuminate the storm anymore.

The rain stopped splashing on my windshield, but the clapping thunder still rocked the shuttle. My legs were cramping up in the tight space. I knew I had to act before it was too late. Then I did something that would either kill me or save my life. I took hold of the cyclic stick in both hands and pulled it towards me to drive the shuttle directly up to the top layer of Jupiter's atmosphere. I fought hard against the strong gravitational pull and prayed that I wouldn't be dragged to the core of the planet. Lightning appeared in a random sequence out of nowhere, following me as I navigated myself upward.

The clouds brightened and the lightning grew quiet. Outer space was clearly visible, and if I continued going up, I would shoot out of the atmosphere. If only that was the way out.

"Fly your shuttle up," I directed to the remaining players. "We'll be able to see the portal from there."

I hoped it was true.

"Which way is up?" Sapphire asked in a panic. "I can't see anything."

Jupiter's great red spot had disoriented her, and with all the flying around, she didn't know which direction to go. Her voice quivered, and I knew she was in trouble.

"I don't know where I'm going," she squealed before her voice was overpowered by the flatlining sound.

"Sapphire?" I asked.

There was a long pause. Sapphire's voice didn't come through the communication system, nor did Anyma's.

"Are you there? Sapphire?" I repeated.

There was no response, only soft static through the communication system and the muted crashes of thunder.

"She's dead, Fate," Anyma confirmed. "You know it. She's dead," she repeated.

"Argh, and she was doing so well!"

The game makers really didn't want any of us to make it through the games. Three players were already dead, and I had no idea if I could make it out alive.

"Anyma, can you get above the storm?"

"I'm already here, Fate," she answered at the same time as I broke through the swirling tapestry of cotton candy.

I couldn't see her shuttle, but I saw what we were looking for from the beginning. The portal, or the beacon at least, activated with a beam of light far in the distance. It was obvious that it was not just lightning. From the beginning, it would have been easier for us to fly over the storm rather than through it. Jaaspar and the others would still be alive if we'd used our brains properly.

"Get to the portal, Anyma," I said as I pushed the cyclic stick forward.

My shuttle jerked, and I had a minor heart attack. But it just needed a quick jumpstart to get going again. Creamy clouds swirled around me with small gusts of wind resisting against my shuttle. The winds were only a fraction of the strength of the ones in the storm directly below.

The triangular portal was clear now. It hovered in the eye of Jupiter's great red spot, almost peacefully, as it waited patiently for players to fly through.

"We're here," I said excitedly, but the excitement slowly faded into the realisation that my friends, and the other worthy players, wouldn't ever see the light of day again.

The portal began closing, which was strange because Moirai said that there was no time limit in this game. It was obvious now that the game makers didn't want any of us to make it through. They just wanted a good show all along.

I pushed the cyclic stick as far forward as it could go, and I knew that I would either make it to the portal in time, or my shuttle would explode.

"Anyma, speed," I said, hoping her shuttle wouldn't explode either.

"But what—"

"No, we need to get out of this game now. Whatever it takes, no matter if it works or not."

I had no idea if what I said made any sense, but the only thing on my mind was getting us out of the game.

The beacon began to fade away, and I pushed the cyclic stick harder, but it didn't do anything. I was only a few seconds away from the exit. The portal flickered, and I screamed as I closed my eyes, hoping that we would make it out. The thunderous sounds around me faded, and I was able to think clearly again.

As I opened my eyes, I exhaled in relief that my surroundings were recognisable. We had made it out alive and unharmed. Second Earth looked the same every time I made it through the portal, and there was no reason it would have changed this time around.

The front of my shuttle sparked up, and I realised there were only a few seconds before it would explode. I pulled the eject lever, and I was flown to the other side of the large holding bay just in time before my shuttle blew up in condensed flames. Anyma's shuttle was perfectly fine, except for the extreme wear and tear all over its outer shell.

The portal finally closed, and the holding bay door opened. Four games down, one to go.

PART III

THE FINALE

# TWENTY TWO

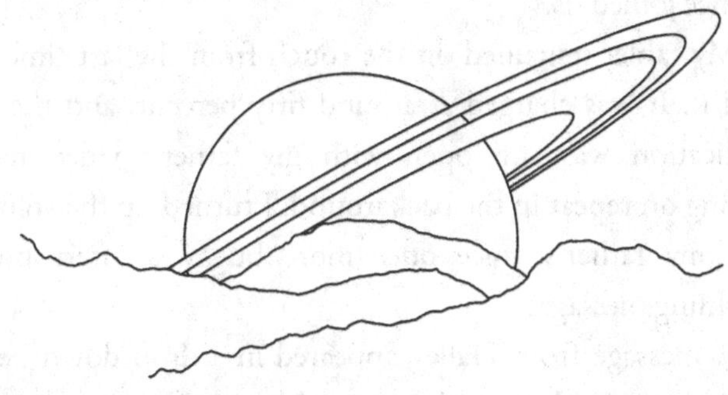

**A**NYMA WENT TO HER ROOM unsupervised, while two gazers escorted me back to my room before the debrief for the final game. Any excitement to play in the Exogames had disappeared with our hope of making it out alive. There was no motivation to win the games. There was no motivation to regain my freedom. There was nobody to encourage me to continue playing.

I entered the Exogames because Jaaspar wanted to. And Anyma entered because of me. I couldn't blame myself for Jaaspar's death, but I had to take some responsibility. The more the thought lingered in my mind, the more it ate me up inside.

The door to my room closed, and I was finally alone. But it wasn't a good thing. Jaaspar's laugh no longer filled the room, nor did his laid-back personality. All his belongings had been removed from our room, which made it seem as though he never existed in the first place. But he was more than a mere memory. I knew Jaaspar for a long time; I'd met him when I first arrived on Mars. We were the original duo before the rest of our alliance joined us.

My tablet remained on the couch from the last time I had used it. It was charged at around fifty percent, and the inbox application was still open with my father's video message playing on repeat in the background. I turned up the volume to hear my father's voice once more but was interrupted by incoming messages.

A message from Halley appeared in a drop down before I was able to finish the video again. I hesitated to open it, but if she was messaging me during the Exogames, then it had to be important. Her message read:

FATE,

I'M NOT SURE IF YOU MADE IT PAST THE FOURTH GAME. I HAVEN'T BEEN WATCHING IT. IF YOU ARE STILL ALIVE, THEN YOU HAVE TO KNOW WHAT I FOUND OUT. I'VE BEEN DIGGING FURTHER INTO YOUR MESSAGE, AND I'VE TRACED IT BACK TO THE WIRELESS NETWORK IT WAS CONNECTED TO. WHOEVER USED YOUR TABLET TO SEND ME THAT MESSAGE WASN'T FROM OUR DEPARTMENT. IT WAS CONNECTED TO THE WIRELESS NETWORK ON LEVEL NINETY-THREE. THAT'S THE GAME

MAKERS' LEVEL. I'LL KEEP DIGGING, AND I'LL LET YOU KNOW WHAT I FIND OUT. GOOD LUCK IN THE FINAL GAME, IF YOU'VE MADE IT THAT FAR.

REGARDS,
HALLEY

It was no longer blood that flowed through my veins or even adrenaline trying to keep me alive. It was pure rage, anger and all things vengeful towards the game makers and the Council of High Judges. Although it didn't entirely prove my innocence, it brought me one step closer to finding some answers. The truth was within reach; I just needed to grasp it with both hands. I couldn't let it go, or it would slip through my fingertips and be lost forever.

I needed to win the final game, and there was only one way to win. I had to play. If I forfeited my position, I would be killed in whatever horrific way the game makers chose. The game makers decided everyone's destiny in the games, whether we were innocent or not, and it was time for the games to end.

I paced up and down the entire room whilst organising my belongings. It was my last night in this room because I wouldn't be returning after the final game. I couldn't imagine the game makers delaying the fifth game any further. But ultimately, that decision wasn't up to me. The fifth game was never broadcast to Second Earth, so in theory, the final game could be ages away. Nonetheless, I packed up all my things and prepared for the final night, alone this time.

My tablet rang twice with the notification of an incoming message. My face contorted because my contact information wasn't freely available. Not even everyone in my department could contact me through my tablet. The message was from an anonymous sender with a random sequence of numbers where their name should have been. There was no subject information or any body text anywhere. There was only a single attachment at the very bottom of the message. I was uncertain if I should press it in case it contained malware, but my tablet was safely equipped with the best antivirus software.

Before I began the video, the thumbnail contained a familiar face and an all too familiar setting. It was Rubie with her face scuffed and marked with small bruises. We were told that Rubie had been taken to the prison on Mars, and it was confirmed by the orange atmosphere that illuminated the familiar interior of the facility.

My finger shook as it inched closer to start the video. Whatever Rubie sent me must have been vitally important, otherwise she wouldn't have gone to such great lengths to reach me.

"Fate, there's something important you must hear," she whispered.

The camera shook as she struggled to hold it up, most likely because the rest of her body was bruised up just like her face.

"Moirai knows I gave you the directions out of the maze," she continued. "Whatever the next game is, they're going to try to get rid of all the players at once. The Council of High Judges wants you all dead."

The message must have been recorded before the fourth game. She wouldn't have known that I already made it out, and she was right, the game makers did try to get rid of us all. The portal had closed early, and we were given false information about the shuttles being able to clock top speeds.

"It's my fault you're all going to die, but you all would have died in the maze without my help," she said with a mix of tears and blood running down her cheeks.

She was wrong. We could have made it out of the maze without her directions. I figured out that the heated tunnels were the correct paths to the portal, so even if she hadn't told me which way to go, we would have made it out. It might have taken slightly longer, but it was a better option than cheating our way through.

"I'm so sorry about Jayde and Thebe. I know you were good friends with them both."

This confirmed that the message was recorded prior to game four because there was no mention of Jaaspar or the other players who died in the fourth game.

"Make the most of the time you have before the next game, or games, if you end up making it out by some miracle. When I recorded your vitals before the first game, your cognitive test was inconclusive. You shouldn't be playing the games in the first place. But if the Council of High Judges found out that information, you'd be instantly killed."

I already knew my cognitive test was inconclusive. Rubie had told me that day, and it had been in the back of my mind ever since. A part of me thanked her for not revealing that information to anybody because my life would have been cut short. But the other part of me despised her because she was responsible for Jaaspar's death, and Sapphire's and Sol's. She was going to be responsible for my death as well, and I couldn't forgive her.

"I hope you make it out alive, Fate. I really do. But if you don't, then I am truly sorry," she concluded, and the video blacked out.

I softly tossed my tablet to the side because her apology was pointless. When Moirai interrogated us, nobody mentioned that Rubie gave me the directions. The only way for the game makers to know for sure was if Rubie told the truth.

I laid back on my bed and gave in to my exhaustion because I couldn't bear it anymore. The games had killed my emotions and took my sanity, and frankly, I didn't care if I won the next game or not. I had nothing left to go back to.

I closed my eyes and let the weight of the world disappear. With every fibre and sinew willing me to sleep, I had no choice but to listen to my body. It wasn't just the game makers who had to pay for everyone's deaths, it was also the Council of High Judges. And I was going to make them pay.

# TWENTY THREE

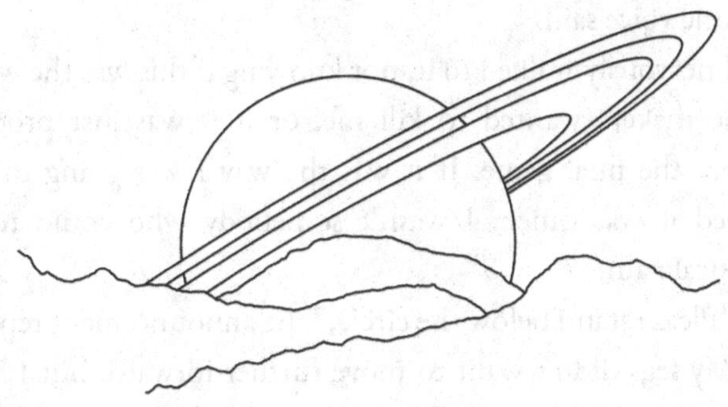

**I** WOKE UP HALFWAY THROUGH THE NIGHT and couldn't go back to sleep no matter how hard I tried. So, I just sat on the couch and stared aimlessly into the black canvas of outer space, which was decorated with a plethora of stars and celestial bodies. I tried to catch a glimpse of a shooting star to wish that I would make it out of the final game, but none passed by, but even if they did, it wasn't up to the stars anyway.

The door shot up, and in walked two gazers, one with a helmet and one without. They grasped my arms and escorted me through the twists and turns of the hallways, before leaving me inside a perfectly symmetrical holding bay. If I were asleep when they'd walked in, I was sure they wouldn't have hesitated to drag me out of my bed in the middle of the night.

The white strip lights on one half of the floor were the exact mirror image of the other half. The lights wrapped onto the walls and met in a fluorescent circle on the ceiling.

"Welcome, Fate Artemis. Please stand below the circle," a robotic voice said.

I nervously walked to it, not knowing if this was the way the game makers wanted to kill me, or if it was just procedure before the final game. If it was the way I was going to die, I hoped it was quick. I wasn't somebody who could tolerate physical pain.

"Please stand below the circle," the announcement repeated.

My legs didn't want to move further forward, but I had to force myself because the game makers were most likely watching. I looked directly up at the white circle above my head, which was pulsing slowly. An opaque force field appeared around me, and I instantly knew what was about to happen because I had experienced it at the commencement of the first game.

The circle above me brightened intensely, almost like the sun was directly overhead. I covered my eyes with one hand and the top of my head with the other forearm. With a lightning-quick flash, the clothing that was once on my body had turned to ash. A small vacuum in the floor sucked the charred fabric into the waste system, and the force field disappeared.

Thankfully, I was not dead. I couldn't see clothes for the final game anywhere, so I was unsure what was actually going on. Another illuminated circle formed beneath my feet, and lights climbed up all over my body. These lights were merely a guideline for a synthetic white material which grew from the floor and wrapped around my body. It was flexible, light and very comfortable against my skin. I liked how it was skin-tight but not so pressed against my skin that it rode in any unwanted crevices. White wasn't usually a colour that complemented my skin tone; however, from the reflection on the shiny black door, I looked good.

As I checked myself out in the reflection, the door opened, and Moirai walked in, unexcited to see me.

"Congratulations, Fate, you've made it to the final round of the ninety-ninth Exogames," he said as he applauded.

The game makers must have been explaining the rules to us separately because Anyma wasn't with me, and I didn't see the gazers escort her out of her room.

"The final game is simple. We like to call it Titan. That is where you will be stranded for fifteen Earth days, equivalent to a single day on Titan."

Stranded on Titan for fifteen days. No food or water. It was a death sentence, guaranteed. The game makers couldn't kill me in the fourth game, but their attempts seemed more promising as Moirai read out the briefing.

"You will need to find a way off Saturn's moon before the time ends or else the nanobots underneath your skin will explode," he explained.

The nanobots weren't exactly a fear of mine when we began the games. I only grew more terrified of them when I knew what they could do, especially after Badru exploded in the first game.

"Titan is a frozen wasteland. It will be impossible to get off it," I said in frustration.

Moirai was sending me to die. It was punishment for what Rubie did. It was her mistake, not mine, and I shouldn't have been the one to pay for it.

"Players have done it in the past," Moirai said calmly, but I sensed that he was lying.

"Nobody has won the Exogames in over thirty-five years."

"Then make sure you're the first."

The rules to the game were extremely vague, but they were simple. I had one Titan day to escape the moon. That was it. And if I didn't get off Titan in time, I would die. I would die regardless, because without food or water, I would dehydrate and run out of energy. I would surely die before the day on Titan was complete.

"The suit on your body will protect you from the cold. Do not take it off or else you will freeze to death. Any questions?" Moirai asked.

"None for you," I answered quietly, almost whispering.

"Alright then. Just push the white button between your collarbone to activate a force field around your head for air. Give me a nod once you're ready to begin."

I did just that. I pushed the white button and nodded my head with no hesitation. A small blue light signalled that the force field was activated, and the refraction of light around my head confirmed it.

"Good luck, Fate," Moirai said as a portal was activated behind me, and a completely different world appeared on the other side.

I almost didn't want to go through. There was no logical reason for me to play the final game because I was sure to die either way.

Moirai stared at me, uncomfortably, until I crossed over. The exact moment my feet touched Titan's terrain, the portal snapped shut. The ground was hard, probably because it was slightly frozen. Chilling wind blew across my face — it was the only thing that penetrated the force field around my head — and my body shivered to keep itself warm. The gravity on Titan was weaker than it was on Earth, but the weighted boots and bracelets made it feel the same.

I didn't know where to begin. The entire moon was lifeless. The atmosphere was tinted orange, almost like it was on Mars, except it was more vibrant here. The sky had few clouds, although it wasn't completely empty and the mother planet, Saturn, was clearly visible as it conquered the heavens.

I walked towards it, curiously, as it tugged me closer. I climbed over rocky slopes and around pillars of clumped dirt. The ground was covered in rocks of various shapes and sizes, which most likely stretched to the pointy mountains in the distance.

The day was about to bleed into nightfall as the sun gradually moved towards the horizon behind me. My body shivered as the temperature cooled drastically, but it wasn't so cold that I would have frozen to death.

The further along I went, the thicker the air became. The force field around my head filtered the air which increasingly thickened, and I knew what I was sensing once I saw the river. Back on Second Earth, we studied potentially habitable planets and moons, particularly Titan. Simulations showed promising results. Before I was born, the aerospace department sent out a large team to survey Saturn's moon, but none of them came back after their communication systems went down. There was no point in sending a rescue team because we assumed they all died. I read a few of the incomplete reports, but they led nowhere. That was why I knew Moirai had sent me here to die. He knew there was no chance at life here. There was no chance at survival, no matter how hard anybody fought for it, and a part of me felt that it wasn't entirely Moirai's decision. There were obviously more players in this game, not just us prisoners.

The river that carved through the terrain was formed of liquid methane, which flowed in the direction of Saturn. It wasn't moving aggressively; it just flowed peacefully into the distance. I couldn't see how far it travelled, so I climbed up a rocky hill that curved beside the river. I almost slipped a few times because I wasn't used to climbing.

The river stretched to the mountains and most likely beyond. The cold winds blew across the river, and tiny droplets bounced up and flew around. Saturn looked so pretty in the sky, unbothered and untouched. I stretched my arm high up, a bit hesitant at first, but then shot it up as high as I could hold it and imagined my palm was touching the surface of the planet. If only I could have grasped it in my fingertips, but that was a power humans couldn't possess, not even the High Judges had such authority.

I held my arm up even through the pain and closed my eyes to accept my death. It took twenty-two years for the leaders of Second Earth to kill me, and the end was only moments away. But something abruptly pulled me back into reality as it grasped my consciousness and tugged at it.

"Fate!" a voice screamed far away, like an echo searching for a place to rest.

I opened my eyes and dropped my numb arm. My blood rushed through it and woke it back up. Perhaps it was my imagination because I didn't see anybody.

"Fate!" the voice repeated from behind me, echoing again as if it didn't have an origin.

I shot around and squinted. The sun was only moments away from sinking below the horizon, but it still blinded me. A figure bobbed up and down from behind some rocky pillars, but I could only see its silhouette. I shielded my eyes with my hands and recognised who'd called my name.

It was Anyma.

"Oh my God," I said in relief as I ran up to her. "Anyma, you're here."

"It's good to see you too."

"I thought they killed you or something worse. I didn't know what happened."

"I'm sorry. I was scared to start the game. I can't believe we've made it. We made it through four games. This is the last one, Fate. We just need to finish it."

"Didn't anybody explain the rules to you? There is no way to get off this moon. It's impossible."

"Nothing is impossible, Fate. You just doubt yourself too much."

Anyma was right. My entire life, all I had done was doubt my abilities. I doubted my ability to get through the Exogames, but already I had survived eighty percent of them. I always used to cower away from success, like a light that was too afraid to touch the darkness, but the light was always the champion. I needed to remind myself that I was the light. I was going to overcome the darkness.

"This is Titan," I said confidently. "It is a lifeless wasteland, cold and empty."

"Yeah, this *is* Titan. And what did our department do many years ago?"

My face brightened with the realisation of what Anyma was referring to.

"The expedition," I answered.

She nodded slowly and pursed her lips.

Finding any of the ships would be a long shot. I had no idea where they landed all those years ago, where on Titan I was, or if any of the ships had survived and were still functioning. But I might as well try to search for something, because I still had one Titan day to get off Saturn's moon. We'd made it this far; I wasn't going to give up when I was so close to the end.

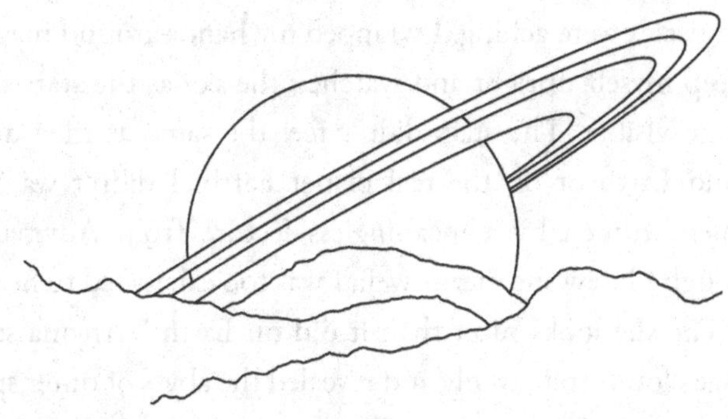

## TWENTY FOUR

ANYMA STARED AT ME, hoping I knew where to begin. I stared back at her and hoped for the same thing. But the simple fact was that neither of us had any clue where to start. Titan was a big moon, and we only had one Titan day to get off it or else our nanobots would explode.

"It's getting dark," I said. "Do you think we should rest and continue again later on?"

When I said those words, it reminded me of the same conversation I had with Jayde during the first game. But Anyma's response was nothing like Jayde's.

"Sure, I'm pretty tired too. We haven't had a proper rest in a while," she answered.

"Let's just sit and watch the stars," I suggested. "Just look how gorgeous the universe is."

"We need to talk, Fate," she said with seriousness in her tone.

I pretended to not hear her because I wanted to have a moment to rest my bones. Once I sat down, I realised that all my muscles were aching. I wrapped my hands around my knees to keep myself upright and watched the sky as the stars slowly became visible. The stars didn't feel the same as they did on Second Earth or on the real planet Earth. I didn't want this moment ruined by a meaningless lecture from Anyma, and although I knew she meant well, I was too exhausted to hear it.

"The sky looks nicer than it did on Earth," Anyma said as orange clouds split evenly and revealed the abyss of outer space.

I doubted her opinion. The sky on Earth was much nicer than Titan's. I found Titan's sky to be too orange for my liking, and it drowned out some of the stars.

"I thought my whole life was headed in the right direction two years ago. It amazes me how quickly that all changed," I said.

"Nothing is permanent, Fate. Even our shadows leave at night. The only difference is that yours will come right back the next day."

I had no idea what she meant by that, and it scared me a bit because she wasn't usually philosophical.

"I can't believe how cool the stars look from here," Anyma said to change the topic of discussion again, and she leaned back onto her arms. "Sometimes, they don't feel real from Second Earth."

"I don't know what's real and what's not sometimes. The

games have fried my mind," I said.

"I know exactly what you mean. None of this feels real at all."

"Sometimes, I look at my life back on Second Earth and wonder what the purpose of it all was."

"Do you think... I am real?" Anyma asked.

I looked at her with furrowed eyebrows, expecting an explanation. "What do you mean?" I asked.

"Fate," she said softly, "go to the lights."

She looked at her hands as her body slowly disintegrated like ashes in the wind. Her fingers were the first to disappear, then the rest of her body. The last thing I saw was her doe eyes staring into my soul and reaching for me to bring her back, but I couldn't save her. There was nothing to save in the first place. Anyma wasn't really there.

I remembered back to when Moirai announced that there were sixteen players, but I had counted seventeen including Anyma. Every time I mentioned Anyma's name, Jaaspar didn't know who I was talking about. None of the players did. It explained how Anyma and I got away with breaking the rules in the first game and why her name wasn't on the roster of players. Anyma's memory would live in my head and heart forever, but it was time for me to move on without her. My mind was no longer her home.

I wasn't sure what she meant by 'go to the lights' until I noticed a tiny luminescence far in the distance that flickered as if a star had fallen to Titan's surface. I had seen it before but completely ignored it. Titan was lifeless, so I ruled out the possibility of fireflies or any other bioluminescent organism. The lights were at the bottom of the mountains where the methane river flowed. It looked very far away, but I promised myself that I was finished letting doubts overpower my will to survive.

I no longer wanted to rest. I needed to find out what those fallen stars were. At this point, they were probably the only things that could get me off this moon, even if the possibility was extremely low.

I followed the edge of the methane river towards the mountains, occasionally running when my legs allowed it. Although my muscles ached as if all the life inside them had been drained, my mind was sharply focused on reaching the lights. The methane river flowed in all sorts of strange bends, but my eyes were locked onto the mountains.

It didn't hit me at first, but as I continued running, the realisation of this being the final game entered my mind uninvited. There were no other players left in the Exogames. All of Second Earth knew that I was the final player if they'd watched the previous four games. This was the only game that wasn't broadcasted to the audience or even to the game makers. I felt strangely alone without the hovering camera. When Thebe died, I was responsible because it should have been me that the lava swallowed. And Jayde saved me from the ice wall in the third game. Jaaspar wasn't ready to die; he was supposed to win the games with me. Anyma wasn't even a real player, but she was a part of me, and losing her meant losing part of myself.

I came to a screeching halt where the river expanded into a

large lake, separating me from the mountains. I almost didn't see it because the sun was no longer in the sky, but the air was at its thickest now, and the lake reflected Saturn.

The lights looked more artificial now that I was closer, but I still couldn't make out exactly what they were. There wasn't an easy way for me to get across to the other side. I required a boat or needed to build a makeshift raft, but without any proper materials, it was impossible. Before I had time to figure out a safe method, my head was enveloped with a black cloth, and the world went dark.

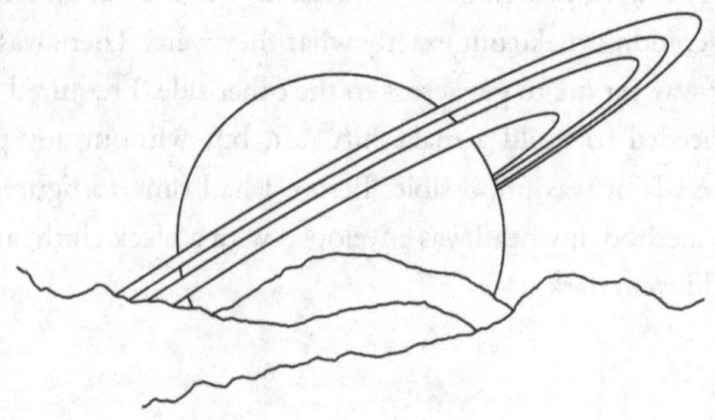

## TWENTY FIVE

**N**OBODY ELSE SHOULD HAVE BEEN ON **TITAN**. I was meant to be the only player in the final game. I couldn't see who had restrained me because my head was still covered with a sackcloth. For all I knew, it could have been aliens who'd found me, planning to digest my body. My hands were tied up behind my back, and I was no longer outside. I knew this because it was much warmer where they kept me.

Someone whispered in the room, but I couldn't make out what language they were speaking. I didn't know if they were speaking to me, so I coughed to get their attention. The whispers stopped, and there was complete silence for a few seconds. I was dead; there was no other ending I could think of.

"Where am I?" I asked.

Nobody answered, but footsteps crunched the dirt in front of me. Something grasped the sackcloth on my head and pulled it off. My eyes needed to adjust to the new lighting, and after a moment, a face was visible. A human face. It was a woman, middle aged, with dull brown eyes and slightly tanned skin. Her hair was tied up with a fraying string, and she wore a black suit. Lines creased her forehead when she looked into my eyes, as if she were examining my soul.

The room was a simple cut-out into the terrain. The walls were made from the orange rock that dominated Titan, and it was completely sealed. It looked like a prison cell of sorts, but nothing as daunting as the facility on Mars which I had been sent to a few years ago.

"What is your name, and why are you here?" she asked intimidatingly in a hoarse voice.

"My name," I hesitated. "Fate Artemis."

Her lines of worry disappeared, and her eyes widened.

"And why are you here?" she asked.

"This is the final game in the Exogames," I said, unsure if she was familiar with the event. "I need to get off this moon immediately."

"Are you alone?"

"Yes. I am the only survivor."

I had just met this woman, yet it was so natural for me to give her all the information she requested. She turned to another person in the room, who I hadn't noticed was there, and stretched her hand out. The man who guarded the door pulled out a knife and handed it to the woman. She grabbed my shoulder with one hand and pulled me forward as she flicked the knife open.

"What are you doing?" I shrieked.

"Shut your whining," she said as she cut loose the rope that bound my wrists together. "Take him to my office," she said to the male guard.

She pulled me up and handed me off to the man, who was well built and walked with his hands behind his back.

"Aries will take you," she said to me.

"Why are you two here? How are there humans on Titan?" I asked, requiring answers almost as immediately as they came out of my mouth.

"All will be explained soon, Fate Artemis."

Aries took me through narrow passageways with artificial lights along the walls in the mountains of Titan. He fit perfectly through the tunnels, but I had to hunch over slightly because my head scraped against the ceiling.

"Hey," I whispered. "What is this place?"

I assumed he would be able to answer the question because the woman wasn't with us anymore — the woman who I had definitely seen before, possibly in photos, because a younger version of her lingered in the back of my mind.

"Libra already told you. You'll find out shortly," he answered firmly.

The name rang a bell. Libra was the name of the leader in the expedition to Titan thirty-five years ago. But Second Earth never heard back from the original crew.

The tunnel opened into an enormous room with no ceiling.

As I looked up, I saw lights climbing to the very top of the room. It was a hollowed-out section of the mountain with scaffolding that stretched to the top. There were multiple entrances to different tunnels the higher the scaffolding went.

People moved about, entering and exiting tunnels. Some even came all the way down to the floor Aries and I stood on. I thought I recognised a few people, but it might have been my mind playing tricks on me again.

Aries took me up the stairs on the scaffolding, and everyone who passed by looked at me with surprise. Perhaps it was because I was the only one in white, while everyone else wore dull clothes. Or maybe it was because nobody had seen me before. But I was just as surprised to see them because there was no known civilisation on Titan.

Aries left me in another room, which had wooden furniture, contrasting with the metallic stuff back on Second Earth. I sat in the chair in front of the desk, while the chair behind it remained empty. There was a lonely bookcase with no books, just a few useless trinkets unevenly spread on the shelves. There were no windows for ventilation, but there was no point because Titan had no oxygen in its atmosphere. Luckily, I had the force field around my head to protect me from the outside elements. I placed my hand between my collarbones to double-check that the device was activated, but it wasn't. The button had been smashed, and there was no light to signal its activation.

I knew I was dead. Without oxygen, I was guaranteed to be dead. I slapped myself across the face to make sure, but I felt it.

Maybe I was still alive.

The wooden door opened horizontally, and the woman from before, Libra, walked in. She sat in the empty chair with her back straight, and she rested her elbows on the desk.

"One question before we get started. How are we not dead? There is no oxygen here," I asked without giving her the opportunity to speak first.

"Right you are. There is no oxygen outside. In here, in this giant bunker of ours, we have plenty of oxygen farms. We've been able to grow plant life on this moon. We are completely safe down here."

"What is this place?"

"We are Titan. This place was built from the ground up more than thirty-five years ago," she answered.

"Were you part of the expedition?" I asked, suspecting the answer to be true.

"Yes, most of us here were part of the original crew," she confirmed.

"What about all the people, where did they come from? Surely the entire population isn't part of the original expedition."

"Some of us are from the original crew, myself included. But the rest, hundreds of them out there, came from the Exogames, just like you. And of course the people had children amongst themselves which added to our population."

"They were all players?" I asked.

"Precisely. A lot of them came at the same time, not just one by one, which is why we have a large population. We haven't had a player come through in a while, which is why we are all surprised to see you."

"Why haven't you gone back to Second Earth? You do want to go back, don't you?" I asked with concern because they had become too comfortable away from home.

"Our mothership cannot be operated anymore. And the smaller shuttles were all damaged upon entry. I came to an agreement with the other leaders to not return to Second Earth. We built a great life here, sustainable too. There's no need to return to Second Earth."

"So, are you the leader of this place?"

"You could call me that. There's nobody higher than me if that is what you are asking. We are all basically on the same level. Although, I have this fancy office, and I call a lot of the shots around here," she answered, smiling with her bright teeth.

"Why didn't you communicate with Second Earth that your crew made it here?"

"Our communication system malfunctioned and stopped working. We couldn't contact Second Earth, and they couldn't contact us. And since our mothership was damaged, and the shuttles were not functioning, we couldn't get back home. Honestly, we preferred it; to not have Second Earth contact us was a dream come true."

"Nobody repaired the communication system or the ship?"

"They were instructed not to repair the communications. We have a team working on the shuttles, but it will be a while before they're able to be piloted."

"I need to get off this moon," I said seriously.

"Now why would you want to do that? You are more than welcome to stay."

"The nanobots inside me will explode if I'm still here after one Titan day."

"Nanobots?" she asked.

"There are tiny trackers under my skin for the Exogames."

"The game makers must have changed the tracking system for the players. The old tracker was a marble-sized device implanted into the player's ankle. They were easy to remove, and the players didn't need to return to Second Earth."

"How long until the day is up?" I asked, afraid my time was almost over. "How long was I knocked out for?"

"You were out for a few Earth days. Was the sun still up when you landed on Titan?"

"Not for very long," I answered.

"There is still some time. Don't stress. We have a solid team of engineers that are repairing the shuttles as we speak. Hopefully, they can mend everything in time. They repaired some of the other mechanical devices we have, so it should be simple for them to fix the shuttles faster."

"Do you think it will make the flight to Second Earth, the shuttle?" I asked.

"I'll get one of the other leaders to take you to the workshop. You can assess the shuttles there and choose the best one to take you home. Your department on Second Earth was aerospace, correct?"

"It was. How do you know that?"

"I was aerospace too. Your father is Scorpius Artemis, yes?"

"You knew my father?"

"I know your father," she corrected. "He is one of the best employees the aerospace department has ever had.

Libra had been here for thirty-five years and was unaware of my father's death. She probably didn't even know that he was incarcerated and that he had entered the Exogames.

"I'm sorry, but my father died about a decade ago. He didn't make it out of the Exogames."

There was a knock at the door — more so a light tap than a pounding strike.

"Come in," Libra said.

"You called for me?" the man who entered said.

I didn't need to see his face to know whose voice it was. I swung my neck around so quickly, I almost got whiplash, and I rose from my chair immediately. When I stood up, I didn't move. I stared into the man's blue eyes, which watered slightly. His mouth quivered as if he were going to say something, but nothing came out.

"That's right, Scorpius. I thought you might want to see your son again," Libra answered.

"You're... alive," I said as my throat tightened.

He threw his arms around me and held my head close to his shoulder. I hoped he wouldn't disappear like Anyma had, but I knew he was really there.

"How are you here?" he asked as he let me go and parted his sandy-brown hair which had begun to recede.

"The Exogames. You were right. I got your video message, finally. They did try to frame me, and successfully, I might add.

I thought you died ten years ago."

"It seems to be a running trend that the final game is here on Titan. I made it through all four games, until I was left here with some other players. We knew there was no way out. We had accepted our deaths until this civilisation found us and we were brought here," he said.

"I thought I would never see you again."

"Your father has been trying to repair the shuttles to go back to Second Earth. He was the only one that wanted to return. To see you," Libra said.

"Is it ready to fly again?" I said eagerly.

"Nowhere near ready. Why?" my father asked.

"I need to get off Titan."

"You just got here, Fate. There's no need to run away so quickly," he said, laughing as if it were a joke.

"You don't understand. If I stay here, I'll die," I briefly explained.

"The tracking system the game makers use has changed," Libra said, hoping my father would understand.

He raised his leg onto the chair and lifted his pants up a few inches to reveal his ankle. He had a scar deep under his skin which looked like it still needed to heal.

"Your tracker isn't in your ankle?" he asked.

I shook my head. "Nanobots. I have nanobots underneath my skin."

"Nanobots was early tech, still in development last time I was on Second Earth. They must have advanced since then. Can we filter them out?" he asked Libra.

"We don't have the right equipment to do that. And it is new technology none of us are familiar with. If we left even one nanobot, it could be lethal when it exploded," she answered.

"I have until the end of the Titan day to get back to Second Earth. We should have enough time to get one of the shuttles up and running. Don't forget, dad, I'm ten years older than when you last saw me. I can help the engineers fix the shuttles," I said, even though I had no engineering experience, only software knowledge.

"Scorpius," Libra said. "Rearrange Sage's and Uilliam's rosters. They're our two best engineers. Get them to help Fate fix the shuttles. Now take your son to the workshop."

She sounded abrupt when she spoke, and I was taken aback. My father wasn't fazed by her reaction at all, probably because it was her natural personality.

"And Fate," she continued as she rose from her chair, "when you get off Titan, don't tell anybody on Second Earth about us," she warned.

"What should I tell them?" I asked.

"Make something up. I'm sure you'll figure it out. Tell them you stumbled upon the wrecked spaceships from the expedition, and one of the shuttles seemed to work. But nobody can know that we are alive, or there will be a great war between Second Earth and us. And Second Earth will surely win."

"A war?"

"Precisely, and it will be very terrible. Not only for us, but for them as well. The High Judges desire total control. Once they know a select number of their population live away from them, they will do anything in their power to make us pay for it, with our lives. We will fight back, but they will win."

"You have my word," I said as I crossed my heart and smiled weakly.

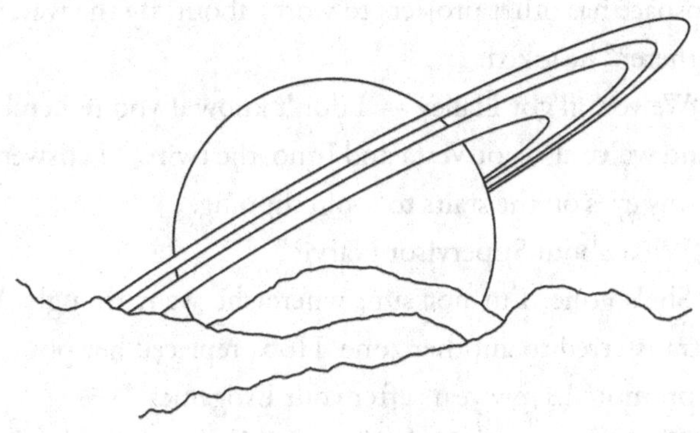

**M**Y FATHER WALKED ME THROUGH the tunnels within the underground bunker of Titan. The walk was quiet, but it wasn't because there was nothing to talk about, it was because I had too much to say and didn't know where to begin. It would have been awkward for him as well because he hadn't seen me for more than a decade, and there was too much of my teenage years that he never got the chance to be a part of.

"For thirty-five years trapped on this moon, Libra has built a real fortress here," I began, trying to break the uncomfortable silence.

"Well, a foundation has to be built on something," my father said.

"What if, one day, Second Earth comes here to search for the shipwreck from the expedition?" I asked.

"Second Earth has no reason to come here. It's been thirty-five years, and they know the expedition was a failure. Aerospace has other projects to worry about. By the way, who is still there?" he asked.

"We've still got Halley — I don't know if you remember her — and we've also got Vesta and Juno, the twins," I answered as I kept my eyes on the stairs to avoid slipping.

"What about Supervisor Narvi?"

"She's gone. I'm not sure where she went though. Maybe she transferred to another zone. Hoba replaced her position; he was promoted a few years after your Exogames."

"They promoted Hoba?" my father said in shock as he swung his arms around. "He didn't deserve it, not for the little amount of work he used to do. There were so many other good choices."

Before we made it to the bottom of the bunker, the entire population of Titan had congregated around the scaffolding. Their voices echoed until they were cut off by Libra, who had stepped out of her office.

"What's going on?" I whispered to my father nervously. I didn't know if her announcement was important or part of the regular routine for the population.

"Citizens of Titan!" she announced with both her arms up and palms extended out.

Her voice projected effortlessly to all our ears. There was no doubt that everyone would be able to hear her.

"Tonight, we welcome a new member of Titan. As most of

you will know, the Exogames were once a method of removing criminals from Second Earth. You were saved from death and brought here, but we haven't had a player come through in a while. The High Judges have hosted another event, another Exogames, another chance to 'cleanse' Second Earth. Only one player made it to the final game of his Exogames, and we welcome him with open arms." She pointed at me all the way on the other side of the scaffolding, quite a few levels below where she stood.

All eyes were on me. I didn't have to look around to know everyone was staring. The whispers began, and I looked at my fingernails as to not appear nervous.

"As many of you may know," she continued, "Scorpius has been mending the shuttles to return to Second Earth for one reason and one reason only. To see his son again. Well, that is no more! Because his son, Fate Artemis, joins us!"

The entire crowd cheered with a thundering roar. The bunker trembled like the beginnings of an earthquake, but the foundation was strong and secure, so I didn't fear that it would collapse.

"Thank you all for joining me in this congregation. You are all free to return to your stations," Libra concluded.

Everybody shuffled through each other to get back to wherever they needed to go. Most people welcomed me to Titan and hugged me with respectful greetings. Some just smiled at me as they walked by. There was no point in all the pleasantries; I wouldn't know them once I returned to Second Earth.

"Why would she announce that?" I asked my father as we manoeuvred through the tide of people.

"It's sort of a tradition. Every time we welcome a new player, Libra announces them to all of Titan," he answered.

"I'm leaving here anyway after we repair the shuttle."

"Not everybody needs to know that, Fate. You still have about a week and a half in Earth time. Try to get to know some people; there's still time before you need to leave," he said, speaking to me as if I were still a child.

The entrance to the workshop was at the bottom of the scaffolding, hidden away from the other doors. If my father hadn't led me to it, I never would have found it.

Noises of drilling and heavy machinery escaped the room as the door opened. It wasn't the only door. There was a second one after that. My father passed me some ear plugs and a pair of goggles for protection, which I put on without hesitation, knowing that we had the same rules on Second Earth. The goggles were blurry, and the ear plugs hurt my ears, but it was safer than permanent damage.

The second door opened, and I wasn't sure if the ear plugs were working because the noise still pierced my brain. I guessed it was because the protective equipment was from thirty-five years ago. If only the people of Titan could see how far technology on Second Earth had advanced. Halley's invention, the afticuvos, would have surely changed the game for the workshop in Second Earth.

My father reached for a lever on the wall closest to him and pulled it down. All the noise quieted to a silent buzzing as the power was stripped away, although the lights remained lit.

"How do you guys have electricity here?" I asked curiously.

"We have generators and solar panels. The generators aren't working as efficiently as they used to, but the solar panels are quite reliable," he answered.

I realised my question was stupid. It was pretty obvious to me that after thirty-five years, the people of Titan would have found ways to create electricity and sustain it. After all, they had an enormous mothership buried somewhere underneath the bunker.

"Alright, team!" he addressed everybody inside.

There were only about ten workers of differing ages and varying heights. They all stared at me with their foggy glasses, probably wondering who I was, then I realised they might not have been at the announcement earlier.

"My son, Fate, has found his way here. If you heard Libra's announcement moments ago, you will be aware that he was the only player to finish his Exogames."

They cheered and clapped, roaring as I stood beside my father awkwardly.

"Sage and Uilliam, you two will help Fate repair one of the damaged shuttles so he can return to Second Earth. The rest of you, take the remainder of the day off," he concluded.

Everyone disappeared out of the workshop except for two people.

"Fate, this is Sage." He introduced me to a girl in her twenties with blue eyes and blonde hair who smiled at me continuously.

"Jealous," Sage said in excitement as she grabbed hold of my arm and felt my suit. "We didn't get these fancy costumes for our games."

"I must be special," I laughed, trying to break the ice.

"And this is Uilliam," my father said as he pointed to the other guy.

Uilliam was of medium build and didn't speak much. The tattoo on his right arm disappeared underneath his sleeve, and he had short, curly black hair that reminded me of cinnamon rolls. His slivery blue eyes looked like they could hold the entire universe.

"Nice to meet you," he said as he shook my hand.

"The pleasure is all mine."

"How many players did you have in your Exogames?" Sage asked.

"Sixteen. We didn't have a lot of players compared to other games," I answered.

"Yeah, that isn't a lot. Uilliam and I came through together, and we had over a hundred players. Most of them didn't make it past the first game, of course. But we had about ten of us—"

"Eleven," Uilliam corrected.

"Eleven of us saved by Titan," Sage concluded.

I swiftly glanced at both of their ankles to find any evidence of scarring from where their trackers would have been removed to confirm that they did play the games. Uilliam had a scar in the same location of my father's, however, Sage's pants ran all the way down to the soles of her boots so I couldn't verify her story.

"I'll leave you two with Fate. Be nice," my father said as he exited the workshop.

"We'll take good care of him. Don't you worry," Uilliam said.

"Uilliam and I formed a great alliance in the games. We made it through all four rounds so easily. Did you have an alliance?" Sage asked.

"I did," I said softly. "There were four of us. The others didn't make it."

"Oh no. Poor thing. I'm so sorry." Sage was trying to sympathise, but it felt distant. "Let's get started on the shuttle, shall we?"

The workshop was smaller than the aerospace department back on Second Earth. There was an array of machinery with what looked like random parts of ships dangling from the ceiling.

"Which shuttle should we get started on?" I asked as I kept my head up.

"None of these," Uilliam answered.

"Your father has been working on a special one. It still needs a bit of work, but it should be fine for the journey," Sage said.

They took me up to a mezzanine with a smaller shuttle, much like the ones from the fourth game. There were wires hanging out of it, and it was split into two parts. The front half sloped over, looking sad, while the back half was attached to the wall.

I walked around and examined as much of it as I could. It looked like my father hadn't done anything to it, but in reality, there was much less work for me to do than starting from scratch. It would have been a pain to start again using the hung-up shuttles on the lower level.

"As you can see, he hasn't got too much to go," Sage said. "He's done pretty well."

"I'm not sure this will get me to Second Earth in time," I began as I inspected the shuttle once more, looking for a specific function. "This shuttle doesn't fold spacetime; it just flies. Getting to Second Earth from here is going to take at least seven years. I'd die without food or water."

Disappointment took over as my body went cold. My father had been here for ten years, and not once did he fathom the time it would take to get back to Second Earth? It was quite rudimentary, and we would have had to start from the beginning.

"Not to worry, Fate. We can check the other shuttles; they might have the ability to get you back home in a few seconds. Those pieces have been repaired already, we just need to join them together," Sage said.

"Ships that fold spacetime were very new when these shuttles were built. It's going to be a miracle if at least one of them has that capability," Uilliam explained.

Sage's words took the disappointment away and replaced it with relief, and Uilliam's statement ripped it away but gave me a tiny bit of hope. Moments ago, I thought there was no chance of getting off Titan, but now that she'd confirmed the hanging pieces were already repaired, I saw the finish line of the Exogames.

"Speaking of food and water, who's hungry?" Uilliam asked as he rubbed his belly.

"I'm starving," Sage answered, sounding exhausted.

"I could eat as well," I said.

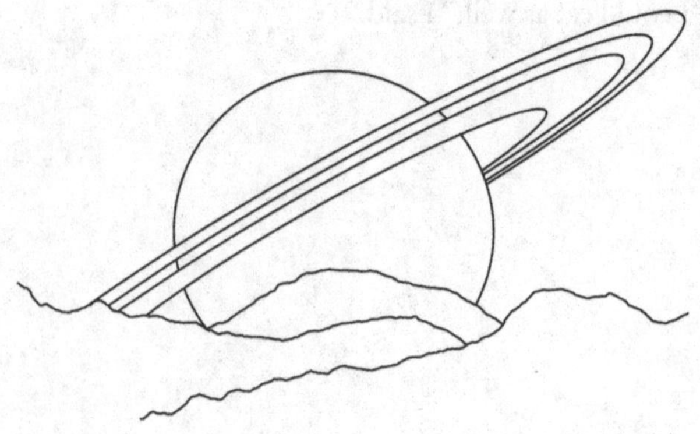

## TWENTY SEVEN

**T**HE FOOD HALL WAS VERY DIFFERENT to the one on Second Earth. Tables and chairs were sort of glued together from old pieces of furniture brought from the original expedition, and everyone would eat whenever they were hungry; there were no assigned time slots for meals.

The hall was barely full when we entered, and there were plenty of seats available, which was surprising because on Second Earth it was lucky if there was one seat left. The cooks served us a mixture of mashed vegetables and a piece of bread, which I hoped was edible.

It wasn't as chaotic as Second Earth's food hall, which was calming because we didn't need to rush to finish our meals. I sat with Sage and Uilliam who introduced me to someone else from their Exogames. Her name was Amethyst, and she had light purple eyes and dark black hair. She explained that her eyes used to be blue, but a medical condition made her corneas bleed which permanently stained her irises, turning them purple.

"So, you must be the new recruit. Scorpius' son, right?" she asked.

"That's me. I'm Fate Artemis."

"I know. All of Titan is talking about you."

"Good things, I hope," I chuckled.

"Always good things. Your father wouldn't stop mentioning you. Sometimes it got annoying, but I understand why he wouldn't stop," Amethyst said.

"Amethyst used to work in the biomedicine department back on Second Earth," Sage said.

"I wanted to move up to medical, but I thought it over too many times and decided to stay where I was. Now I'm one of the schedule supervisors here, and there is nothing better I could ask for," Amethyst said.

"Biomedicine?" I asked eagerly.

She nodded to confirm.

"Did you work with someone named Jaaspar?"

"Jaaspar Nosna?"

"Yeah, that's him," I said as my eyes brightened.

"I did. He was actually one of my superiors. I reported all my work and project concepts to him for approval. Why, do you know him?" she asked.

"He was in my alliance these games. He died in the fourth game," I said miserably, regretting bringing up his name.

"I'm sorry, Fate. He didn't deserve to die."

I just smiled at her so she wouldn't feel that she brought the mood down.

One of the cooks brought us a tray of metal cups and a jug filled with a thick green liquid. He then smiled at me and welcomed me to Titan before he walked back to the kitchen.

"What's this?" I asked, looking at the drink with caution.

"Lime vodka," Amethyst answered as she poured each of us a full glass.

"It's not really vodka. Don't tell the cook," Sage laughed.

"Bottoms up!" Amethyst said.

I took a sip and immediately spat it back into the cup.

"Yep, that's definitely not vodka, and it doesn't taste like lime," I said in disgust.

The others laughed at me as they chugged the rest of the drink. Uilliam had the rest of the jug, and he tilted his head back to drink the remainder of it.

"It will take a while to get used to it," Sage said as she packed our cups back onto the tray. "It's not for everyone."

"Nobody I know would be able to drink that," I said.

"Not even Jaaspar?"

"Not even Jaaspar," I repeated.

"Have you taken him to the hall of players yet?" Amethyst asked Sage and Uilliam.

"What is the hall of players?" I asked curiously as its name sparked interest.

"Come with us," Sage said.

All four of us walked through a narrow passageway that wasn't normally open to anybody. I assumed it was alright to show me because I was new, and also because I was Scorpius' son. My father clearly had some form of authority here since he was able to change Sage's and Uilliam's schedules, and everybody in the workshop listened to him when he addressed them all.

The tunnel opened to a domed room with four warm lights bright enough to fill the entire space. Words were etched on the wall, names that stretched to the ceiling.

"This is the hall of players," Amethyst said.

"Were all these players in the Exogames?" I asked, feeling the inscriptions deep in the rock.

"Everybody from the past thirty-five years that didn't make it here," she answered.

Sage walked over to the opposite side and placed her hand on a group of names.

"This was my alliance," she said.

Uilliam looked up to the names on the ceiling as his eyes followed them down to the ground. I don't think he'd ever had the chance to examine all the names before.

In the very centre of the room, propped on a pillar, was a sharp flint big enough to hold firmly in one hand. Amethyst dragged it off the pillar and walked slowly to an empty spot on the wall with purpose. She dug the flint into the rocky foundation and etched a new name.

"Here," she said as she held the flint out towards me after she finished.

When I moved closer to her, the name 'Jaaspar Nosna' was inscribed into the wall.

"Write everyone's name from your Exogames," Amethyst said. "We'll leave you so you can remember them in peace. Do you know how to get back to the workshop?"

I nodded slowly as all the players' names flooded back into my brain. Of course, I started with my alliance. I scratched the names Jayde and Thebe in a group with Jaaspar. Then I placed the other names around them with the number ninety-nine underlined for a heading because they were the games we played. I included everyone. Even Badru, who tried to steal my portal pieces in the first game. Even Kuiper, who killed Cobalt out of spite. Even Neon, who the rest of us found annoying. Although some of them shouldn't have had the honour of being remembered as an important player, I also didn't want them to be forgotten. Everybody knew that death was a possible outcome, and they took the chance because of how desperately they wanted their freedom which was stolen from us.

Lastly, I carved Anyma's name at the bottom of our group, because even though she wasn't really a player, she helped me get through the games.

Beside the names of the players in my Exogames, there was more empty space on the wall. The numbers ninety-seven and ninety-eight had no players beneath them. Libra had mentioned that I was the first player to be rescued in a while, but I didn't want to believe it when she said it.

"The hall of players is quite something, eh?" My father's voice echoed as he entered the hall.

"All these players, there has to be hundreds of them," I said emotionally.

"Nine hundred and seventy-eight, last time I counted."

"Almost one thousand deaths that the Council of High Judges are responsible for."

"Be thankful that you weren't one of them, Fate," he said, trying to stop my rage from erupting.

"I'm about to die if I can't get off Titan, Dad. None of the players in my Exogames had to die, and I'm sure you can probably say the same about yours."

"I had alliances too, with many of the players in my Exogames. And most of them ended up dead, burnt up or lost in deep space. There were things I did in the games that I'm not proud of, Fate. But I did them to get my freedom back."

"There's never any freedom when it comes to the Council of High Judges. Second Earth is a false paradise. You know even if we won the Exogames, they'd never give us our freedom back." I wasn't quite yelling, but my throat was scratchy. "What did you do anyway, that got you into prison?"

"The Comett is what got me into prison."

"The ship that was meant to be the largest of the fleet? I'm familiar with it. That is what sent me to prison as well."

"It had many technicalities that nobody was prepared for. I needed to prevent it from leaving Second Earth or else it would have exploded."

"The Comett is no more. It already exploded."

"That would have been impossible, because I took out the stop switch."

"Nobody knew the stop switch was missing because the Comett was never used for voyages. It would have been the first time the Comett left Second Earth. That stop switch would have prevented the deaths of seventy-seven passengers and crew. Do you know what you have done?"

"I prevented the ship from imploding and destroying all of Second Earth."

"Don't call yourself a hero."

"I didn't say I was, Fate."

"You implied it."

"What about you then? Why did you get sent to prison?"

"I told you already. I was framed. My name was on the passenger list for the Comett before it exploded."

"Lucky you weren't on it."

"The problem is that I never requested to be on that ship. And with the stop switch missing, the investigators put together a strong case against me."

"I knew they'd try to frame you, but why?"

"That's what Halley and I are trying to figure out. She only recently started believing my innocence."

"You wouldn't have been in the Exogames if you didn't go to prison, and you wouldn't have gone to prison if you were proven innocent," my father said. "Is Moirai still the head game maker?"

"Yes. Well, not head game maker, but he is still one of the game makers."

"Do me a favour when you go back to Second Earth. I want you to kill him."

I gulped and widened my eyes because I had never seen my father this way, not when I was younger or since I'd reconnected with him on Titan.

"He's not in charge. He's just following the orders of the High Judges," I said.

"He would've had a part to play. Nobody with that much authority is innocent. As long as he is around, the games will continue."

"As long as the High Judges are around, the games will continue," I corrected. "They can always get new game makers."

"They all deserve to pay for what they have done. For all these deaths," he pointed around at all the names on the wall, "and for getting you involved with my crimes."

"Don't worry; they will pay. When I get back to Second Earth, I will make sure of it. But I am not going to kill a man because it's not in my nature."

<h1 style="text-align:center">TWENTY EIGHT</h1>

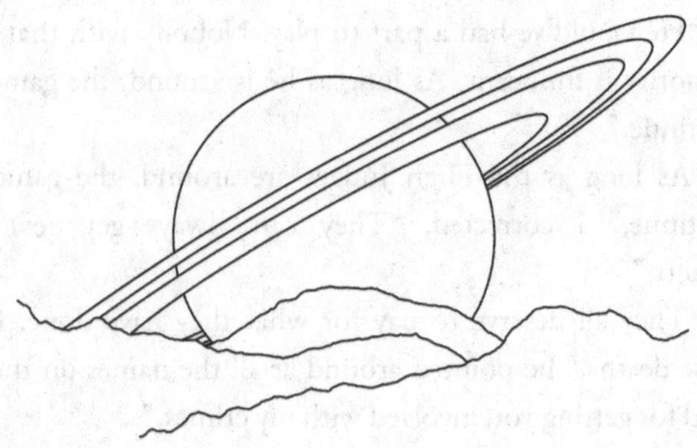

**T**HE SCHEDULING SYSTEM was confusing because the Titan civilisation broke up the day into a simple twenty-four hours. An actual day on Titan was made up of almost sixteen Earth days, making it difficult for my body to adjust. The bunker had a good artificial lighting system, which helped with keeping track of how many Earth days had passed, but it just didn't feel the same. When I was on Mars, the facility was almost identical to Second Earth, so it was much easier to adapt to the new days there.

Libra had given me a pocket watch with a countdown timer of how long I had left until my nanobots exploded. She had set it forward two Earth hours so that I had time to exit Titan's atmosphere. The clock showed seventy-two hours remaining, and I wasn't sure I was ready to leave this incredible place.

I had met some amazing people with talents from beyond this world, people that didn't deserve to play in the Exogames but chose to do so because there were no other options available.

It wasn't just the emotional connections that kept me on Titan. I wasn't sure the shuttle was ready to fly again. I didn't doubt Sage's technical advice or Uilliam's expertise in engineering, but I doubted my own. I feared that I would be the death of myself.

My father always came to collect me before we went to the workshop to make sure I was still alive. Sage and Uilliam worked overtime every day to ensure the shuttle would be up and running in time. They didn't have to help me, and I knew Uilliam was slightly hesitant at first, but Sage was genuine from the beginning. Uilliam warmed up to me eventually; he was just reserved the same way Jayde was when I first met her.

"So, I've noticed you and Libra are pretty close," I said to my father as we walked down the scaffolding.

"What?" he said shyly. "We are just co-leaders here. There's nothing more to it."

"Okay," I teased. "Since Mum died, I know it's been hard for you. Have you tried dating again?" I asked, hoping he would open up about his private life.

"I'm not sure this is a conversation we should be having."

"I'm not twelve anymore. I think you should give it a go with Libra and see where it takes you. You never know; she may be waiting for you to ask her out," I said as I shrugged my shoulders. "Did you work with her back on Second Earth?"

"Yes. But I never really spoke to her. She was too high up,

and I was nervous when she came near me."

"Like an excited nervous or a terrified you might die kind of nervous?"

"Your mother was really special to me, Fate, and I don't know if I'm ready to jump into a relationship again," he said softly, hinting that he didn't want to speak about it anymore.

My mother died a very long time ago. It ate up my father for many years because it happened so quickly. He deserved better, everybody around him knew it, but he was the only one who didn't see it.

By the time I became aware of my surroundings, we had arrived at the workshop door again.

"Hey, bestie," Sage said with excitement as I walked in.

I laughed as I danced towards her. Sage and I grew very close instantly, and it was like we were the same person whenever we were together. Uilliam just smiled at me and didn't join the group, but I dragged him into the dance huddle that Sage and I had started.

The shuttle we had all be working on was strung up in the very centre of the workshop. Some mechanics soldered metal pieces on the shuttle's underbelly and others worked on the internals.

Once Sage, Uilliam and I had finished our little dance, we got back to work. Sage and I continued working on the technical aspects of the repair in a separate room where it was quieter, whilst Uilliam returned to the heavy lifting.

Every time we turned on the system, it took a while to reconnect to the shuttle. I hoped it wouldn't take that long on my last day because I was already running out of time. While we waited for the connection to strengthen, Sage began a conversation.

"Is this what you had to deal with every day back on Second Earth?" she asked.

"Pretty much. I focused mainly on the software of the ships. I could never do any of the physical work," I laughed.

"Me too," Sage laughed as well. "I am not somebody who would do what they're doing over there," she said as she pointed to the mechanics working on the shuttle.

"What was your department back on Second Earth?" I asked as I wiped away tears of laughter.

"I was mechanics, level forty-four," she answered after she regained her breath.

Sage never spoke to me about her past life on Second Earth. Perhaps she wanted to move away from it all. Most people on Titan did, especially after almost dying in the Exogames.

"Oh, so you would have worked with Jayde Edaj. She was in my alliance through the games," I said.

"Not really," she clarified. "The mechanics level was sort of split into two zones. I worked on all the software of the internal systems on Second Earth. Jayde's section did all the physical stuff. I did get to work with her a few times, but I didn't speak to her all that much. I was scared of her."

"I was the same," I said as I grasped her wrist. "I was so scared to talk to Jayde. But I warmed up to her after I got to know her. I wish she was here. I wish the others were here, too."

"If you don't mind me asking, how did she die? How did

the others in your alliance die?"

Sage asked a question I didn't want to answer. It was emotionally too much for me to handle. But I answered it because I wanted to stay on good terms with her.

"Thebe was the first in my alliance to die. She was killed in the second game. We were on Venus, and a wave of lava swept over her. Jayde was second; she drowned in the third game, and Jaaspar was the last of my alliance to go. His shuttle exploded on Jupiter," I answered, and a few tears fell from my eyes.

"I'm so sorry, Fate. That must have been difficult seeing them die one after the other," she wrapped her arms around me and squeezed my slim body. "We will make sure that doesn't happen to your shuttle so you can live to tell the story to Second Earth."

I didn't want to repeat the story again, not when I returned to Second Earth, and not to anyone on Titan. Those memories were locked in a special part of my heart to which only I had the key. If anybody wanted to know who I played the games with, all they had to do was look in the hall of players.

The computer beeped as the connection regained its strength. Sage and I looked through the coded software to search for any corruption or incorrect formulas. I guessed the systems on the mechanics level of Second Earth were very different to aerospace because a lot of the time I couldn't understand what Sage was looking at. She had changed the software to one that she understood because she was faster at coding than anyone in the workshop, myself included.

The ships that my department worked on used the systems

that I managed. However, the systems on the internals of Second Earth would have been run from the mechanics department where Sage had worked.

"What got you sent to prison?" I asked Sage, knowing that the question was invasive.

"It's a bit of a long story."

"We've got time," I lied as I checked the timer in my pocket.

"Well, alright then," she joked before she continued. "I was working on a software update for the entirety of Second Earth, and I realised that there was a dangerous flaw in the system. To fix it, I had to reconfigure the system, which should have worked perfectly. I erased the old system and dug myself a deeper hole because I didn't realise that it was impossible to update it. Luckily, my supervisor cancelled the process and restored it to its original firmware. I still faced a trial for almost destroying Second Earth," she answered while working through the computer.

"Wow, you almost brought chaos upon all of us," I laughed.

"It's not my fault. I thought it was going to work."

"At least someone was there to stop the system from being erased. Imagine if the High Judges couldn't host their Exogames," I mocked, and we both laughed at that thought.

"And the thing is that it wasn't supposed to erase the entire system on Second Earth. It was only supposed to erase one section at a time."

"Would there have been a way to permanently erase only specific systems?" I asked curiously.

"Yes," she answered. "Each level has its own code system

with its own identifier. Within that, there are codes for specific rooms. For instance, the room I worked in back on Second Earth was the seventeenth, so that number would be four-four-one-seven, the level and the room number."

I was very confused, and my face definitely showed it because she tried to explain it again, with simpler terms this time.

"Above every door in small writing is a series of digits. That is the identifying number for the systems in that room. Does that make sense?"

"Sort of."

"Were you taught nothing in your department? This is pretty much general knowledge for software workers. That's you," she emphasised.

I shook my head and contorted my mouth weirdly.

"Okay, say I wanted to erase the system for my room, four-four-one-seven. I would type in those numbers with a hash key between every digit and hold the delete button until the screen turned blank. The option to erase everything would appear, and it's that simple."

It was a bit too much information for me to have all at once, but when she explained the entire process, I understood that erasing an entire system wasn't too difficult.

The hum of heavy machinery and tools stopped vibrating through the cracks in the door. Uilliam walked in after knocking twice and told us that the shuttle had been put together perfectly, and the physical aspects were all finalised. Sage and I just needed to test if the system was ready to handle flying again, especially folding spacetime.

"Okay," I said softly. "This is really happening."

For once since arriving on this barren moon, I saw the end of the Exogames. I didn't expect it to come so quickly because I was still adjusting to my new life on Titan.

"Alright, let's make sure this code is all correct," I said excitedly, propping my face closer to the screen to the point where my eyes became irritated from the artificial light.

Sage laughed uncontrollably as she grabbed my arm. Her eyes narrowed as she giggled.

"I've already done it, Fate," she said. "I just need to run a system software checker, and it will notify us if there are any faults within the system."

"How long is that going to take?" I asked.

"A few hours. There's a lot of code that the checker will have to go through. Why? Are you eager to leave Titan? You're wanting to leave us all right now?" she laughed in a way that suggested she didn't want an answer.

"I don't want to leave at the last minute. The quicker I get off this moon, the safer I'll be."

"Second Earth isn't the safest place to be. You'll be much safer here," she said.

"I know. But I can't stay here or else my nanobots will explode."

"Aw," she said as her eyebrows lowered and pulled closer together. "I don't want to you leave." The corners of her mouth were drawn downwards. "I've had so much fun with you here."

I knew exactly how she felt because I enjoyed working with

her as well. I never had that much fun in aerospace; everyone back in my department was always so serious, except for the two troublemakers — Vesta and Juno.

"I'll come visit once in a while, once it's safe for me to do so. Who knows what'll happen once I return to Second Earth?"

She didn't say anything in response. Instead, she kept her sorrowful face on me before she began the software check.

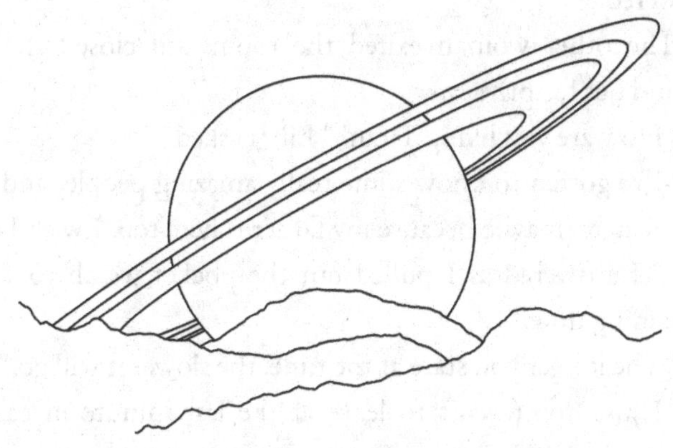

## TWENTY NINE

**T**HERE WERE TWELVE HOURS LEFT to get off Titan. The software checker took longer than expected, but Sage made sure there were no faults within the system.

I made my way to Libra's office, skipping a few steps on my way there. I no longer required anybody to escort me around Titan's bunker. I was so used to the locations of all the rooms that it became like muscle memory.

Libra's door was closed, so I knocked softly. There was no response, so I knocked again after a few seconds.

"Come in," she called.

There was someone else in the office who I didn't know the name of, but she looked familiar. Perhaps she played in one of the Exogames that I had watched before my father was arrested.

"Am I interrupting something important?" I asked slowly.

"Not at all, Fate. We were just finishing up here," Libra answered.

The other woman exited the room and closed the door behind her for privacy.

"How are you liking Titan?" Libra asked.

"I've gotten to know some really amazing people, and I feel so safe here, maybe because my father is here too. I wish I could stay," I answered as I pulled out the pocket watch to see the remaining time.

"The longer you stare at the time, the slower it will go."

"I just don't want to leave at the last minute in case the nanobots explode."

"You don't have to wait until the timer ends, you know. You were free to go as soon the shuttle was ready. Sage and Uilliam tell me the shuttle has been repaired. So, what's stopping you from leaving?"

"No need to rush me out so fast," I joked.

She took it well, cracking a smile and narrowing her eyes slightly.

"I'm not sure I'm ready to leave just yet. I have nothing to go back to. There's nothing left for me on Second Earth. All my friends betrayed me, and my new friends died in the Exogames. I just got my father back, and if I say my goodbyes, I'm not sure I will ever see him again."

"Don't let it be goodbye," she said.

I tried to believe it would be that easy, but the more the thought lingered in my mind, the more difficult it seemed.

"Shall I announce your departure to all of Titan?" Libra asked. "It will be a nice way to send you off."

"No," I said simply. "I would rather you announce it after I've left Titan. I don't want to see everyone's disappointment."

"Alright, that isn't a problem," she said. "It's been real nice having you around. Your father is so proud."

"Thank you for letting me stay."

I smiled with watery eyes and walked back out in the direction of the workshop. I crossed paths with Uilliam on the scaffold, who was leisurely walking upstairs.

"Uilliam, can you please find my father and bring him to the workshop?" I locked my eyes with his like some bizarre hypnotic spell, and I spoke very fast.

"He's already there," he responded. "Is everything alright?"

"I'm..." I hesitated to tell him. "I'm leaving now."

"Right now?"

"Yes."

Uilliam yelled out to everybody on the scaffold to stick to the edges so that he and I could have a clear path to the workshop. I followed him there, breathing quickly and smiling every few seconds.

The mechanics and engineers inside the workshop finished moving the shuttle into an airlock at the same time as we jogged inside.

"Why are you running?" my father asked me.

I ceased all movement immediately in front of him and didn't say anything. My mouth quivered, and the words were about to come out, but I couldn't speak. Instead, I threw my arms around his torso. He knew what was about to happen without me saying.

Sage, who stood close by, began to tear up and sniffle as she realised the same thing.

"It's time," I whispered to both of them.

My father bolted to the mezzanine level where his shuttle was originally kept. I couldn't look Sage in the eyes, not because I didn't want to say goodbye, but because I couldn't bear it.

"Promise me you'll come back," she demanded, croaking out the words.

Every time I made a promise, I could never keep it. It was too big of a request, but I lied to keep her happy.

"I promise," I said, realising that she would hold onto my words until the day she died. It was an unfair white lie that ate me up inside.

"No. Say it like you mean it, Fate."

"I promise," I repeated in a more believable tone.

"You better mean it." Uilliam came out from behind me and gently nudged my shoulder. "I want to see you again."

"Well, since you asked nicely, now I have no choice." I chuckled.

It was our last moment of fun before I was ripped back into reality. My father returned from the mezzanine holding a bundle of charcoal-grey nylon fabric. He shook it out and held it in front of him. It was a spacesuit, probably too big for me and too small for him. I took it out of his hands and held it against my body.

"I was going to wear it when I returned to Second Earth," he began as he sniffled his way through his sentence. "It probably smells a bit; it hasn't been washed in a while. But it should fit you. You will only need to wear it until you get back home."

"Thank you," I said genuinely. I'd completely forgotten that I needed bodily protection in outer space — it was too risky to go without, especially in an ancient shuttle we had repaired so quickly.

The four of them walked me to the airlock while the other mechanics in the workshop stood in a single row on either side of me. I didn't expect a guard of honour because I was only here for a few Earth days, but it was a touching moment.

The spacesuit my father gave me was loose and baggy, but it was very comfortable. The mechanical door to the airlock opened, and the completed shuttle was the only thing inside, clean and repaired, as if it were a brand-new spacecraft.

"So, this is it," I said.

"This is it," my father repeated softly.

"I'm going to miss you, Dad."

"Don't forget what I asked of you when you get back," he whispered into my ear as he hugged me one last time.

I hugged the three of them individually and stepped into the airlock. The door sealed in front of me, and all the noise from the workshop was cut off. I saw my father's tears form in his eyes even though he tried to be strong. Sage bawled her eyes out and wiped her face with her entire palm. Uilliam smiled asymmetrically, and his eyebrows were miserably tilted towards each other.

The shuttle's roof closed over my head, and the cabin

darkened. The control panel was exactly the same as the training simulations, and the cyclic stick was similar to the shuttle in the fourth game.

When I pushed the button to fire up the shuttle, it shook and rattled. I hoped, prayed even, that I would make it to Second Earth safely. I didn't care about the time anymore; I just wanted to get back home unharmed.

The other side of the airlock opened, and for the first time since I landed on Titan, I saw the outside again. I had forgotten what it looked like after all this time. My eyes adjusted to the orange tint of the air and the rocky surface. Saturn was still gracefully observable in the sky, claiming its territory.

The shuttle hovered off the ground and whizzed out of the mountainside. It took around three minutes to reach outer space, and Saturn looked much larger in full. The creamy gas giant occupied more space in our solar system than I ever imagined, and its thin rings spun around in an elegant dance.

Sage had preloaded the coordinates to Second Earth before the software check. All I had to do was push a green button whenever I was ready to go back home. But I hesitated. I wanted to stay.

The end of the Exogames was within reach — my freedom was within reach. I hoped the shuttle didn't explode once I pushed the button. But if it did, it would be alright, because I had nothing left on Second Earth waiting for me. I had nobody to celebrate this win with.

I pushed the button a little too hard, hurting my finger, and sleeping gas filled the cabin. In less than ten seconds, my eyes shut, and I lost consciousness so that the shuttle could fold spacetime without destroying my brain.

When I opened my eyes, I wasn't entirely sure if I was still alive. Saturn had disappeared from view, and all I could see was the moon, Earth's moon, appear from behind the silhouette of an enormous structure hovering above the blue planet. Once my eyes adjusted, I recognised the entity as Second Earth.

The Exogames were over, and I was home. But deep down in my heart, it didn't feel that way.

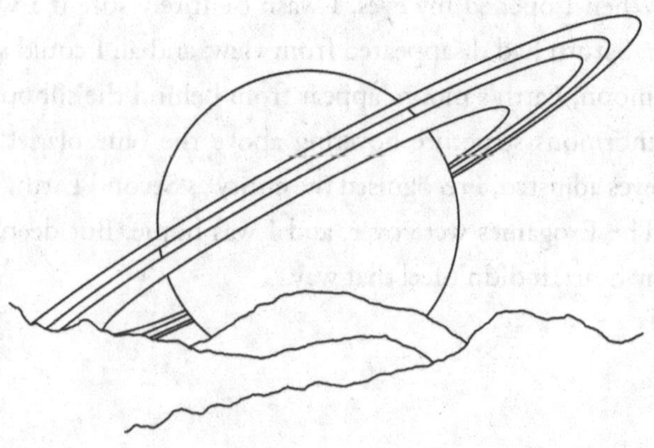

## THIRTY

**T**HE GATES TO SECOND EARTH automatically opened when the shuttle was detected nearby. Without looking at the number painted on the wall, I knew this was level eighty — aerospace. All incoming ships entered through this hangar, which was located on the opposite side of where I was usually scheduled.

The hallways were eerily quiet. It was as if the entire population of Second Earth had disappeared. I checked my side of the aerospace department, and nobody was there. Not even Pallas, who spent most of her time working at her desk. In fact, her desk was cleared out entirely. The room felt empty without Vesta and Juno's usual ridiculous cackles.

The drop pods were still operational, so I took one to the players' dorms on level ninety-five to find someone. I didn't know what I was expecting when I arrived back home, but it definitely wasn't this. I hoped there would be a celebration, although I was unaware of the procedure because I was the first winner in over thirty-five years.

The door to the dorm I had shared with Jaaspar opened automatically, and the entire room was empty. All my belongings had been cleaned out, just as Jaaspar's things were removed after he died in the fourth game. The room was spotless and smelled fresh as if it was sanitised only moments ago.

Something sinister was going on in Second Earth. I felt it deep in my stomach, churning and twisting. I just needed to figure out exactly what it was before something terrible happened.

I remembered the path to the rooms where the gazers had taken us for the first game and made my way there to look for clues. Like the dorm, the preparation room emitted a strong smell as if it had been freshly cleaned. Laser guns hung on the wall, and gazer helmets were placed on the shelves beside them. The room had been turned into an armoury, and I was unaware as to why.

I placed a helmet over my head and attached a belt to my waist to magnetically holster a gun. The armoury door shot open, and I hid behind the helmet shelves. It was only one person, a gazer, who came in to replace his gun.

I did something completely stupid, but it was pivotal for my survival. I waited for the door to close behind the gazer, grasped my gun tightly in one hand and pointed it at him. I'd never used a gun before, and I'd picked the worst time to learn.

"Where is everyone?" I demanded as I slowly come out from behind the shelving.

The gazer was too stunned to speak. He tried to grab a gun but fumbled his grasp and knocked a few of them down. He gave up and surrendered to me because I had the gun pointed towards him. He raised his hands and pleaded for his life.

"What happened to everyone?" I repeated, slowly this time.

"They're... in the atrium," he answered.

The atrium was only used to announce the winner of the Exogames, and it was always the same announcement: that nobody had won.

I fired the gun without looking, and a small white laser beam was shot into the wall by the door. The gazer flinched, so I fired another shot, with my eyes open, into his upper thigh. He fell to the ground with a loud smack and held his wound tight as blood bubbled out.

"So you don't follow me," I justified, before running out of the armoury and taking the nearest drop pod to level forty-seven, the bottom of the atrium.

The atrium expanded at least fifty floors up. It was illuminated by an enormous light strip, which curved horizontally across the wall. The entire population of Second Earth filled up all levels to the very top, and there was no room for anyone else.

Four of the High Judges were seated on the balcony, which was an extension of level sixty-eight. The fifth High Judge stood near the edge and addressed the audience. He was the oldest of the five and most likely the wisest.

"Citizens of Second Earth!" he announced without a microphone.

The atrium was designed in a specific way so that the speaker's voice would echo right to the very back, to the very top and to the very bottom. This meeting only occurred every other year; it was basically the event everyone cancelled their plans to attend.

The drop pod that brought me here was one of the closest ones to the High Judges, so my view was the best anyone could get. Since I wore the helmet of a gazer, people moved out of my way, not because they wanted to, but because they were frightened. Gazers had a lot of authority on Second Earth, and it felt good to possess it for a while. Although, the power went to my head quickly so I had to remind myself that too much of it would have been dangerous.

"Today marks the end of the ninety-ninth Exogames," the High Judge continued.

All eyes were on the High Judge as everyone waited eagerly for him to announce the winner. Luckily, I was close to the front, so I could be taken to the balcony to accept my freedom. I wasn't sure if I was supposed to go up there beforehand or if someone would take me there after my name was announced, but it all happened so suddenly. Nobody congratulated me on making it back to Second Earth when I arrived, and Moirai was nowhere to be seen. Surely, they knew I was here because my nanobots would have connected to Second Earth's systems by now, and the drop pods had scanned my body multiple times.

"It is a well-known fact that there have been no champions in over thirty-five years, and this was the year we hoped that would change."

The entire atrium was dead silent. Nobody breathed or moved a muscle as they anticipated the announcement. The High Judge raised his arms and let his bony hands droop on his wrists.

"Unfortunately, that has not changed," he announced as if he already knew all the players were dead.

The uproar from the audience was thunderous, and disappointment filled the entire atrium. The High Judge's announcement made no sense. I was alive and well. I made it out of the final game. I won the ninety-ninth Exogames. But nobody knew, and something deep inside me told me not to reveal that I had won just yet. The gazer helmet stayed on my head, and my mouth remained closed.

"Settle down!" the High Judge yelled as he raised his palm to stop the commotion.

The people listened and shut their mouths.

"The next Exogames will be the one hundredth since the first, and we plan to make it worth your while."

Suddenly, the people of Second Earth seemed to forget the disappointing news and cheered as the announcement for a better game was revealed. Every Exogames was the same, with the same rules, but there were minor tweaks like the introduction of the advantages. There was no telling how difficult the hundredth Exogames would be. The High Judges had the capabilities to put on a stunning show, which was what they wanted, to entertain the audience. Without a doubt, if the High Judges wanted it to be a show-stopping Exogames, they would do everything in their power to make it possible.

"We will see you again in two years for another wonderful Exogames." The High Judge concluded his announcement.

I took the drop pod up to level ninety-three, the floor of the game makers, in hopes of making them aware that I was alive and that finally there was a winner of the Exogames.

Technically, there were more winners from previous games. They were all living on Titan, but I wasn't about to risk hundreds of lives by sharing their secret, especially because Libra warned me not to reveal it.

The entirety of level ninety-three was empty and quiet, except for beeping noises from the computers. The floor was enormous. Perhaps it was because there were fewer walls to make spaces feel small. The light strips on the ground moved in one direction through the entire level. I had been here before. This was the floor where we had our examinations prior to the commencement of the games. It was the level where our initial briefing was given.

I followed the lights to a spacious room with a white circular desk in the centre. On a billboard-like screen embedded into the wall opposite the entrance were portraits of all the players in the Exogames I'd just won. They were listed in alphabetical order with a red strike through all photos except for mine. Beside all the portraits was the word 'terminated' in bright red letters. Beside my portrait, however, was a countdown with zero hours, forty-two minutes and nineteen seconds remaining.

I had no idea what would happen once the timer reached zero, but I suspected it wasn't anything good.

"You're supposed to be dead, Fate Artemis." Moirai's voice emerged from behind me like a ghost long-awaiting its haunting.

Second Earth had its fair share of ghosts, none of which I believed in, and they roamed around, forgotten as quickly as they revealed themselves. But Moirai wasn't one of them.

I slowly turned around and took off the helmet. There was no point in keeping it on since he already knew who I was. I went to reach for my gun, which was magnetically attached to my belt, but he already had a gun pointed at me.

"How did you get off Titan?" he asked, angry and confused.

I couldn't reveal that the expedition crew had survived and that the previous players were living there, so I lied and used Libra's explanation.

"The expedition from many years ago. I found their shuttles and used one to come back here," I said.

He shook the gun towards me as if he were about to fire a shot. I flinched and took a step back to maintain as much distance as possible between us.

"The shuttle still worked after thirty-five years?"

"Yes. I was just as surprised as you. What do you mean I should be dead?" I asked.

"The games were difficult. Nobody's won in thirty-five years. The High Judges just announced no winner," he hesitated between his sentences.

"Don't lie to me. Why did you say that I should be dead?" I

repeated with more frustration.

"In thirty-nine minutes, you're going to explode, so I might as well tell you. You'll be dead either way," Moirai said as he pointed to the billboard with the gun in his hand.

The timer was a countdown until my death. There was no way I was getting out of the situation alive because either Moirai was going to shoot me, or the nanobots would explode.

"There is a reason the final game is never broadcasted," he began. "There is a reason why the final game is impossible. Nobody wins the final game; nobody gets off Titan."

Thankfully, he was unaware of the surviving players.

"Why leave me stranded on Titan with no possible way of getting off? You've rigged the games," I said, infuriated at his meagre excuses.

"The games were never meant to be won. All of you were criminals who needed to be killed off one by one. Once we realised that nobody returns from Titan, we changed the meaning of the games and made sure nobody survived."

"None of us were guilty. I was framed," I yelled. "Jayde, Jaaspar, Thebe, everybody in these Exogames was innocent."

"No," he said softly. "None of you were innocent. Especially you, Fate Artemis."

I furrowed my eyebrows at him and shook my head.

"Do you think we were unaware that you and Jayde snuck around this floor? We knew what was going on, but we didn't penalise you for it. But we did make sure that eventually, in one of the five games, you would all die. See, you weren't innocent. Just like your father."

"You're wrong!" I shouted as my blood boiled through my veins.

"Let me explain it to you," Moirai said. "Your father, Scorpius, is responsible for the death of seventy-seven passengers and crew. He took out the stop switch and prevented the Comett from beginning its journey. He delayed it by eight years."

He was right about one thing at least: my father's crime.

"That wasn't my fault though. Why punish me? My father prevented the extinction of the human race. The Comett would have exploded inside Second Earth if he didn't take out the stop switch," I defended.

"Your father wasn't a hero. He was a coward who tried to run after he knew he made a mistake."

"Don't talk about my father like that," I said angrily.

"You are the legacy of a criminal, and so were the other players. Crime flows through your blood, and Second Earth has no room for criminals."

"So the Exogames are a way of removing criminals from Second Earth? You gave us false hope of regaining our freedom. Why not round us up and kill us all at once?"

"The High Judges wanted a show, and the Exogames are a way of cleansing Second Earth. I just do what they command," Moirai said. "We have to teach criminals a lesson, and if they die along the way, then so be it. The Exogames work; crime rates are low, lower than they have ever been."

"Then you're a puppet. They're using you for their own gain."

"Nobody uses me. The Exogames are for criminals, just as they always have been. But we made these Exogames different. The ninety-ninth Exogames were for all you legacies. That was the theme. When Kuiper asked what the theme was back at the dinner, I couldn't reveal it to all of you. It was a surprise."

"That is so cruel! Most of us were so young with our entire lives ahead of us."

"Hey!" a female voice shouted from behind Moirai.

I couldn't see who it was because I was standing on a lower platform, and Morai was blocking my view.

"This is for messing with my friends," she said as a laser was shot through Moirai's body.

He fell to the floor with a loud thud, and Halley stood at the entrance with a gun in her hand and her hair messily fallen in front of her face.

"Fate, you're alive!" She ran to me and threw her arms around my neck.

"I got your message about the wireless network before the fifth game."

"The fake message was sent from here," she said as she let go of me.

"Why aren't you in the atrium?" I asked.

"I had to find out *who* sent that message. While everyone was distracted by the announcement, I snuck up to this floor to look through their systems. It's been difficult to crack. Even when I came up to see you after the third game, I struggled to get the drop pod to go any higher. I've been planning this for more than a week. I'm so glad you're alive."

"Barely," I said as I looked over at the countdown. "I'm going to die in half an hour. Once that timer ends, the nanobots in my blood will explode."

"There might be a way I can override that timer," Halley said. "I can try adding more time to the countdown. It should be easy. I managed to get into the system to look through the cameras and see who sent the message."

"Did you find out who it was? Do you know who framed me?"

Halley looked at me with a glint in her eye as if she'd solved the investigation all on her own. She pretty much had, because I was too busy trying to survive the games. She turned and looked at Moirai, who coughed out splotches of blood. My father wanted me to be the one to kill him, but I wouldn't have been able to bring myself to do it.

"Moirai framed you," Halley answered. "He framed all the players. The game makers are responsible for the deaths of everyone who played."

"Liar," he tried to scream but blood filled his lungs.

"There is one thing I'm not, and that's a liar," she said as she fired another shot at Moirai, this time through his beating heart.

# THIRTY ONE

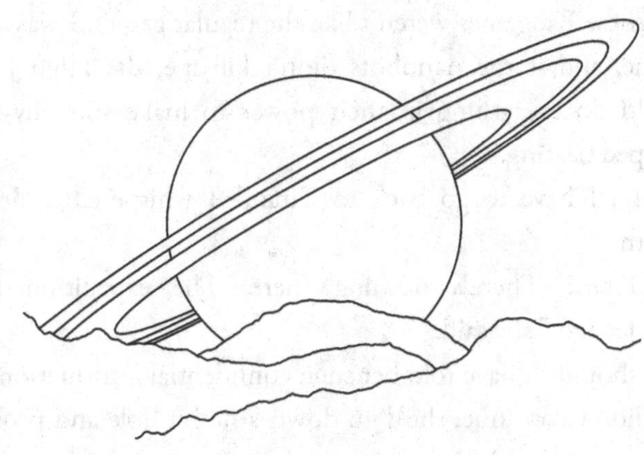

**H**ALLEY SAT IN ONE OF THE CHAIRS around the white circular table and asked me to join her. My eyes were glued to the countdown, which had less than half an hour until it reached zero — less than half an hour until my death.

She bypassed the password, which was a randomised series of numbers and letters, and looked through the code to try to increase the time until the nanobots exploded. My foot tapped the floor, and my hands shook as my breaths became quick and short. Every possible scenario ran through my mind and all of them led to death.

"The High Judges want me dead," I said as I helped her look through the system.

"I'll extend the time, and you won't die. You'll be alright,

Fate," she tried to reassure me, but she didn't understand that it wasn't just the nanobots threatening my life.

These Exogames weren't like the regular games. I was about to die, and if the nanobots didn't kill me, the High Judges would do everything in their power to make sure my heart stopped beating.

"I... I have to go back to Titan," I whispered under my breath.

"Titan? There's nothing there. The expedition failed decades ago," she said.

I shouldn't have told her such confidential information. But if I didn't continue, she'd go down a rabbit hole and probably find out the truth the same way she uncovered the person who framed not only me, but the other players as well.

"Fate, is there something you're not telling me?" she asked the moment I looked away from her.

She pulled out her afticuvos from her pocket and handed me half.

"The expedition was successful," I said softly, after I confirmed the afticuvos was activated.

"No, the communication system had gone down moments after the crew landed on Titan. Haven't you read the report?" she tried to correct me.

"There's a civilisation there in a ginormous bunker with the remaining crew and hundreds of surviving players from previous Exogames. They're the reason I got off Titan."

"We have to tell Supervisor Hoba."

"No!" I shrieked. "Nobody can know, or all their lives will

be at risk," I warned.

"Second Earth has a right to know that Titan has life."

"Please," I begged as I widened my eyes and didn't break my eye contact with her. "It is not something you have to share."

"If your father was here, you know what he would say."

"He already told me what to say. He's on Titan with the others. He wanted me to kill Moirai but you got to that first."

"Your father is alive?" she asked in disbelief and genuine confusion.

"Yes. That's why nobody can know."

"Right then, we have to get you back to Titan," she said as she typed out a new code on the keyboard, which was a simple hologram on the table.

The timer sat at twenty minutes, but the countdown continued. As the clock ticked the seconds away, my heartbeat increased. My hands were so sweaty that I couldn't look through any more of the code with Halley because I would have accidentally typed something incorrectly. After all, Halley was the expert, and I had very limited knowledge of the software used on the space station itself.

Halley's eyes tracked each new letter and number on the screen as she threw all her knowledge into the system. Two years ago, I was certain she was not on my side, but now she was risking her own life to save me.

"It's done," she said in relief as the countdown stopped and flashed on the same digits.

"It's not giving me more time," I said with concern.

"The system didn't let me increase the countdown, but I've

stopped it. It was easy."

"If you could stop the countdown, then anyone could just override it and continue the timer." I panicked and pulled on my hair, trying figure out another solution.

"Nobody can override the new code. I've put a system lock on it," she said.

"I'm sure the game makers have a master key that can override your lock. I'm a dead man."

"There's no other way to cancel the countdown, Fate. The only way to do that would be to erase the entire system, and I don't know how to do that."

The brightest light bulb lit up in my head. There was a way to delete the entire system. Sage had given me the instructions because she had done it before. It was her crime that sent her to the Exogames.

"I can do it. I can erase the system," I said confidently, trying to convince myself that I was a simple task.

I bolted to the entrance of the control room, hopping over Moirai's dead body, and scanned the top of the doorway with my eyes. Sage had said that the identifying number would be at the entrance of any room on Second Earth. She was right. The digits nine-three-eight-one were etched in small writing on a plaque at the top of the doorway; I had to squint to see it clearly.

Halley tilted her head quizzically as a look of puzzlement crossed her face. I almost fell off the chair as I went to sit back down, but Halley caught me with one arm. I paused just before my fingers could touch the keyboard, but knowing that it was the only way to guarantee my safety, I typed out the code to erase the system.

Nine, hash. I stopped and looked at Halley before continuing. Three, hash, eight, hash. I stopped and looked at Halley once more. I nodded slowly. One. I pushed the final digit and held the delete key.

Halley gasped when the screen turned off, but I remained calm because Sage had said it would happen.

The screen turned back on, and only two options appeared: erase or cancel. Without hesitation, I pushed the erase option, and the entire room went black. All the lights blinked uncontrollably, and the screens made static noises as they flickered as well. The portraits of all the players on the board rearranged themselves and disappeared one by one as the system's brain was being wipes clean.

"We need to get you out of here," Halley said.

We sprinted out of the control room, and we took one of the joint drop pods to aerospace. When the drop pod opened, two gazers stood at the entrance with their backs facing us. I froze. Halley froze. We didn't move a muscle. They turned their heads when they heard the door open and immediately reached for their guns.

The shorter gazer pointed her gun at Halley, and the taller gazer pointed his gun in my face. Halley and I shot our arms up in the air and slowly stepped out of the drop pod, pausing slightly between steps.

"Moirai said you returned to Second Earth," the male gazer said.

"You're going to prison," the female gazer said to Halley. "Helping a convicted criminal escape. Pathetic."

"He's innocent!" Halley responded. "You don't understand."

"Nobody's innocent."

"The Exogames were rigged. Did Moirai tell you that? Or did he lie to you as well?" I said, trying to convince them because they were most likely brainwashed.

"Shut it!" the female gazer said.

The male gazer in front of me jolted his gun, and I flinched. The two of them laughed, but it wasn't for long. A quick laser blast shot through the male gazer's neck and hit the female gazer in the head. Both of them fell to the ground with a hard thud. Halley and I stepped further out of the drop pod to see who shot them, and out of the side wall came Juno. I was relieved to see him because it was the first time he had done something for someone else.

Juno worked with me in aerospace with his twin sister Vesta. But when I saw him now, he looked different. Dark patches circled his eyes, and his nostrils flared up as his sight locked onto the two dead gazers. Juno wasn't his usual self; the person who laughed at random jokes and never took anything seriously was gone. It was the first time I ever saw Juno without a smile.

"Juno," Halley said as she reached for his hand. "Thank you."

"Fate." He acknowledged me as his eyes welled up, but no tears fell. "Congrats on surviving the games. I'm glad you made it out. It must have been very difficult for you."

"It was." I nodded.

"Go now! Before anyone sees this. I'll clean it up."

Halley pulled me by the arm through the corridors, and we stopped when we were farther away from Juno.

"What happened to him?" I asked. "That is not the Juno I remember."

"You're not the only one who hates the game makers. Immediately after your trial, Vesta was arrested for accidentally messing up one of Pallas' projects. She chose to enter the Exogames in the hopes she would win, but she was killed in the second game. Juno lost a part of himself that day, and he's never been the same," she answered.

"Oh no. I understand exactly how it feels. I lost so many friends in these games. The game makers were so cruel. I assume he hasn't been able to forgive Pallas for turning in his sister."

"Pallas no longer works for aerospace. She applied for a game maker role. I don't know if she had any part of your Exogames, but she left our department soon after you were arrested."

"Pallas turned me in as well, the day before my trial. It probably made my sentence worse. I don't know why she hated me."

"She was a broken girl, and some people just cannot be fixed. Come on, we have to get you out of here."

This part of the aerospace level looked different, as if I had never been through it before. Perhaps it had been remodelled, and I was unaware. I mostly stayed in the software zone.

"Which shuttle do you want to take?" she asked as we jogged towards the hangar.

"I need one that folds spacetime," I answered.

The white light strips on all the walls turned off and reilluminated the level with a red glow, and a siren wailed throughout Second Earth. The sirens weren't activated very often, if ever, and there was only one purpose for them: to notify all of Second Earth that a criminal was on the loose.

"Run!" Halley said.

The drop pods around us whirred as gazers rushed to this level. The hallway shrank as a solid metal wall dropped behind us. We were going to be trapped if we didn't move. Walls came down behind our backs, missing us by mere millimetres. It reminded me of the third game, and I accidentally called Halley 'Jayde' a few times.

"We're not going to make it!" I yelled, trying to keep up.

"Just keep running, Fate. We're almost there."

The door to the entrance of the hangar slowly came down. I pushed all my energy into my legs and raced Halley as fast as I could. Halley was slightly faster than me, and she made it to the hangar first. The door was about halfway down, and I calculated in my head that I wouldn't make it there in time. I sprinted until I couldn't feel my legs anymore. The door was three quarters of the way closed. I leapt forward and slid on my stomach to fit underneath the door, which snapped shut millimetres behind my toes.

"We made it," I exhaled in relief.

I had only been to this hangar once, and that was to verify a malfunction in one of the spacecrafts. The hangar was filled with ships of all shapes and sizes, all crammed tightly together.

When I arrived back on Second Earth from Titan, my shuttle didn't bring me here; it took me to a smaller entrance on the other side of this level.

"Halley, you have to come with me. Come to Titan," I said.

"My life is here, Fate. You know I have to stay. There is so much I can't leave behind."

"Once they catch you, you'll be thrown into prison. I'm a convicted criminal, and you'll be responsible for my escape."

She didn't have to think about it for too long. Once she realised I was right, she agreed to join me.

"What about Juno? He'll be captured for the deaths of those two gazers."

"It's too late now. There is no way for him to get here safely," she answered.

There was a pounding bang at the door as gazers tried to force their way into the hangar.

"It's locked, but they'll be able to get inside soon," Halley said as we looked for a big enough shuttle to fit the both of us.

"This hangar is airtight, yes?" I asked.

"Correct. The ships leave through the ceiling."

"If the gazers get inside, they'll die when the roof is opened," I said empathetically.

"It's not your job to worry about the people who are coming to kill you, Fate. If the gazers get in here, yes, they will die, but that's not our issue," she reassured.

The ships in the hangar were all fastened to the floor with incredibly strong magnets so that when the roof opened, none of the ships would be sucked into outer space.

The moment Halley and I climbed into one of the shuttles, the door to the hangar opened, and ten gazers marched in with their guns ready. The shuttle was desirably sleek and more spacious than the previous two I'd piloted. Halley slipped one of the spacesuits over her current clothes and fiddled with the control panel. We stuck tiny earpieces in our ears because the rumbling of the engines would have been too loud when the shuttle took off, and Halley forgot the afticuvos back in the game makers' room.

"Computer," she spoke to the shuttle. "Take us to Titan."

The shuttle was programmed to take the passenger anywhere in our solar system, which was an immense upgrade from my previous spacecrafts.

"Confirming launch to... Titan," the computer said.

"Confirm."

"T-minus three minutes until launch," the computer said.

The gazers looked through all the spacecrafts to try and find us, but luckily, we were in one of the shuttles at the very back of the hangar. I recognised one of the gazers who limped as he held onto his thigh with one hand and his gun with another. He was the gazer I shot earlier and warned not to follow me. Obviously, he hadn't listened, and unbeknownst to him, was about to face a death he wasn't prepared for.

"Halley," I said as panic began to overtake me. "They're still going to track us when we leave."

"There is no way to disable the tracking system. The only way to do that would be to remove the tracker from inside the motherboard."

"Is it possible to do it in less than three minutes?" I asked.

"No way! You're dreaming!"

I looked at her with my jaw clenched, mouth closed, and so much seriousness in my eyes that she had to do something. Halley pried open the hatch underneath the screen and stared at the array of wires and chips she had never seen before. The gazers were close; their footsteps were getting gradually louder.

"There's another problem," I said as I looked at the entrance of the hangar. "The door is open."

"For fuck's sake," Halley said in frustration. "All of Second Earth will be torn apart from the inside out."

"T-minus two minutes," the computer said.

The glass roof of the shuttle began to close, and Halley quickly slipped outside before it shut tight.

"Halley! What are you doing?!" I screamed.

"Be not afraid," she said as she placed her hand on her earpiece. "Get to Titan for me. Get out of here."

She nodded and smiled as her eyes filled with tears. Then she took out the earpiece and crushed it under her foot. There was a piercing flatlining sound before I ripped out my earpiece and threw it to the back of the shuttle.

"No!" I screamed. "Halley!" I wailed, but she couldn't hear me.

"T-minus one minute."

I pulled myself together and blinked the blurriness away.

"Computer, what does the tracker look like?" I asked.

"I'm sorry, I don't understand," the computer answered.

I looked for Halley, only catching glimpses of her as she

stealthily dodged gazers and hid behind ships on her way to the entrance.

"Computer." I spoke slowly so it could thoroughly understand my words. "Tracking system."

"Would you like me to disable the tracking system?" it asked.

"Yes!" I said excitedly because it wasn't meant to be that easy.

"Tracker disabled," it confirmed. "T-minus thirty seconds."

Before Halley reached the door, she fell to the ground after she was hit with a sharp white laser blast. A gazer walked towards her slowly with two guns at the ready, but she managed to slide herself across the floor with great difficulty, and she pushed the button which closed the door to seal the hangar.

"T-minus ten, nine, eight," the countdown continued.

Halley looked back at me and nodded before the gazer fired another shot at her. She fell back and hit her head on the hard ground. Her body spread out into a star, and her blood emptied onto the floor.

"Halley!" I cried out and my throat tightened as my lungs struggled to take in air.

"Four, three, two, one."

The ceiling opened, and all the gazers looked up as they were pulled out and outer space swallowed them. Halley's body disappeared into the darkness, and the shuttle flew out of Second Earth. I wanted to believe she landed among the stars the same way Jaaspar did. It was easier to find closure that way. And one day in the future, wherever it took me, I would be able to join them.

The cabin filled with sleeping gas, and I lost consciousness as my eyes fell shut.

All of my friends died for me. They chose to give up their lives so I could have my freedom back. Nobody else would have done that in my department. Technically, I won the ninety-ninth Exogames. Technically, we all won because we were all innocent. None of us were meant to play.

I went back for my father who was still alive, and for Halley, who sacrificed herself so I could see him again. I went for Jayde and Jaaspar, who both should have been with me because they deserved it most, and for Thebe, who was too young to die but still found the courage to play. And for Anyma, who still lived on in my head and heart. Titan was the safest place to go, and I went back for the ones that got me there.

## THE END

# ABOUT THE AUTHOR

"Everybody can write a story. Not everyone can tell your story the same way you do." — G. A. Jøhn.

When he's not writing young-adult fiction, G. A. Jøhn watches movies, plays video games, and reads all the books he can. He lives in Sydney, Australia and is currently working on more exciting stories to share.

Visit him at www.gajohnbooks.com for all news and updates.